continued . . .

DEADLY DAGGERS

"The Lavene duet can always be counted on for an enjoyable whodunit . . . Filled with twists and red herrings, *Deadly Daggers* is a delightful mystery." —*Midwest Book Review*

"Never a dull moment! Filled with interesting characters, a fast-paced story, and plenty of humor, this series never lets its readers down." —*Fresh Fiction*

GHASTLY GLASS

"A unique look at a Renaissance Faire. This is a colorful, exciting amateur-sleuth mystery filled with quirky characters, who endear themselves to the reader as Joyce and Jim Lavene write a delightful whodunit." —*Midwest Book Review*

WICKED WEAVES

"This jolly series debut . . . Serves up medieval murder and mayhem." —*Publishers Weekly*

"A creative, fascinating whodunit, transporting readers to a world of make-believe that entertains and educates." —*Fresh Fiction*

"[A] terrific mystery series . . . A feast for the reader . . . Character development in this new series is energetic and eloquent; Jessie is charming and intelligent, with . . . saucy strength." —*MyShelf.com*

SPELL
BOOKED

Joyce and Jim Lavene

BERKLEY PRIME CRIME, NEW YORK

THE BERKLEY PUBLISHING GROUP
Published by the Penguin Group
Penguin Group (USA) LLC
375 Hudson Street, New York, New York 10014

USA • Canada • UK • Ireland • Australia • New Zealand • India • South Africa • China

penguin.com

A Penguin Random House Company

SPELL BOOKED

A Berkley Prime Crime Book / published by arrangement with the authors

Berkley Prime Crime Books are published by The Berkley Publishing Group.
BERKLEY® PRIME CRIME and the PRIME CRIME logo are trademarks of
Penguin Group (USA) LLC.

For information, address: The Berkley Publishing Group,
a division of Penguin Group (USA) LLC,
375 Hudson Street, New York, New York 10014.

ISBN: 978-0-425-26825-4

PUBLISHING HISTORY
Berkley Prime Crime mass-market edition / December 2014

PRINTED IN THE UNITED STATES OF AMERICA

10 9 8 7 6 5 4 3 2 1

Cover art by Mary Ann Lasher.
Cover design by Lesley Worrell.
Interior text design by Laura K. Corless.

CHAPTER 1

Candle flame burning bright,
With your flame on this night,
Trap the evil, seal it well, in this stone, make it remain.
Never to be free again.

"Can you *see* her?" Olivia fussed with her lipstick. "There's no use in having spelled binoculars if you can't *see* anything."

"I can see just fine," Elsie snapped back, refusing to allow her friend to take the binoculars from her. "She's not out there yet. If she were, I'd tell you. Why don't you get me another cup of tea?"

Olivia gave me *the look*, a frown between her eyes, her nose wrinkled like she'd smelled something awful.

Her smooth blond hair looked perfect, as always. Her gray eyes were impatient—*as always*. "Do something, Molly. Do we want to check out this new girl, or what?"

I smiled at her, amused as anyone would be with the comfort of long years of friendship. "I'm sure Elsie can see her as well as you could. She's facing in the right direction."

"Thank you, Molly." Elsie inclined her head, and her large pink hat slid down into her face. "Oh dear. There must be something wrong with the spell. Everything has gone pink."

I laughed, and Olivia grabbed the binoculars from Elsie.

"Let me see those." She put them up to her eyes and adjusted the lenses. "Oh yes. There she is now. Pretty Dorothy Lane, librarian. She dropped her bag again. That girl needs some fashion sense. Why is she carrying a purple bag with those blue tennis shoes?"

"That's not why we're watching her," I reminded Olivia. "Do you see anything around her?"

"Not yet. She's still picking up the books, and her cell phone."

She put down the binoculars that had been spelled to see *through* the buildings that were between our shop and the downtown branch of the New Hanover Public Library. "Why don't we just go talk to her?"

"Oh no. No. No. No." Elsie clicked her tongue as she said it and then righted her hat. "You know we can't do *that*. We can summon her a little and keep feeding magic her way. When she gets the glow about her, we'll know she's ready."

Olivia gave back the binoculars with an impatient sigh. "Ladies, we are *never* going to get to Boca this way. We'll be hundreds of years old before Dorothy Lane even realizes we're looking for her. Is this the *best* we can do?"

Elsie rolled her expressive green eyes before putting the binoculars back up to her face.

It was a discussion we'd had many times before. The three of us needed Dorothy Lane, who was an orphan and a librarian recently graduated from East Carolina.

She was also an earth witch, with no knowledge of her abilities. She was powerful for a witch with no training, but she had no idea.

Elsie, Olivia, and I had grown up in the practice of magic, with our mothers and grandmothers—along with a few aunts and uncles—showing us the way.

Dorothy had no one. It made a big difference.

Normally a small coven like ours wouldn't have been interested in an unschooled witch, but we were desperate.

There comes a time in every witch's life when she realizes that it's time to retire. For me, it was when I meant to zap a ding out of my new car before my husband saw it and asked what happened. Instead, I changed the color of the blue car to bright purple. Even worse, I couldn't change it back. How humiliating!

Like everything else, even magic fades with time. Those little things you could once do with a snap of your fingers are now big things that can't be done at all. I have been reduced to putting dishes in the dishwasher. *Manually.*

It's shocking. *Shameful!*

But it happens to the best of us.

"You know it's all we can do," I reminded her. "If we approach her in any way, it could be very bad for us. She needs to come to us on her own. Those are the rules."

Olivia got up and paced around the counter in our shop, Smuggler's Arcane. She filled the kettle and then whispered a few words beside it. It only took an instant before it started whistling in her hand without touching the hot plate.

"See there? Things aren't as bad as we make them out to be."

Our three signature cups—my goldfish, Elsie's flamingo and Olivia's star—were already on the table where we sat. Olivia put some tea into each cup and poured in the hot water.

Elsie picked up her cup to have a sip. She put down the binoculars. "Whatever did you do to this tea?"

Olivia picked up the binoculars again to have another look at Dorothy. "What do you mean?"

"Why is the tea coming out of the cup?"

We all stared at Elsie's cup. It looked as though the tea leaves had grown tendrils and were reaching out over the edge.

"Oh my heavens!" Olivia knocked the cup out of Elsie's hand. "What is that?"

I caught the cup, Elsie's favorite for the past fifty years, and kept it from smashing on the floor.

"It's nothing." Elsie chuckled. "I think Olivia got her growth spell mixed up with her warming spell."

"You see what I mean?" Olivia's voice was high-pitched in her moment of stress. "How can we live this way? Yesterday, I almost shaved the fur off Harper's body."

Harper was Olivia's twenty-two-pound, gray and white cat. His spirit was that of a British sailor from the 1500s. He told some fascinating tales of his sea voyages.

Elsie glanced at me, her lips quivering. I did the unforgivable and laughed back.

Olivia took all three of our cups to the little sink behind the counter. We'd only recently begun using it to wash our cups and other utensils. Too many were being mangled by our cleaning spells.

"I didn't even have a chance to take a look at my tea leaves!" Elsie complained.

"I can tell you what you would've seen in those tea leaves," Olivia said. "It's not going to get better by itself, you know. We need to find those three witches to take our places and hand off our spell book. That's the only way our lives are going to get any better."

"Have we thought *how* things will be better?" Elsie asked. "We won't have any magic. What's that going to be like?"

"Better to know a toaster isn't going to work than to keep trying to use it!"

"I'm sorry, Olivia," I apologized. "You're right. But Elsie is right too. We have to be patient. We have to be like spiders, waiting for the right flies to come our way."

Olivia dropped the kettle she'd begun to fill again. She shook all over. "Why did you have to say such a thing,

Molly? You know how I feel about spiders. Being compared to one is only slightly better than that time you actually turned me into one."

Elsie chuckled. Her chubby, pink hands—covered with rings she'd collected—flew up to her mouth. "Oh yes. I remember that. *Funny.* I never saw such an angry little spider."

"You'd be angry too." Olivia was defiant. "I can't remember what you were trying to do, Molly. What was it?"

"I was only five, like you," I reminded her. "We were trying to make butterflies from cocoons."

"And you turned her into a spider instead." Elsie rocked from side to side. "It was fun being your babysitter back then."

Living in a small town, and being witches, the three of us had known each other while we were growing up. Our families had spent time together trying out new spells and looking for magic artifacts.

"Let's have another look at Dorothy, shall we?" Olivia picked up the binoculars and faced Chestnut Street, even though the old brick wall of our building was only the first obstacle between her and us. "Oh, look! She's walking now. You know, I think she glanced this way."

"Really?" Elsie snatched the binoculars and took a peek. "Oh, Molly! She's *right.* Dorothy's looking our way, and I think she has a slight glow about her."

"All right. Let me see." I hated to get between the two of them and the game they'd made out of watching Dorothy leave the library each day. I had a good time just *watching* them!

I peered through the lenses and saw the tall, gawky girl in her early twenties. She was as plain as bread pudding with her brown eyes and brown hair. But I could feel the power in her. It was as strong as mine had once been, even though she was a water-locked earth witch.

I had always been a little more powerful than Elsie or

Olivia, even though Elsie was older and Olivia was an air witch. Air is powerful, but being surrounded by the Cape Fear River *and* the Atlantic Ocean in Wilmington, North Carolina, worked nicely for me as a water witch.

"You know, I think the spell is beginning to work." I smiled as I handed the binoculars back to Olivia. "We may see some success in the next week or so."

"She's still raw material," Olivia said. "We're gonna have to train her before she's any use at all."

"Yes," Elsie agreed. "But think how strong we'll be with an earth witch to complement us. Maybe we won't have to give up our magic entirely."

"We've been through this before," I reminded her.

"That's true enough." Olivia took one last pass with the binoculars. "The spell is fading. All I can see is really big bricks."

We put the binoculars away, just in time too, as a customer came into Smuggler's Arcane.

"I'm looking for a love spell." The handsome young man's eyes roamed across all the items that we'd collected and stored, both to sell and for our enjoyment.

The mummy wrappings and scarabs we'd found on a trip to Egypt, and the rune sticks we'd brought back from Peru. There were also more generic items of snakeskins and wasp stingers to be used for potions and poultices.

"What do you plan to do with the spell?" Olivia went around the counter, twitching her green skirt.

"Oh, here it comes," Elsie complained. "If she sees a good-looking young man, she can't help but flirt. Good thing she's an air witch instead of fire. I'd hate to think what *that* would've done to her."

"You have to admit she looks good for being in her fifties," I said. "Doesn't look a day over thirty. I don't know if it's still magic working or because she's taken such good care of herself."

I wished I could say the same. I wasn't a former high school beauty like Elsie was with her red hair and green eyes. I wasn't sexy and provocative like Olivia with her natural blond hair and flirty gray eyes.

I was a little on the plain side, like Dorothy. My brown hair and blue eyes were nothing special. I'd sacrificed my figure to have a child, and never completely got it back. I was a fifty-eight-year-old homemaker, mother and wife. I felt as though I looked the part.

"She's still got some mojo!" Elsie nodded as Olivia slipped her arm around the young man's back to show him some powdered eyebright that could be used to improve his vision.

"He seems to be enjoying it." I watched as the curious young man smiled and slid his hand across Olivia's butt. She squealed and giggled.

"She's playing games while we're trying to keep everything together." Elsie's eyes roamed the store that we all loved. "I'm older than you two. I don't know how much longer I can go on. I can feel the fire dying inside me. It used to burn so hot and bright. I don't want to give up my magic. I want to bring in some new members and make it strong again."

I put my arm around her shoulder. "It's going to be fine. I know the idea of having no magic is scary, but magic that flickers on and off, that we can't control, is even worse."

Elsie wiped a tear from the corner of one eye. "A witch's tear. Powerful medicine. Too bad we already have so many stored up. I hate to waste it."

"I'm going to leave now with Brian." Olivia looked up at the young man, adoringly. "I'll see you girls later. Keep an eye on Dorothy. Tomorrow could be a great day for us."

Brian waved and smiled before the old door to the shop closed behind him and Olivia. He was a witch, of course. I don't think Olivia had ever dated anyone without magic.

I couldn't explain it, and didn't mention it to Elsie—she might take it the wrong way—but I had a sense of melancholy and foreboding.

Perhaps it was only the slow loss of everything I'd held dear in life, not only the loss of my magic. For the first time in my life, I was worried about what the future would bring.

Whatever it was, I left Smuggler's Arcane with a heavy heart that evening. The weather seemed to mirror my emotions, as frequently happened. Water witches are known as harbingers of changing weather. A large storm was rolling in from the Atlantic. I was afraid what it might bring with it.

CHAPTER 2

Power of the witches rise.
Come unseen across the skies.
Come to us, we call you near.
Come to us and settle here.
Blood to blood, I summon thee.
Blood to blood, return to me.

I woke up at two A.M. There was a loud crash of thunder—lightning struck close by, illuminating the night.

I looked around my quiet bedroom with my heart pounding. Nothing *seemed* wrong.

Then I saw a small glowing ball float across the room. I threw back the blanket and slid my feet into slippers.

"What's up?" my husband, Joe, muttered sleepily.

"I don't know. Something's wrong."

He patted the empty spot beside him. "It's only the storm, Molly. Come back to bed."

"I can't right now. Go back to sleep."

I could tell by his breathing that he'd already fallen asleep again. I kept my gaze locked on the ghost ball that flitted from room to room. I followed it silently, watching as it went through the house. *What is it searching for?*

The orb spent a few minutes in my son's bedroom. Mike had already gone back to school for the fall semester. He was in his sophomore year at East Carolina University, majoring in engineering. The school was far enough for him to feel independent and close enough for me not to worry so much. He probably wouldn't be home until Christmas.

My cat, Isabelle, pushed her head under my hand. I could hear her thoughts as clearly as I heard my own. I stroked her soft gray fur and tried to calm my rapidly beating heart. We both knew something was wrong.

Isabelle was convinced nothing good could come of following a ghost ball in the middle of the night, but she tended to be a little negative at times. It wasn't surprising since her spirit was that of a fourteenth-century witch condemned to die at the stake.

I watched the ghost ball until I heard Joe's cell phone ring in the bedroom. He was a homicide detective. A phone call at this hour rarely brought good news.

Isabelle twitched her tail, reminding me that she'd told me so.

When I looked back, the ghost ball was gone. It had disappeared as quickly as it had come.

My heart was still pounding when I met Joe as he was coming out of the bedroom. He was trying to push his long legs into worn jeans and pull on a black T-shirt at the same time.

"What is it?" Dread filled every fiber of my body.

Olivia.

It was a shadow that floated across my brain as the ghost ball had flitted through the house.

"There's no easy way to tell you this, Molly." He put a hand on each of my arms. His black hair was threaded with silver now but was as thick as it had been when we were married thirty years ago. "Your friend Olivia has been found dead in an alley off Water Street."

"Are you sure it's her?" My mind grappled with what he'd said, but I already knew the answer.

"Yes. There's ID. It doesn't look like a robbery. That's all I know right now."

"You're going down there?"

"Yes."

"I'm going with you."

"Molly, you can't do anything for her now. And I can't take you into an active crime scene. You wouldn't want to see her this way. Why don't you call Elsie, and the two of you get together."

"I'm going with you." I repeated the words in a way that let him know I was serious. "I can be ready as fast as you."

He nodded. "Okay. Let's go."

It had never been easy being married to a homicide detective. Our lives had been made up of late-night phone calls that led to dead bodies—and Joe leaving parties to answer leads that helped find killers.

This was the first time his job had involved someone I knew.

Olivia. How was it possible?

I took a moment after my shoes, jeans and sweatshirt were on to take a deep breath, close my eyes and say a few words of peace for my friend. It was difficult to find that time, between silence and fear, when I could concentrate on her.

Who killed her? Where were her protection spells?

I wanted to call all the magic that I knew was available to a skilled practitioner—magic I had never called upon before. I could feel the roar of the ocean surging through me, wanting me to reach out and pull in that strength. My heart ached with the need to find and destroy whoever had killed my lifelong friend.

"I have to go, Molly," Joe called.

"I'm ready."

He seemed surprised to see me there beside him. "Are you sure about this? I think it's a bad idea."

I didn't have to answer. I knew he could see the determination in my eyes.

"All right."

We walked out of the house together. The storm had receded from Wilmington, but lightning still flashed over the dark swells of the ocean.

Elsie was standing by Joe's SUV in the drive.

He was startled when he saw her. "Oh, it's you! Did Molly call you?"

She took my hand. "She didn't have to."

Joe complained about taking both of us to the crime scene. "You're not going to like what you see." His voice was raspy in the damp night air. He'd given up smoking twenty years before, but still had that husky smoker's voice. "This isn't your friend out there in the alley. Olivia is gone. You have to understand that."

Elsie and I sat together in the backseat. We held hands and stared into each other's eyes. We knew exactly what we'd find.

He drove us to Water Street, next to the river in the old part of town, not too far from the Cotton Exchange, where Smuggler's Arcane was located.

Here it was said Blackbeard the pirate once roamed the coast of North Carolina. Some of the older houses still had escape tunnels under them. The good folk of Wilmington had gone to hide there until the late-night raids and terror were over—always with their valuables in their pockets.

There were several police cars with blue lights flashing. A crime scene van was already there. As Joe got out of the SUV, several officers came to speak to him. His partner, Lisbet Hernandez, walked up slowly, blue gloves protecting her hands.

"Hello, Molly." Lisbet nodded to me. "Joe told me this woman was your friend. I'm so sorry for your loss."

She was a good partner for Joe. Lisbet was younger and

liked to joke around. I worried about him getting too serious from the things he witnessed every day. They'd been partners for ten years. She was good for him.

"This is Elsie Langston. The victim is a friend of hers too," Joe explained to her.

Lisbet repeated her words of condolence to Elsie. "They aren't going over there, right? It's *terrible*."

"I couldn't talk them out of it."

She shrugged, her thin shoulders covered by a brown leather jacket that matched her knee-high boots. "It's okay with me. As long as you explain to the boss—and *you* write up the report."

"Yeah. Whatever. Talk to me." Joe put on his protective gloves too.

Elsie and I were still holding hands. Lisbet explained the basic details of what they thought had happened that night. Joe nodded as we walked toward the crime scene. Uniformed officers acknowledged them and moved out of the way.

"She hasn't been dead long," Lisbet said as we reached the spot where Olivia had fallen. "Her throat was cut. Nothing was taken. Like I told you, I don't think it was a robbery."

Joe approached the scene with a grim face. "You might want to look away," he warned us before he pulled back the green sheet that covered Olivia's body.

I wanted to look away. I didn't want to be there. I wanted all three of us to be home in our beds.

But here we were, together at the end. I wished we could've been together when Olivia had died.

Her still-pretty, proud face was smudged with dirt from the street. Her expensive clothes were dirty and torn. Both of her new shoes were gone. The bottoms of her feet were dirty, as though she'd walked without them for a while.

"Any sign of sexual assault?" Joe asked Lisbet.

"The medical examiner said he didn't see any indications of it, but he won't know for sure until after the autopsy."

Joe glanced around at the old buildings that surrounded the spot. There were several restaurants and a tavern, along with some tightly closed boutiques. "Let's see if we can get any camera footage. Have the nearby restaurants and the tavern get theirs for you too. We might get lucky. Maybe she went in and out of one of the local places with her killer."

"You got it." Lisbet wrote down what he said.

"Witnesses?" Joe asked.

"Only an old man who was sitting by the river. He said he didn't see anything, but he heard a woman scream."

Joe and Lisbet glanced at me and Elsie.

"Are you two okay?" he asked.

"I think we've seen enough. Thanks for bringing us. We'll get a taxi home." My mouth felt like it was carved from wood.

"You don't need to do that, Molly," Joe said. "I left the keys in the SUV. Take it home. Lisbet can give me a ride. Maybe Elsie could stay with you. I don't think either of you should be alone right now."

I nodded, not able to find words. Elsie and I walked away from the scene of Olivia's death.

"What can we do?" Elsie whispered. "There must be something. Maybe a locator spell to find the killer."

We got in the SUV and sat there for a few minutes, trying to take it all in.

"It won't be easy to do anything," I reminded her. "Even with Olivia's magic and ours working together, we've been having a difficult time getting mundane things done. How are we going to find a killer?"

"We have to do *something*." Elsie's voice trembled, as did her cold hand in mine. "Someone murdered her out here in the street, Molly. She shouldn't have died that way. We have to find out who did it."

"I know."

"You know it was *her* turn to have the spell book," she

reminded me. "You don't think it had anything to do with her death, do you?"

"She wouldn't have had it with her. It's too big and bulky. I'm sure it's still at her house. But we should go and check."

"I couldn't sense a thing magical about her death, could you?" Elsie wiped her eyes and blew her nose.

"I'm not sure that I could have sensed *any*thing." I was tearless, but my head was reeling with the knowledge that Olivia was dead. It was a tight compression in my chest that wouldn't allow me to take a deep breath. "She reached out to me as she was dying. There was a ghost ball at my house right before Joe got the call to come down here. I knew it was her."

"Harper!" Elsie put on her seatbelt. "That poor dear thing! We have to go and check on him and the spell book. I don't like to think what he's going through right now."

I started the SUV, and we drove to Third Street. Olivia had lived in the same house that had been passed down to her through her mother's family for several generations. It didn't have the safeguard of an underground tunnel to hide from pirate raids, but its magic protection was ingrained in every foot of lumber and every iron nail.

The porch light was on. Olivia's silver Mercedes was still parked in the driveway.

"Was she still out after leaving the shop this afternoon?" I asked. "I wonder if she was still with that young man."

"What did she say his name was?"

"Brian. She didn't say his last name. She's seen him before, I think. He didn't buy anything, or we'd have a receipt we could use to track him down."

"No." Elsie nodded. "But he *did* touch a few things. That might be enough of his essence left to find him, at least for us. It won't do the police much good."

"Let's go inside first and talk to Harper."

"And find the spell book."

Years before, Olivia had spelled the front door to allow us entrance, but it took both of us to use the incantation.

"It may have been easier using the key under the rock," Elsie muttered.

"That wouldn't have helped with the alarm system." I opened the door and turned on a light. "We're in now. That's all that matters."

"Oh my goodness!"

Everything had been ripped apart in the handsomely decorated foyer. Antiques that Olivia had collected through her life had been needlessly destroyed. A carpet was shredded near the stairs, and an original Gainsborough painting was torn from its frame, though not stolen.

We carefully proceeded through the rest of the house. Everything was ransacked—from flour bins in the kitchen to Olivia's lingerie drawers. The clothes were thrown out of her closet, and the walls inside it were ripped open. Every piece of furniture in the entire house was sliced open and broken. It seemed as though there wasn't a single spot left untouched.

"How could this happen?" Elsie demanded in pain and sorrow. "The doors and windows are spelled. How could anyone get in?"

I showed her the kitchen door, which had been pushed in almost to the point of ripping off its hinges. The wires to the alarm system were cut too. "Someone *physically* broke in, probably after she died. Olivia's death weakened the spells on the house, or it wouldn't have mattered."

"Then why did *we* have such a hard time getting in?"

"We didn't use a crowbar." I stared at the devastation around us. "It still took a witch to get inside, but why cut the alarm and break the door? Magic should have gotten them inside without all of this damage."

"We should look for the spell book."

Harper called to us from the cellar. Even though he didn't belong to either of us, we could still hear his frightened thoughts. We flew down the old stairs as quickly as we could. His loud cries continued, even after we'd located him behind the washing machine.

"Poor thing." Elsie gathered the large cat to her and hugged him close. "What happened here? When did someone break into the house?"

Harper was clear in his response that it had happened after Olivia's death. He'd been devastated, knowing instantly when she'd died. Their bond had been strong.

"Whoever did this knew her spells were weak and waited until it was possible to cut the alarm and break down the door."

Elsie snorted, startling Harper into jumping down. "They must be a good sight better than us. We could barely open the front door, and it was spelled so we *could* get in."

"Did you recognize the person who broke in?" I asked Harper as I looked into his blue eyes.

He was regretful that he hadn't recognized the man who was there. He wished he had, and that he could've killed him. It was going to be a sorrowful life for him without Olivia.

"And the spell book is gone." I glanced into the safe behind the washer again.

"Why would someone want to steal our spell book?" Elsie asked. "There must be dozens of them more powerful than ours."

"Maybe. Still, we're talking about more than a hundred years of spells and incantations, counting back from our grandmothers and great-grandmothers. That's nothing to fool around with. We may not be the most powerful witches in the world, but we have been well documented."

Elsie shook her head. She knew what I was talking about. Generations of practical witchcraft lore were housed in that tome. Maybe it wasn't as powerful as some of the more well-known witches in the Grand Council, but it probably wasn't guarded as well either.

Harper lay on the concrete floor, not moving. He didn't want to go on without Olivia, requesting that we leave him there to die.

"I understand your feelings," I told him. "But the police will be here soon, searching through the house. If they find you trying to kill yourself, they'll hand you over to a shelter. It would be best if you come with us."

"What are we going to do with him?" Elsie's thin red brows went up to a point. "Barnabas won't have him. He hated sailors when he was alive. I doubt he'd feel much different now."

Barnabas was Elsie's cat. I knew Isabelle would feel the same. Familiars tended to be one cat to a house. Anything more messed up the whole environment.

"We'll take him to Smuggler's Arcane. He should be all right there."

"We're taking Olivia's staff with us too, right?" Elsie asked.

"Yes, if we can find it. We should look around anyway. There might be something unusual we'd see that the police would miss."

Olivia had lived alone. She had always preferred it that way. She was happy collecting antiques and traveling to exotic getaways. She took a lover when she needed one and got rid of him when he became too attached. No man had ever been allowed in her home.

That made it a little easier to locate her staff—no other personalities to sort through.

Because she was an air witch, the staff was her tool. It was a limb from a rowan tree that had been carved with magical runes down through the years that she'd had it. It carried strong magic that only Olivia could wield since she had no descendants.

My tool was the cauldron. Mine was large and heavy, forged from cast iron by a master cauldron maker. It had three legs and was inscribed with water symbols. It spent all of its time in the cave we used for rituals below Smuggler's Arcane. I had a tiny likeness of it that I wore around my neck. It was cast from the same iron.

Elsie's tool was the sword. She'd had hers made for her in Toledo, Spain. The hilt was silver and inscribed with fire symbols. It was as sharp as a razor—almost as thin and light. She still sometimes carried it with her, beneath a cloak.

Each of these was useful in helping focus our practice. They meant nothing on their own, but they retained some of our magic after we'd used them for so many years.

Harper could have led us right to the staff, but he was refusing to leave his spot on the cellar floor where he was pining for Olivia. Not that I didn't understand. Part of me wanted to do the same thing.

But I refused to allow Olivia's murderer to get away with what he'd done to her—not to mention taking our spell book. It gave me purpose in the face of misery. It made me feel that Olivia still needed me. I was there for her.

We found her rune-carved staff in her bedroom. She'd had a rune carved for every spell she'd ever cast. It had imbued the staff with great power. When I picked it up from behind the pink drapery, I could feel her strength.

"I'm surprised they didn't take this," Elsie said. "I've noticed all sorts of magical items, some with real power, that were left behind. I would've taken those too."

"I know what you mean. Whoever broke in here *knew* about our spell book and was only interested in it."

"But how could someone know this was Olivia's month to keep it?" she asked. "That's private information that we never share. It could've been me or you, Molly. How did her killer *know* she had the spell book?"

CHAPTER 3

Craft the fire, weave it higher.
Weave it bright, of shining light.
None shall pass this fiery wall.
Answer now this witch's call.

After we'd searched unsuccessfully for further clues to who'd broken into Olivia's house, I called Joe to let him know what was going on.

"What are you doing there?" He sounded a trifle exasperated. "I thought you and Elsie were going home?"

"I couldn't leave Harper here alone. We came to get him."

"Harper? Is that one of Olivia's relatives?"

"Harper is her *cat*."

Joe is a sweetheart, but he didn't know about my practice—or my magic relationship with Elsie and Olivia. I had no plans to tell him either. He was too pragmatic. I wasn't sure if he'd even believe me. Too many relationships between witches and those without magic ended badly.

I'd been successful so far covering up my magical mistakes. I'd had the car repainted and paid a neighbor to get the bike down from the roof (another mistake). Joe had been to Smuggler's Arcane a few times, but he just thought we sold herbs and antiques. He wasn't really interested.

"Oh. Her cat." He wasn't really okay with it, but he understood. "I hope you didn't touch anything."

"Nothing. I'm a detective's wife. I know better. We're going home now. I'll see you later."

After I'd shut off my cell phone, Elsie said, "But we aren't going home. Not yet, are we? We have to take Harper to the shop."

She was clutching the large, unhappy cat to her bosom. He was making feeble attempts to get away so he could go back to the cellar and die.

"We're going to the shop first," I confirmed. "We have to put Olivia's staff there too. We don't want it to fall into police custody either. I just thought it was best for Joe not to worry about what we're doing. He's got enough on his mind."

"What will we do with the staff? We can't use it. She has no one to leave it to."

I sighed as I started the SUV. "I suppose we'll hang on to it in case we find another air witch to help us retire. Then we could give it to her, if she wants it."

"I wonder if we'll be able to retire now at all." Elsie drew in a deep breath as she stared out the window. "It didn't seem that we were very close when Olivia was alive. Now that she's dead—"

"We'll make it," I promised her. "Joe only has five years until he retires. That's our deadline too. We have to stay focused."

"My dear, I haven't been focused since I was *twenty*. You can ask Aleese. She swears I have no focus at all."

Aleese was Elsie's daughter. The two of them had lived together since the death of Aleese's husband a few years back. Elsie's husband—also a man with no magic—had died about ten years before that.

Aleese, like my own dear son, had absolutely no magical inclinations at all. They were wonderful, loving children, but the gift had passed them by.

That was what had put the three of us into this position in the first place. When my grandmother was ready to retire, she'd passed on her spell book to my mother. My mother had done the same with me.

Without children who were involved in the practice, we had to go outside the family, which made it much harder, and had led us to stalking Dorothy Lane.

The streets were so quiet. I hadn't been out this late in so many years, I'd almost forgotten. Not that traffic here could be compared, even at its height, to Atlanta or even Charlotte.

Wilmington had all the refinements of a large city but none of the drawbacks. The old city was still full of charm and kept its vigil along the Cape Fear River with grace. There were no pirates now—no wars fought here. Still the city waited patiently, should it ever be needed again.

The Cotton Exchange was quiet too. The old red bricks had mellowed in the sun and rain for the last fifty years as people came and went. It had once housed the largest exporter of cotton on the East Coast. Now it held restaurants and shops. Ghosts flitted between the shadows near the river where pirates had once walked.

Elsie brought Harper, and I brought Olivia's staff. The door to the shop was also spelled to open at the touch of one of our hands. It worked for a change. We went quickly inside, then locked and spelled the door behind us.

Harper got away from Elsie and found a dark corner to mourn Olivia's loss. Elsie pulled up the rug and the trapdoor that led to the cave beneath the shop.

"You know, we've been meaning to get these stairs repaired for the last ten years," she said. "I think *now* is the time."

"No!" I cautioned as we stood on them.

Too late! Elsie had used her fire magic to "repair" the broken, rickety stairs.

Before we could get off them, the stairs became a steep ramp. We slid down on our butts to the hard-packed sand and rock at the bottom of the cave.

"Whee! What a ride!" Elsie came down with her hands up in the air as though she'd been on a roller coaster.

I had a few other words I would've liked to use to describe the experience, but my magic wasn't always reliable either. I knew Elsie had meant well—even though I was covered in sand and my backside hurt.

"I hope you have something in mind to fix that." I got to my feet and helped her up. "I think it's too steep for us to get out now."

"Don't be so sweet about it. If Olivia were here, she'd give me a piece of her mind." She bit her lip and took a deep breath to control her emotions. "I wish she were here to do just that."

"I wish she were too, but we can't dwell on it. We'll have to mourn her later, *after* we find her killer. Let's see what we can do with the stairs."

The cave under Smuggler's Arcane was different from the other underground areas in the city. Smugglers and pirates had created it to sneak in from the river without being noticed. It gave them the opportunity to ransack at will. The cave opened at the edge of the water. We had spelled the opening years ago to keep intruders out.

Being so close to water gave me an extra boost of magic. Between us, Elsie and I were able to re-create the old stairs that had been there for the past twenty years. They were better than the steep ramp that was little more than a slide, though they were still not entirely safe.

Elsie sat down on one of the carved chairs we'd brought when we first purchased the shop. Olivia, Elsie and I had spent a lot of time here.

We had a fire for our potions and spells, not to mention a

place away from prying eyes. Being a witch in Wilmington wasn't a hanging offense any longer, but we'd always observed the Grand Council's rules of keeping magic out of laymen's lives.

There was always a small fire going here, kept alive by Elsie's fire energies. I put in a few small logs and sat opposite Elsie's carved chair.

Olivia's matching chair was conspicuously empty. Both of us glanced at it from time to time as the fire crackled and grew. The smoke went out through the end of the passageway to the shore. The tunnel hadn't been used much in dozens of years. But I could still feel the power of the old river and smell the odor of the water. Its energy surged through me.

A piece of wood dropped down, sending sparks into the air around us. For a moment, the cave was brightly illuminated, showing the outline of every rock and speck of sand around us.

"You don't think—" Elsie began, but there was no need to finish.

The bright light became a shape. No doubt who that was.

"Ladies."

"Cassandra." Elsie and I said her name with equal amounts of lackluster welcome.

Cassandra Black was a herald of the Grand Council of Witches. She was very tall and very thin to the point of being skeletal. Her long black hair hung below her waist, and her eyes held the night in their depths.

She was at least a thousand years old—or so she'd told us many times. The Grand Council might have put their faith in Cassandra, but we didn't trust her. Of course, we liked to stay away from everyone who was part of the council.

"I am so sorry about your loss." Cassandra sat in Olivia's chair, making Elsie and me wince. "It's a tragedy. The Grand Council sent me to extend their deepest sympathies."

Elsie was more than a little unhappy with the herald's presence—the fire flashed up without any tending. "What do you *really* want, Cassandra? You didn't even know Olivia."

Cassandra smiled. I didn't know a single witch who wasn't offended by that smile. It was more a condescending smirk that said she was superior to the rest of us. She knew more. She could do more. She probably never had to worry about *her* magic waning.

"You're so wrong, Elsie. I *knew* Olivia. We spoke many times. I feel great sorrow at her passing."

"Thank you for that." I decided to end the conversation before things got really heated between Cassandra and Elsie.

Elsie's abilities were erratic. She might not be able to light a birthday candle on a cake, but she might be able to set Cassandra's elegant white gown on fire.

"The Grand Council also wanted me to remind you that it does not tolerate revenge magic. What happened to your friend is terrible, but lashing out with magic would be against the rules."

"Thank you for reminding us," Elsie said. "We might otherwise have forgotten."

"*Exactly.* That sort of practice is against all policies. We hope you will grieve for your friend and get on with the task of choosing three other witches to assume your practice and receive your spell book."

Elsie put a hand over her lips and shook her head.

I continued. Cassandra didn't need to know that our spell book was missing. "We will do the best we can to get on with our task. We need some time to mourn our friend before we get started again. I hope that's all right with the council."

Cassandra laughed. It was a tinkling sound that I'd always believed she'd been cultivating for the entire thousand years she'd been alive.

"Of course. The Grand Council is not without understanding

of this terrible time in your lives. Please feel free to call on me if you need help finding witches to take your places."

The light in the cave rose up again, and Cassandra was gone.

"Help with finding someone to take our places." Elsie shook her head. "I would rather die right now, with no one to receive our spell book, than to ever ask *her* for help."

I sniffed the air. Cassandra always left the scent of roses behind her—another interesting trick. "Don't worry. We can find our replacements."

"I hope so. Now that we need *four* witches, that's going to be extra hard."

I puzzled over my friend's statement. "Why would we need four witches now?"

"Well, obviously because Olivia is dead. We needed three before her death. Now we have to find another witch to replace her." Elsie wiped tears from her eyes.

I didn't have the heart to tell her that nothing had changed. Tomorrow would be soon enough for that.

"Let's go home. Is Aleese out of town?" I didn't want to leave her alone in her big, empty house. Not that Barnabas, her Manx, would ever consider her being alone while he was there.

"She's there," Elsie said. "I wish I could tell her what's happened. She'll know about Olivia's death, of course. But sometimes keeping our secret from people who don't have magic can be very difficult."

"I know exactly what you mean. Let's both get some sleep. We can start looking for Olivia's killer tomorrow. I don't know about you, but I think we should do that before we start calling Dorothy Lane to us again."

We went slowly up the creaky old stairs and said good night to Harper before we went outside into the cool, foggy night.

"Molly!" Elsie pulled at my arm. "You should see this."

"Let me lock the door."

"No. Really, Molly. *Now!*"

I turned around, and there was Dorothy Lane standing on the stairs right in front of us.

CHAPTER 4

Knowledge gained by deadly mean,
leave thy vessel, sight unseen.
The heart which burns with stolen flame,
Never to be seen again.

"Hello." She looked nervous and unsure of where she was. She was still wearing slippers with ears on them and red flannel pajamas under a black raincoat. "I'm Dorothy. I'm not sure why I'm here. I woke up and suddenly knew I had to come—wherever this is."

Elsie nodded, and smiled at me. "The summoning. It finally worked."

I was so surprised to see her that I almost couldn't think what to say or do. Many times magic has that effect. You don't think anything is happening, and then it is.

"I'm sorry. Where are my manners?" I unlocked the shop door. "Won't you come in and have some tea?"

Dorothy walked in first, with a zombielike expression on her face.

"I thought we weren't going to search for her again until after we find out who killed Olivia." Elsie's voice came out in a mock stage whisper.

"We may never have this chance again," I reminded her.

"Even finding one other witch will keep Cassandra and the council off our backs for a while."

"Did you say 'witch'?" Dorothy turned and faced us as I closed the door.

"How about some mint and chamomile?" Elsie asked with nod in my direction. "There's mint for the disposition, and chamomile to relax. Mint always makes me want to giggle."

"Okay."

I could see Dorothy was trying hard to piece all this together. She'd come out on a rainy night, alone, to visit an odd shop on the waterfront. Not her normal lifestyle—we'd been watching her long enough to know.

"Come and sit down." I encouraged her to sit at the little table where we'd watched her yesterday with the spelled binoculars.

"I don't think I should." She began to walk toward the door. "I don't know what I'm doing here. Maybe I had a stroke or something. I'm not feeling very well. I should probably go home."

"Well, if you've had a stroke or something, you probably shouldn't drive right now." I tried to rationalize the situation for her. "Sit here. Drink a little tea. We can call an ambulance for you if you need one."

She sat awkwardly with a panicked air about her. "My pulse is racing. This can't be good."

"Oh my dear." The teakettle began whistling, almost interrupting what Elsie wanted to say. "Most good things in life come with a racing pulse."

Dorothy's frightened brown eyes met mine across the table. "Where is this? I mean, where are *we*?"

I patted her hand. "This is Smuggler's Arcane, our shop in the old Cotton Exchange. I'm sure you've been here before."

She glanced around the shop at our oddities. "Not here.

I'm sure I'd remember. But I have been at Two Sisters Book Store. We're next to the river, right?"

"Exactly."

Elsie brought three cups and the teakettle. She strained some tea leaves through the hot water. The cup she placed in front of Dorothy was new. We'd bought it especially for her—so we could appeal to her earthy nature at this moment. It had come from a local potter who'd created the design of leaves and tree on the handle.

"This is nice." Dorothy smiled, as we knew she would. Earth witches love pottery and any kind of nature scene that involves trees.

She sipped her tea. Elsie and I watched her like she was drinking poison and we were waiting for her to fall over. I gestured to Elsie, and she quickly took her chair.

Dorothy seemed calmer after a swallow or two. She got up and inspected our books, potion bottles, spell charts and magic tools.

"What is it you do here?" She sat down again.

"We supply items to local witches." I had no choice. We were forbidden by practice to lie when we were trying to recruit her. It had to be up to her—what *she* wanted. We could summon, and throw our hopes her way, but nothing further.

"And sometimes to witches who come from as far as Cleveland to purchase unusual items from us." Elsie giggled a little. "Sorry. I told you, mint makes me light-headed."

"That's what you were talking about before." Dorothy put down her cup. "You're witches, aren't you?"

"Yes. We are." I included a large, friendly smile with the truth.

"*Bad* witches?" She was immediately wary. "Because you don't look bad. You look like someone's grandmothers."

Elsie's red eyebrows went up. "Well, you're lucky Olivia is dead. She wouldn't like you calling her a grandmother."

Dorothy wrinkled her nose. "Olivia? Is she a witch too?"

"She was a very dear friend of ours." I danced around the truth, trying not to overwhelm her.

"She was a witch too," Elsie blurted out. "She was murdered tonight."

"Murdered?" Dorothy got up quickly, knocking over her cup of tea.

The cup was about to roll onto the floor. I concentrated on changing that situation. Instead of falling on the hard floor and breaking into dozens of pieces of useless clay, it jumped right back on the table where it had been.

I was fortunate the spell had worked. It could just as easily have sent the cup flying across the room. It probably helped that there was still water inside it and we were very close to the river.

"Oh!" Dorothy backed away and almost tripped over Harper.

He'd come out for a snack and to see what was going on.

"I thought you were going to pine away from missing Olivia," Elsie teased him. "She hasn't even been gone a day and here you are, looking for treats."

"Who are you talking to?" Dorothy's fragile peace of mind rapidly deteriorated. "Are you talking to the *cat*? Can you talk to animals? Is this what happened to Olivia? You turned her into a cat?"

"Of course not." I tried to coax her into sitting again and drinking a little more tea. "Harper was Olivia's cat. That's all. We brought him here because he had nowhere to go."

"I have to go." Dorothy backed away from us, one eye on the front door. "I have to go to work in the morning. I can't be up all night."

Elsie nodded. "Of course not. Librarians need their rest, don't they?"

That was it. Dorothy was a blur of long legs and frightened eyes as she streaked across the squeaky wood floor and out the door.

"That went well, don't you think?" Elsie always saw the good in everything.

"Maybe it could've gone better. But she was here. She won't forget us. She'll be back."

Elsie yawned as she put out some treats for Harper. "I should probably be getting home before Aleese misses me. I don't want her out driving around searching for me at this time of night. It could be bad for her health."

I agreed. We locked up—this time with *no* surprises—and went home.

Joe came home a few hours later, as the sun was rising across the city. He closed the bedroom door behind him and yawned, running his hand through his hair.

I turned on the lamp beside me. "Good morning. I'm glad you made it home at all after last night." I'd been awake, with Isabelle draped across my lap, since I'd come home from the shop.

"Me too. We had a couple of leads from the man who heard Olivia scream. We followed them up." He shrugged.

"Nothing?"

"Have you been up all night too?"

"I couldn't sleep. Would you like some breakfast?"

"How about I make my special omelets for both of us?" He grinned at me. "Guaranteed to get you through the rest of the day—if washed down with several gallons of coffee."

I laughed and put Isabelle down on the floor, despite her complaints against moving. We went into the kitchen, and I got on a stool at the counter to watch him make breakfast. Watching your man cook is always a treat.

Before he got started, he took my hand. "I'm so sorry about Olivia. I know how much she meant to you."

Tears welled in my eyes. "Thank you. It was a horrible way for her to die."

He took out eggs and green bell peppers. "Any idea what she was doing down there by herself at that time of night?"

"I don't know." I wanted to tell him about the young man she'd met at the shop, but it was better for Joe not to get involved. Brian was a witch. Joe couldn't investigate him—that would be up to the Grand Council.

He put a dollop of butter in the omelet pan and took out his notebook. "Was Olivia seeing anyone?"

"Not as far as I know." I didn't enjoy lying to him, but it could be dangerous for him to investigate this any further.

"Come on, Molly—she was always seeing *someone*, wasn't she?"

"No. Your butter is browning."

He cracked some eggs into a bowl. "Olivia's house was trashed when we got there. I'm assuming it was the same when you were there. Any idea what someone was looking for?"

"Not really. Olivia had some very expensive antiques and jewelry. Do you think the same person killed her and ransacked her house?"

I couldn't tell him about the spell book. This was as close as I ever wanted him to get to magic. I'd always protected him and Mike from it. This was no time to stop.

The council was waiting to pounce if we did something wrong. The penalty for telling him that I was a witch wasn't pleasant.

"Would you know if something was missing?" Joe flipped an omelet and put bread in the toaster.

"Maybe. Would you like me to take a look?"

He shrugged. "We'll see. Let crime scene take a whack at it first. Let's see what they come up with."

I got off the stool and poured coffee into two cups. I'd made it earlier so we could drink it and talk when he got home.

The cups reminded me of our encounter with Dorothy. I'd purchased them at the same shop earlier in the year.

Despite Elsie's optimistic take on the situation, I wasn't sure at all if Dorothy would dare come back to the shop again. We weren't prepared. I wasn't sure if it would've helped if Olivia had been there—although it would've stopped Elsie from talking about her being dead.

It was enough for someone completely unacquainted with witchcraft to deal with that idea without thinking that we had killed Olivia too. Witches have a bad reputation that isn't deserved.

The omelets were done, and the toast was buttered. It was a cool, sunny, fall morning. We took our plates out to the patio and ate there.

"Are you sure Olivia wasn't meeting someone? Has she mentioned anyone in particular lately?" Joe's eyes narrowed against the sunshine filtering through the trees. "I don't want to speak ill of the dead, but she could be a little on the wild side."

I sipped my coffee and looked at my overgrown patch of rosemary. It was badly in need of a trim.

"I don't think Olivia has been all that wild in the last ten years. She may have been dating someone and not said anything. It's possible." I didn't want to say too much, but I had to say something.

Joe knew that Elsie and I were very close to Olivia. He was bound to ask questions. "I know. Sorry I had to ask. She doesn't have any relatives, right? No one who might want to get rid of her and inherit a little faster?"

My hand trembled as I cut into my omelet. "No. She was the last of her line."

"So who does the house and everything go to? You and Elsie?"

Witches have an inner knowledge when death is coming—at least natural death. Murder, car wrecks—we weren't always good at seeing those. At least not for ourselves.

But the three of us had a pact about unforeseen death. Joe was right. Everything Olivia owned would go to us, if the council allowed it. It was a little trickier for me and Elsie since we had family, but it was always agreed that whoever was left out of the three of us would inherit any magic items we owned—such as Olivia's staff.

"It would surprise me if Olivia had a will, if that's what you're asking. She never planned to die." I couldn't tell him that distribution of her belongings would probably be decided by the council since she had no will or heir.

He frowned as he bit into a slice of toast. "A wealthy woman like Olivia, with no family. It seems odd she wouldn't want to safeguard what she owned."

"I know. That's the way she was." I dabbed my lips with a napkin. I couldn't eat the breakfast Joe had made.

He saw my movement and recognized it for what it was. "I'm sorry, Molly. I'm acting like a homicide detective instead of a husband. No more questions. Do you need help setting something up for her funeral?"

"I guess there's no real hurry, is there? The medical examiner will have her for a while."

"That's true. I'll let you know how that goes. She tried to fight off her attacker. I hope we'll have some DNA to help locate him."

"Thank you for whatever you can do. If Elsie or I can be of any use in the investigation, let us know."

He squeezed my hand as I got to my feet. "Don't worry, sweetie. We'll find him."

"I'm going to take a quick shower and get dressed. Are you going to get some rest before you go back out?"

"No. Lisbet is already waiting for me. We're gonna go over and see the ME. You should probably try to get some sleep. Did you have something planned for today?"

"Not really. I'll probably open the shop for a while. I have to check on Olivia's cat."

"Why don't you bring him here? I'm sure Isabelle won't mind. We could take care of him."

Of course he had no idea. Isabelle hissed at the very thought as she listened to us from the screen door.

"We'll see," I promised. "I'll talk to you later."

I took a quick shower as Isabelle sat on my bed and promised dire consequences for any cat I brought home. She still knew plenty of spells, she told me, from her time as a witch. She could use them if necessary.

"It won't be necessary." I dried my brown hair. I could still manage to keep it that shade without a trip to the hairdresser, although once it had turned pink. My son had thought it was cool. I'd had some explaining to do.

I took out one of my favorite outfits, one that Olivia had given me for my fiftieth birthday. It was exactly the color of my blue eyes, a cornflower shade. I asked at the time if she'd spelled it, but she'd sworn that she'd found it in a little dress shop at the Outer Banks.

The dress fit like a well-worn glove. I loved it, and the tiny matching jacket that had puff sleeves. I put on my cauldron and chain, the symbol of my power as a water witch. That had come from Elsie the same year.

That had been eight years ago, a good year for me. My magic was still strong, and Mike was still living at home. He was always practicing basketball in the driveway and playing video games until I yelled at him to go to bed.

Sixty wasn't looking as promising as fifty had. I had dreaded it for a while. Now with Olivia gone, the dread had become reality.

I slipped my feet into worn, but serviceable, black pumps—would Olivia's ghost ball return? It was unusual for a witch to avoid moving on after her death. Sometimes there was unfinished business.

Olivia's death had certainly left a lot of questions unanswered. There was no time to prepare. She might decide to defy the laws of nature to find some peace.

Joe kissed me quickly on the cheek when he had changed

clothes and was ready to go. "Be careful today," he warned. "We don't know yet what happened to Olivia, or if it might affect you in some way. You and Elsie watch your backs. Don't take any unnecessary chances. Call me right away if either of you think of anything that could help us find her killer."

I hugged him tightly and gave him a proper kiss before I put on my makeup. "You don't have to worry about us. Elsie and I know how to stay out of trouble."

CHAPTER 5

Show yourself now to me,
Man of unknown identity.
Let your light be clearly seen,
So we may find where you have been.

I picked Elsie up at her house. She hadn't driven in years.

Aleese answered the door. She had the brilliant copper red hair in tight curls that her mother had passed down to her. She also had Elsie's diminutive height and petite build. But she had her father's mournful brown eyes.

"I can't believe you're here today, Molly." She closed the door after I'd walked inside the foyer of the old house on Grace Street. "You and Mother were out very late last night. I don't know if she's even up yet."

"Of course I'm up." Elsie bustled down the stairs, her purple hat with green flowers matching her dress. "I haven't slept past six A.M. since before you were born, Aleese."

Aleese was an accountant—very good with numbers but not much of a people person. She tended to be very serious and didn't see the world as her mother did, with humor and tolerance. The death of her young husband hadn't helped matters.

"I really don't think the two of you should go out today,

especially to that terrible shop. Mother told me what happened to Olivia. Do you think it's a good idea to hole up in that dusty old place after that?"

"I don't think it makes any difference," I replied. "No matter where we are today, Olivia is still dead."

"Besides, it will be better at the shop," Elsie added. "That's where the three of us have always gone. And there's Harper to check on, you know."

Aleese gave in with a heavy sigh. "Molly is much younger than you, Mother. She can recover from these things much faster than you can."

Elsie picked up her purple bag. "I'm not dead yet, dear. I think I still know when I can go out. I'll see you later. Have a nice day at the office."

We marched out the door together.

"I believe Aleese is thinking of herself as your mother again," I remarked as we got into my car.

"She's always thought of herself that way." Elsie held on to her hat as she got in. "It's her most annoying trait. How is Joe doing?"

"He's been very kind and careful around me—when he isn't asking me dozens of questions about Olivia. He even made breakfast this morning after he worked all night."

"Wasn't that considerate?" She pulled on her seatbelt. I fastened it, as I always did, since she could never find the clip. "You know, my husband couldn't even make food on the grill. I wouldn't have considered it much of a kindness to have to eat his breakfast."

I laughed at that. Elsie's husband, Bill, had been a lot older than her and had strong traditional ideas about the roles of men and women. He wouldn't have cooked or cleaned if it had meant his life.

"So, what are we going to do today to find Olivia's killer? You're the detective's wife. I assume you have some ideas."

"I've thought a lot about it. We should start at the shop

and do a locator spell from there. If Brian wasn't careful and left some of himself there, we should be able to find him."

She nodded. "That sounds like an excellent place to start. And very ambitious. Do you think we can pull it off?"

I wasn't sure and changed the subject. "Joe asked about Olivia's will and what would happen to her belongings."

"I'm assuming they'll come to us." Elsie shrugged. "I'm sure she didn't have a will. I can't imagine who else would get her things."

"I can." I glanced at her as we stopped at a red light. "Can't you? Remember what happened with Darla Linsky?"

She looked confused for a moment and then her green eyes sharpened into focus. "Oh, that witch from Morehead City who moved here and wanted to join our coven. I remember her! She was an earth witch, so it would've been a perfect match."

"But she was struck and killed by that woman driving a pink Cadillac. She died with no will, and the Grand Council took everything. That could happen with Olivia."

"*No!* That would be terrible. There has to be something we can do to keep that from happening."

"I don't know. We can talk to Olivia's lawyer. He might have some idea of a relative, however distant, who could be her heir."

"That's a good idea. Let's do that after we find Olivia's killer and convince Dorothy that she's the witch for us. Sounds *easy*." She laughed at her simplification.

I laughed at *her* as we pulled into our parking space at Smuggler's Arcane. There was already a mud-colored Volkswagen Beetle parked in the space beside us. To our complete surprise, Dorothy Lane got out and waited for us. She was dressed in street clothes this time and appeared more coherent.

"Well, I declare." Elsie slapped her thigh. "Will wonders never cease?"

Dorothy didn't look any less afraid than she had last night. She was trembling as we approached her. Her smile was tentative.

"Good morning," Elsie greeted her. "Don't you think morning is the best time of the day?"

"Not really." Dorothy hunkered down in her jacket. "Can we talk?"

We went inside, not caring if our companion saw us open the spelled door without a key. Thank goodness it worked. That would have been embarrassing since were trying to recruit her.

"That was kind of cool." Dorothy smiled a little, a chipped tooth exposed. It made a whistling sound with her *s*'s. "Can you do all kinds of little tricks like that?"

"Oh, that's not a trick, dear." Elsie was quick to point out. "It really happened. These aren't parlor gimmicks magicians do."

"Why me?" Dorothy took off her coat and put her enormous multicolored bag on the table. "Why were you stalking *me* to be a witch?"

I took off my coat too and stowed my bag behind the counter. "We weren't stalking you exactly. Our friend—"

"The dead one?" Dorothy asked.

"Yes. Olivia Dunst. She saw you one day at the library and recognized you as an earth witch. We observed you for a while, until we could get a sense of who you were and what you were like. Not anyone would do, you know."

"That's kind of creepy, even for a witch." She peered closely around the shop again. "So you two are *really* witches? Good witches, right?"

"Don't be silly," Elsie said. "There are no good or bad witches. Just witches. Like you."

"Me? I'm not a witch. Maybe I look like one." She peeked in an antique mirror. "What's an earth witch?"

"An earth witch gets her strength from the earth," I

explained. "You'd feel strongest in a forest, for instance. I'm a water witch. I feel strongest around the river and the ocean, so Wilmington is a good place for me."

"Not so good for me," Elsie added. "I'm a fire witch. In this town, there's so much water that it's a little suppressive. I'm strongest with a fire close by."

Dorothy nodded, taking it all in. "What kind of training are we talking about to be a witch?"

"There's no training. I mean"—Elsie stumbled in her explanation—"there are spells and incantations to learn, and some herb lore. It helps to understand the natural world because our abilities derive from nature. Otherwise, you're either born a witch or not."

"If I was born a witch, how could I not know after all these years? Nobody ever said anything."

"You were orphaned," I tried to explain. "The chances are good that your mother and grandmother were witches too. Most girls get their information from the women in their families as they're growing up. In your case, there wasn't anyone to teach you."

"And what do you want me to do? Do we dance around naked in the moonlight? Do we ride goats or something?"

I gazed into her haunted, questioning eyes. "Why did you come back, Dorothy?"

She shrugged. "I don't know. After I left here last night, I kept thinking about you, and this place. I had some really freakish dreams. When I woke up this morning, I knew I had to come back."

"There's a bond between witches that can't be broken once you become aware." I put my hand on her shoulder. "You learned that there was something else in the world yesterday—something you didn't know was possible. You'll never be able to forget it. You may choose not to practice magic, but it will always be part of you now."

She bit her lip. "You didn't answer me. What do witches *do*?"

"We observe and protect the laws of nature. We interact with the natural elements of the world. But Elsie and I have been witches for a long time. Our abilities are fading. We need new witches to take our places and to continue adding spells to our spell book."

As Dorothy digested all of that, Elsie went off describing the history of witches, of how they had helped defeat Hitler in England during World War II and had kept terrible things from happening all over the world. It was a rich and heavily embroidered tale, but one I could see had impressed our new recruit.

"That sounds awesome." She grinned. "Who *wouldn't* want to do that? Where do I sign up?"

Elsie and I exchanged glances. I knew we were both thinking the same thing.

As much as we needed Dorothy, things had become rather complicated to try to take in an uneducated witch. Our hunt for Olivia's killer could get dangerous.

"We would definitely love to have you with us," I assured her.

"But now is not a good time," Elsie continued. "We have to track down Olivia's killer. It could get very sketchy, not the best opportunity for a new witch."

Dorothy shrugged. "I'm not afraid. I want to help. How was your friend killed?"

Elsie went into detail on Olivia's death in the alley. "You see, you wouldn't want to be involved."

To her credit, Dorothy swallowed hard and made her decision. "I want to help. I'm sure I'll learn a lot about being a witch by helping."

"Okay," Elsie agreed. "If that's what you want."

"I don't think it's that easy," I interrupted. "We'll be using magic that she won't be able to use for years. It's not a good idea."

"Please, Molly." Dorothy put her hands together like a

child, her large brown eyes beseeching my approval. "Let me help. Even if I can't do the magic, I'll know it exists."

Elsie played with a reddish ringlet near her ear. "And there's always the chance that we'll be able to tap into her fresh, young *magic*."

I sighed. This was really not in any plan we'd ever formulated for a new recruit. But neither was Olivia's death. As with many things that seemed to happen out of order, sometimes it was best to go with what you had. That was part of the natural way of the world.

"All right. Don't blame me if things get a little strange."

Dorothy squealed and hugged me. She took a step back. "Is that okay? Do witches hug? I wouldn't want to do something I wasn't supposed to."

"That's fine." Her naïve enthusiasm was refreshing. I felt jaded beside her.

"No," Elsie said. "It's not fine if you don't hug *both* witches. Otherwise the other one—*me*—might get offended."

Dorothy hugged Elsie too, and we sat down.

"We need to start here at the shop. Brian was here with Olivia. We know he touched certain things, which left behind part of his essence. That will be our best way to track him."

Elsie was already brewing the potion that would allow us to see where Brian had been in the shop. The steam from it began to rise and slowly fill the room.

"Do we need special glasses?" Dorothy whispered. "Like 3D or something?"

"No." She was going to have to learn to keep still. "What we need is quiet so we can concentrate on finding our strengths to add to the potion, which will make it work. No tool or herb will work without the magic we give it from inside ourselves."

"Okay." She closed her eyes tight and wrinkled her nose as she concentrated.

The steam continued filling the shop. Harper hid in the back room where we kept some of our rarest artifacts and medicinals.

"How long will this take?" Dorothy whispered. "I only ask because I haven't had coffee yet, and I'm afraid I'll fall asleep."

"Shh!" Elsie frowned.

Another few minutes passed. The steam was beginning to pick out Brian's footprints on the hardwood floor. As it rose upward, it would show his fingerprints—and hopefully more about him that we could use.

"It might help if I knew what Brian looked like," Dorothy said.

"It has nothing to do with that." I didn't open my eyes. "It has more to do with patience and quiet."

"Sorry. I guess I'm a little fidgety."

By this time, it was possible to see everything that Brian had touched. The steam showed dark places where he'd fingered books and touched vials and powders in paper.

"Wow!" Dorothy opened one eye and looked around. "I can see it. How awesome is that?"

"It would be a lot more awesome if you didn't tell us about it until the potion is finished," Elsie snapped.

"Sorry." Dorothy closed her eyes again and sighed.

The steam reached out for the image we needed, creating a ghostly replica of Brian. It was an odd picture since the strongest image of him was when he was standing with his arm around Olivia right before they left the shop. With his arm up around empty space, he looked as though he might fall over.

"We've got him!" Elsie sneaked a peek. "Now we have to make it last for a while."

I broke the circle and took out a vial of Everlast. The name was misleading since it only made an image last until it was committed to memory. There was no way to capture it with a camera or any other device.

The steam began to evaporate, but it left behind all the places Brian had been as well as the full image of him. Elsie walked around and around, trying to be sure she'd know him if she saw him again.

Together we muttered a spell that would show us some personal details about him. It took only another twenty minutes before we had his address and last name.

"Brian Fuller," Elsie said. "He lives near Cape Fear Community College."

"He's a full-time student," I added. "Not a very good one either."

"And he smells like pizza." Dorothy sniffed. "Old pizza at that."

Elsie smiled. "She's good. Exactly what I'd expect an earth witch to pick up."

"Yeah?" Dorothy was obviously pleased. "High five!"

We gazed at her serenely.

"Fist bump? Come on, you two. Celebrate a little. This is what you needed, right?"

Elsie timidly bumped her fist into Dorothy's. I did the same.

"All right. That's what I'm talking about!" Dorothy was satisfied. "Now what?"

CHAPTER 6

I now invoke the law of three,
What once was lost return to me.

The community college wasn't very far. We took my car since neither Elsie nor I could imagine trying to get into the backseat of Dorothy's Beetle.

Using our knowledge of Brian, it was easy to locate him in a small apartment complex. It was an older building with rooms leased by college students.

Dorothy was able to pinpoint the apartment Brian shared with some other young men by the smell.

"I am rather impressed with our new witch." Elsie was smug as we followed Dorothy upstairs.

"She's surprising," I agreed. "She's had no training at all. Her family must be very powerful. When there's a strong bloodline—"

"There's a strong witch." Elsie finished the quote.

We reached the floor where Brian lived. Dorothy knocked on his door.

A different young man answered—this one wasn't a witch. He said that Brian wasn't there. "He's got some classes this morning. You're welcome to come in and wait for him if you like."

We agreed—it would be good to have a look at Brian's possessions—but we couldn't step foot into the apartment. Brian had thoroughly spelled the entrance so that no witch could enter without him.

I hastily told the young man that we'd be back. One glance into the apartment behind him sent us all quickly back down the stairs.

"How can anyone live that way?" Dorothy held her nose. "The stench was enough to gag me."

"I have a son at East Carolina. I know what you mean. My husband, Joe, and I never visit his dorm room. We always meet somewhere else."

Elsie cleared her throat and adjusted her purple hat on her fading red curls. "You know, it's only a matter of them growing up. They don't smell nearly so bad once they're adults."

Dorothy laughed loudly. "That's a good one."

"It was clever for him to spell the apartment," Elsie said. "We'll have to find another way to get to him."

"Who is he anyway?" Dorothy asked.

"He's our best suspect in our friend's death since we know he left the shop with Olivia yesterday. We may need to spell those binoculars again and go back to the crime scene."

"Really?" Dorothy sounded excited about the idea. "You know where Olivia was killed?"

"Molly's husband is a homicide detective," Elsie explained. "We went with him to see her this morning. It was extremely unpleasant. I'm not happy about going there again."

"You can stay in the car, Elsie," I told her. "But we need to take another look at the alley. There could be something that we missed. If we can find some real proof of Brian's involvement in Olivia's death, we could ask the council to take over."

"What about the police?" Elsie asked. "What are you going to tell Joe?"

"As little as possible," I replied. "I don't want him involved."

"Not much you can do about that *now*," Elsie reminded me.

"So you have magic binoculars?" Dorothy asked as we headed back to Smuggler's Arcane.

"We used them to watch you from the shop," Elsie said. "Olivia loved to watch you going in and out of the library. She was a little selfish about holding on to them, but we worked it out."

Dorothy frowned. "How could you see the library from Smuggler's Arcane? There are buildings between your shop and the library."

"That's why we spelled the binoculars." I turned in to the parking lot at the Cotton Exchange.

"I can't wait to see them!"

We went inside the shop, but Elsie couldn't remember what she'd done with the binoculars. In the meantime, two customers came in.

"I hope your monkshood is fresh." Adriana, a witch from Kure Beach, stuck her face into the paper bag and drew back quickly. "Yeah. That's *fresh*."

"Anything else with that?" I was eager for her to leave so we could take another look at the alley. There was no reason to be impatient though—Elsie was conjuring a spell to find the missing binoculars. It wasn't working very well.

"I'm looking for a new boline," a woman with blue hair told me. "Someone broke into my house last week and stole mine."

"Really?" I thought about the ritual white-handled knife. "Are you looking for a curved blade on that?"

"That would be okay." She looked at our selection and

chose one. "If I ever find out who took mine, look out. That boline belonged to my family from several generations past. My granny is gonna kill me when she finds out it's gone."

"You could put up a notice on the bulletin board by the door. We have lost-and-found items that end up here."

"This wasn't lost, it was stolen," she assured me. "But I'll try it. Thanks."

The next customer wasn't a witch. We tried not to discriminate—so long as the person wasn't doing something that could hurt them or someone else.

"I have several nice cauldrons over here." I pointed them out. "What size are you looking for?"

"I'm not really sure," the woman admitted. "I'm trying to bring forth a werewolf. Maybe it should be extra large, huh?"

"Bring forth a werewolf?" Elsie overheard our conversation. "Why ever would you want to do such a thing?"

"I was hoping he could be the father of my child. You know, sire a wolf puppy." She giggled.

"That is *completely* ridiculous," Elsie declared. "Where did you get such an odd idea?"

The woman shrugged, a little less confident about her "odd" idea. "I read a lot of werewolf and shape-shifter romances. I thought it sounded cool."

"I guess I've heard everything now." Elsie went back to trying to find the missing binoculars.

"Do you have a werewolf-sized cauldron?" the woman whispered, keeping an eye on Elsie.

I smiled and remained professional. "I think you might have to order that online. I appreciate your business. Good luck with your project."

Nora came in as the other customer was leaving. She was a practicing witch who came by regularly to refill her supplies. She knew of our dilemma and picked up on Dorothy's emanations right away.

"You finally found a witch to take one of your places," she said. "Too bad you lost Olivia. What was that about anyway?"

"We don't know yet," I admitted. "We're looking into her death."

"You know the *real* way to get power quickly is to kill a witch," she carelessly suggested. "You can mess around collecting magic tools all you want, but it takes forever and the magic doesn't last."

I didn't ask how she knew. "If witches start killing each other for their power, that could be the end of us all."

"That's right." She nodded, tight-lipped. "Armageddon."

We were all quiet for a moment after that. I bagged her supplies and handed them to her. "Thanks for stopping by."

"Will you hold a memorial for her—for witches to attend?"

"I'm not sure yet. The Grand Council wants this kept quiet. I suppose we'll wait, and find out if she was really killed by another witch."

"Spooky times we live in." She shuddered. "Magic artifacts disappearing and witches being killed." She walked out of the shop with her bag.

"*Eureka!*" Elsie called out a moment later. She held the binoculars above her head. "I found them."

Dorothy, who had been reading through an old, generic spell book, shot to her feet. "Are we going to the crime scene now?"

"I don't see why we should wait any longer." I came around the counter. "The longer we wait, the weaker the impressions will become."

We closed the shop again and got back into my car.

"Don't you have to work today?" Elsie asked our new witch.

"I took the day off. I could take *weeks* off, if I need to. I've never taken any vacation or sick leave, so I have a lot of time accumulated."

We approached the alley where Olivia had been killed. The yellow crime scene tape at each end of the old street flapped forlornly in the breeze from the river. There were no police officers working, but it appeared to be safe.

Still, the evil deed that had been done had left its shadow. There was a gray pall over the entire area that only witches could see and feel. Going into that alley wasn't a task any of us did without reservation.

"Maybe we should talk to the man who heard Olivia scream," Elsie suggested. "We might be able to pick up something more from him than he thinks he can remember."

"Is that like hypnosis?" Dorothy poked her head between the front seats.

"Something like that." I parked the car at one end of the alley. There was no point in letting Dorothy get too far ahead of herself. It would be confusing. "We should also consider trying to find out which bar or restaurant Olivia came out of before she was killed. Joe is looking for videotapes. We should be able to follow her energy signature."

Elsie shook her head. "There are only a few places around here that Olivia *would* have walked into. You know how particular she was. That narrows the search considerably."

She was right. This was an old part of town. There were unpleasant memories embedded in the broken and dirty cobblestones. Not many people with finer awareness would want to be there for long.

I took a deep, cleansing breath and gathered my thoughts around me. I felt the power of the river close to where we stood.

Elsie did the same, except I knew she had to banish the water influence from her thoughts. We were standing next to a spot that advertised flame-grilled food. I hoped she could tap into some of that fire.

Dorothy closed her eyes and tried to emulate us. She opened them quickly and stood off to one side, looking a little forlorn and embarrassed.

"You gave up," I said. "Did you try to feel the earth and the power of living things around you?"

"Kind of hard standing here between these buildings."

I noticed a small patch of velvety green moss with several tendrils of climbing weeds struggling up into the watery sunshine.

"Close your eyes," I said. "Lean down and put your hand here on the moss. Let yourself feel the strength and power of the earth. Strip away the brick and cobblestones—though they're also made of earth. The living earth fills you, Dorothy. Draw it into you and let it go."

She did as I suggested and then stood up quickly and looked at her hand.

"What was *that*? It felt like an electric shock, only different."

"That is power you can draw from the earth to help balance nature. You can call it inside you whenever you need it."

I covered her hand with mine and felt the earth magic surge inside her. The water magic had once been strong like this in me. I could still call on it, but it was weak. I knew someday it wouldn't be there at all.

"All right." I tried to keep myself from trembling. "We have to go into the alley now. Hold hands. Elsie and I will focus on Olivia. Dorothy, you focus on us."

We walked timidly under the yellow tape and proceeded to the area where the police had found Olivia's body.

There was nothing there except for a few dark stains on the wet ground that could've been blood—or grime that had been tracked around during the night.

"I can see her." Elsie's eyes were closed, but tears slipped from them. "I can *feel* her. She was so afraid. She panicked and forgot who she was, what she could do. She called out, but it wasn't a scream for help."

I saw Olivia too. She was fighting someone much stronger than she was. She knew she had no chance of winning. At the end, she was calm, and had left a message for us.

"Dorothy Lane." Dorothy was first to say it. "She called my name!"

We opened our eyes, sniffling a little from the experience. It was a sobering moment, watching helplessly as our friend was struck down.

"Why did she call for Dorothy?" Elsie pulled out her lacy purple handkerchief.

"I don't know. Maybe that was what she was thinking about. Maybe she was using her last bit of power to call Dorothy to us."

"Maybe." Elsie blew her nose loudly. "She knew we were going to need her more than ever. Trust Olivia to look after us even as she was dying."

"Was she that sure I'd want to be a witch with you all?" Dorothy shook her head. "This is very strange and scary. I didn't even know her, but I felt—*something.* I couldn't see her, but it was like I knew her. Whatever it was broke my heart."

Dorothy started sobbing. I knew it was time for us to get out of the alley. I put my arm around her and turned to leave.

Joe was standing behind us. "You shouldn't be here, Molly."

CHAPTER 7

Bless this plant and let it grow,
Hiding here, no one will know.
Strong and green, earth's tapestry,
Let it thrive, so mote it be!

I couldn't speak to Joe. My emotions were too raw. I urged Elsie and Dorothy to leave the alley. The three of us hurried under the yellow tape and out on the sidewalk.

"Molly?" Joe called after me before his long strides caught up. "I need to know what you're doing out here."

"We were putting flowers on Olivia's last place on earth." My voice cracked with tears. "We came to say a prayer for her. I'm sorry if we got in your way."

"Flowers? I didn't see any flowers." He looked back, and there was a bouquet of pink wildflowers growing from the patch of green moss. "Oh. Sorry. I didn't mean to doubt your word."

Dorothy stopped crying long enough to take a peek and mouth *Wow!* at me.

It was the combination of our magic that had made it happen. I wouldn't normally do something so flashy, but this wasn't a normal situation. I thought our grief added to the strength of the spell too.

"Listen, I'm sorry to rush you out of there that way," Joe

said. "The crime scene team is on their way to go through the alley again. I didn't expect to see you here."

"They didn't find anything the last time they went through it?" I asked.

"No. Not a thing. It's as though someone scrubbed the alley after they killed your friend."

"What about the videotapes from the bars and restaurants?"

"Nothing there either. If Olivia was in any of these places, there was no sign of her."

That was good, and bad, news.

I'd hoped we'd be able to find Olivia's killer or at least prove who it was. Most certainly the witch who'd killed Olivia had wiped away all trace of having been there. Even we hadn't been able to feel any magic left behind.

The good news was that Joe was pushed further away from Olivia's death. I knew that would be frustrating for him, but it eased my mind.

Two cars pulled up that were marked "Crime Scene Investigation." Lisbet arrived too and started walking toward us.

"Just don't go back in there again, okay, sweetie?" Joe put his arm around me and kissed my forehead. "Let *us* figure this out. Stay out of her house too. It's different now. You can't wander in and out like she's still there."

"Of course." I smiled and kissed him back.

Lisbet waved to me as Joe met her. They walked back toward the alley together.

"No sign of *anything* in the alley," Elsie muttered.

"And nothing on any videotape," I added.

"What does that mean?" Dorothy whispered.

"Combined with what happened at the house, it means magic *was* involved." I opened the car door. "It's what we feared."

"I hate to think that another witch killed Olivia for the spell book." Elsie took out her handkerchief again.

"Or the spell book was secondary, and she was killed to collect more magic."

"I wonder what part Brian Fuller played in it, if any." Elsie tried to get herself together.

"Do you think that's why she called for me when she was dying?" Dorothy didn't get in the car right away. "Maybe she needed my magic."

"I don't know." I got behind the steering wheel. "We'll have to figure that out with the rest of it."

"How are we gonna find the man who heard Olivia scream?" Dorothy finally got in.

"I'm not sure yet." My brain felt crammed too full of problems that didn't have answers. "I might be able to get Joe to tell me who he is."

"Look!" Elsie pointed in the direction of the dock. "Doesn't that look like—?"

"Brian Fuller!"

Dorothy turned her head to see where we pointed. Brian was getting on the old-time steamboat that took tourists on narrated trips of the river.

"That's him." I unfastened my seatbelt. "Let's go."

"What are the chances that he'd be here now?" Elsie queried. "It could be a trap."

I agreed, but we couldn't give up the chance to talk to him about Olivia.

"But isn't your husband going to think something weird is happening?" Dorothy asked. "He's still standing right over *there*."

I bit my lip. She was right. He was not only standing at the opening to the alley as the crime scene techs went back in, he was staring right at us.

"Does he know you're a witch?" Dorothy asked.

"No. He doesn't," Elsie answered for me. "My daughter doesn't know either. The council frowns on telling family members who aren't witches that there is magic."

"Does that mean you *can't* do it?"

Elsie shrugged. "It can be dangerous for the family. The council can get very nasty. It's probably for the best anyway. Your family might think you're a little cuckoo. My mother used to call it *touched*. Either way, you end up in therapy."

"We have to get on that riverboat." I drummed my fingers on the steering wheel. "Let's not panic. We'll work this out."

I started the engine and drove slowly past the spot where Joe was standing, even waving as I went by. I made a sudden left as soon as I'd passed him. That took us behind one of the older buildings. We parked there. "He won't see us get on the riverboat from here."

"I don't have any money for a ticket," Dorothy said. "Sorry. Librarians don't make much money, you know."

"Oh, don't worry about *that*." Elsie picked up her bag and righted her hat. "We're going to be standing right next to the old river. We have a water witch and an old ticket stub. We'll be fine."

I went up the gangplank first, feeling the depth and flow of the Cape Fear River beneath me. The young man at the admissions counter took the old ticket stub that Elsie had saved from a previous trip.

"There are three of us today." I muttered a charm as I gave it to him. If I could stand in or by the river all the time, I wouldn't even notice my waning powers.

He saluted me. "Of course, ma'am. Happy to have you on board."

We went up to the top deck and watched the activity on the boat. There was no sign of Brian Fuller.

"We saw him get on the boat," Dorothy said. "He has to be here, unless he jumped overboard."

"I don't think that happened." I was actually keeping a closer eye on Joe. He was still standing outside the alley. It would take only a turn of his head for him to see us.

In my experience with the natural world, the best way to call attention to yourself is to invite trouble by looking for it. I turned away from my husband and put my back against the rail. He was certainly more likely to see us if I kept staring at him.

"What do we do now?" Elsie asked. "This is a *big* boat."

The riverboat blew its whistle twice and cast off from the dock.

"Isn't there a spell or something you can do, Molly?" Dorothy wondered.

"It would take more preparation than I have time for now. Our best bet is to wander the boat slowly, like we're enjoying the ride, and find Brian."

"What are we going to do when we find him?" Elsie compensated for the wind blowing at her hat by sticking a large pin into it.

"We'll bind him so he has to stay with us," I replied.

"Can we do that?" she whispered. "You know I'm not at my best on the water."

"I know." I patted her hand. "But you still have something you can put into the pot. Dorothy's earth energies should be fine—even close to the water. We should be able to manage a binding spell. We'll take him back to the shop and question him."

We all agreed with the plan and started walking slowly around the top deck as the history of Wilmington unfolded around us.

We passed the USS *North Carolina* battleship as she lay at anchor for school tours and private visits. She would never set out to sea again, but the ship had faced many battles during World War II and deserved her cushy retirement.

There was a replica of a tall, three-masted sailing ship in harbor. It was modeled after one of the American blockade runners that had kept the Confederacy alive during the Civil War. At that time, the daring captains had outmaneuvered much larger ships to deliver supplies to the desperate citizens of the city.

It was painted bright blue, red and green—one of the old runners would never have wanted to draw that much attention. Hundreds of seagulls were perched on its masts.

We'd reached the bottom deck by that time. Several other passengers were going up to the top deck for a better view. There was only one other person on the bottom deck. It had to be Brian.

"He's dressed differently," Elsie noticed. "Was he wearing that cloak when he got on board?"

"No." Dorothy sounded worried. "Where did he get *that*? Is it a witch thing?"

"Slowly," I advised in a whisper as we approached him, ignoring their chatter. What difference did it make what he was wearing? "I know you don't know a binding spell yet, Dorothy. Concentrate on what we want to do. Think about Brian not walking away from us. Envision that he's bound to us by a rope. Got it?"

"I've got it."

Elsie and I repeated the binding spell that had been in our spell book. I could hear the words in my head as I thought them. It was easy to recall since I'd used it many times for various purposes—none like this one.

He was standing at the railing, looking at the city, his back to us. The large, hooded cape he wore billowed around him. It should have been simple to catch him unaware.

But I was so caught up in trying to make the binding spell as strong as possible that I didn't question anything until it was too late.

There was no face—no form that I could see—inside the cloak. If Brian had been there, he was gone.

"Molly?" Dorothy's voice was shaking as we faced the empty cloak.

Before I could reassure her, I heard a muttered spell, and in the blink of an eye, we were falling from the bottom deck of the boat and into the cold river water.

CHAPTER 8

I am invisible to my enemies.
They will not see me until it is too late.
I will bring them to their knees.
For their defeat, I wait.

I could happily have drifted in the river forever. There was no sense of panic or worry about survival. I felt more at home in water than I did on land.

Something rapped on the top of my head. It was Elsie. She pointed toward the surface, her cheeks puffed out with air, and started kicking her feet.

I became aware that my lungs were burning. It was one of those cases where the spirit was willing, but the flesh was weak. I started kicking my feet too and surfaced right next to her.

Dorothy's head was already above the water. "What was that? Did someone throw us overboard? All of a sudden, I was in the water."

"That"—Elsie spit out brown river water—"was a powerful witch."

"He saw us coming," I agreed. "He'd already worked his spell. We were too close to do anything about it."

"Well, let's face it—we've never had a run-in with a witch like him." Elsie splashed around. "I think I've lost my shoes."

It was funny in a way because she was clutching her bag, and the pin still held her drooping hat on her head. It looked like a sodden purple pancake, but it was still there.

"Is there a spell that can protect us from powerful witches?" Dorothy asked with a wealth of fear in her voice.

"I'm sure there is," I responded. "But you have to realize what you're up against first."

"And then you have to be strong enough to deal with it." Elsie gave me a look that said I shouldn't be too encouraging with our new witch.

The captain of the riverboat had made a distress call to the Coast Guard vessel that was in dock. He'd already thrown out life preservers. They floated on top of the river close to where we'd surfaced.

"Oh dear." Elsie shook her head. "This is going to be a mess."

It was more of a mess than she realized. Joe had jumped on the Coast Guard vessel—that's what comes of focusing your thoughts on someone you don't want to notice you. I'd never seen his face look quite the way it did that day. I couldn't tell if he was angry or scared.

The Coast Guard crew helped us on board and gave us blankets. They were polite and deferential. They offered to call an ambulance if we needed one.

Joe sat beside me. Somehow, I'd become separated from Dorothy and Elsie. They were laughing and talking with the crew about the experience. I was stuck with a slightly angry husband who didn't understand what had happened.

"What in the world is going on?" His dark eyes were full of concern. "What made you decide to take a trip on the riverboat when you were headed home or to the shop?"

"I can't really explain." My mind was racing. We were

walking a thin line between the truth and what I could get him to believe.

"Is it the new girl? What's her name? Dorothy? Is she forcing you and Elsie to do things you don't want to do?"

"Of course not. Dorothy is a librarian, and a very nice, sensible person. She probably has trouble collecting overdue book fees."

"Then what is it, Molly?" He gently moved a strand of hair out of my eye. "You can trust me with whatever is going on. Are you in some kind of trouble? Is that why Olivia was killed?"

What could I tell him that would throw him off? I was in the middle of the river, strong with the water, but had never felt so helpless. My mind was still trying to wrap itself around the attack on the boat. I didn't know what to say.

"You know I trust you, Joe." I took a deep breath. I was going to have to jump in with at least a partial truth. "We thought we recognized a man on the boat. He might have been dating Olivia. But it wasn't him."

He looked almost comically surprised. "And you were going to tell me this when?"

"I wanted to surprise you. I thought *we* could solve Olivia's murder together."

It was almost too much for him to take in. "*What?* Where did you get such a crazy idea? The police will be lucky if *we* can find Olivia's killer. How did you even think of such a thing?"

I shrugged. He was angry, but he was a safe distance from magic.

"You're my husband. It's not like we haven't talked about some of your cases. I taught you how to make an omelet. I was thinking that I had probably heard enough to solve this case."

He struggled to get his emotions under control. "You

need to tell me everything, Molly. I hope I'm clear about that. I need to know all about this man on the boat, and anything else you can tell me that could help."

I nodded and promised that I would. My blanket was slipping down. As I reached to pull it up, our hands met.

Joe pulled the blanket more securely onto my shoulders. His gaze softened. "Don't *ever* do this again, sweetheart. You just took ten years off my life that I didn't have to lose. If that man had killed you—I don't know."

I put my arms around him, sorry that I had hurt him, but more determined that we should find the killer before him.

If Brian was the witch who had killed Olivia—which seemed more possible than ever—he was very strong. He was probably stronger than the three of us had been in our prime. He would have killed Joe without thinking. The only thing that had saved Elsie, Dorothy and me was my affinity with the water.

Joe could never find this man. We were going to have to take care of it and hand Brian over to the Grand Council. There was no crime worse than killing another witch. They would act appropriately.

"I'm sorry, Joe." I smiled and kissed him. "I love you. Let's sort this out later."

He held me close for a long time. We were still together when the Coast Guard vessel docked again. The crew helped Elsie and Dorothy off the boat. I got off with Joe.

I saw Lisbet waiting for him on the dock, a puzzled expression on her handsome face. No doubt Joe would tell her my story. She was his partner, and that tended to make people close. I was sure she knew all about our lives together.

I didn't like that she'd think I was a little crazy, trying to solve Olivia's murder myself. It couldn't be helped. It kept Joe away from my reality and left us free to continue our search. Now that we had a better idea of what we were facing, I hoped we'd be better prepared.

"I'm going to take everyone to their houses and then go home and change clothes," I told Joe. "Maybe we could have lunch somewhere and talk about everything that's happened."

"That would be fine," he said. "But I need Elsie and the new girl—if she knows anything about this man who might have been dating Olivia—to come with you. We'll have to interview all of you."

"It was only me and Elsie. We met Dorothy later. She's going to help out at the shop."

Smuggler's Arcane had always been the perfect cover for our magic. It gave us a reason to be together at all hours. Joe had never questioned how important the shop was to me. I'd always supposed that he was glad I had something to do during the long hours he spent at his job.

"Maybe this isn't the best time to talk about it, Molly, but I think you should consider giving up the shop. We don't need the money—if you've ever made any money at it. Olivia's death might be the right time to call an end to it. Elsie certainly isn't getting any younger. Maybe the new girl would like to buy it."

It was like a sword to my heart. The shop had been more than a distraction, it had been a place to store all the magic artifacts that I hadn't wanted to bring home. I knew I was going to have to say good-bye to the place when we retired and moved to Boca, but I wasn't ready yet.

"You're right. This isn't a good time to talk about it. Not so soon after Olivia's death. I'm sorry, Joe. I can't think about that right now. I'll bring Elsie for lunch after we've changed."

He caught my arm as I would have walked away. "I'm sorry, Molly. I didn't mean to hurt your feelings."

"I'm fine." I was very conscious of Lisbet watching us. "Can you have lunch with a suspect?"

He laughed and kissed me. "You're *not* a suspect. I just need to know what's going on in your head. Let's meet at Riverboat Landing. Give me a call when you leave the house."

We separated as we walked down the dock to the shore. I didn't want to know what he said to Lisbet or her opinion of me.

"Is everything okay?" Elsie whispered as we walked back where the car was parked. "You didn't tell him, did you?"

"Of course not. I love him. I don't want *anything* to happen to him."

"Good." She let out a relieved breath. "What now?"

"We go home and change clothes. Joe wants to talk to us about what's happening with Olivia and a man she might have been dating—no name. I had to tell him something. A little truth seemed like a better idea than the whole truth."

"I see." Dorothy looked out over the river with a mournful expression. "So your husband can't help us with Olivia's killer."

"No. It would be too dangerous for someone without magic."

"I thought you said there *weren't* good and bad witches," Dorothy accused. "Just witches. That seemed like a very bad witch to me."

"It was a very bad witch," I agreed. "We've never known someone like this before. It was frightening for us too."

Elsie took off her hat and shook the water out of it. "What do we do now, Molly?"

"We lie to Joe, I'm afraid. I kept him out of the magic part by telling him we were trying to solve Olivia's murder by ourselves."

"You did *what*?" Elsie made a hissing noise like a cat.

"All I can say is that we'd better be having lunch someplace *really* good."

Dorothy shivered and got in the car. I could see she was deeply shaken by what had happened. I wished I had a better answer for her.

Riverboat Landing was a quaint, historic restaurant that faced the river. It had private balconies and the best flatbread pizza in Wilmington.

You'd think I'd have been tired of the water after the dunking I'd received, but it was still pleasant to look out and see the river. The weather had cleared a little, and a few artists were out on the riverfront, painting the beautiful scene.

Elsie didn't feel the same way. She turned her chair a little so she didn't have to look at the water. She also had chicken salad because pizza upset her stomach.

"How are you feeling?" Joe asked her.

"I've felt better, thanks. I didn't think Aleese was ever going to let me out of the house again. Sometimes that girl goes a little too far trying to protect me from myself."

Joe sipped his water as we waited for our meals. "Maybe she's trying to protect you from Molly."

Elsie's red eyebrows went up. "I would hope she'd know better than that by now too."

"It was probably a little startling seeing you come home soaking wet," he continued. "Did you tell her you fell off the riverboat?"

Elsie glanced at me as if to say, *Is that our story*?

"I told Joe about the man we think could have murdered Olivia," I filled in for her. "And then we fell off the riverboat."

"Oh yes. *Yes*." Elsie picked up her glass of red wine and mumbled into it.

"It must've been hard for all *three* of you to fall off the boat." Joe seemed like he was musing about the experience, but I knew he was fishing for more information. It was the way he thought.

"It all happened so fast," I added quickly. "We didn't expect anything like it."

That was certainly the truth. While I'd been home changing clothes, I'd confided what had happened to Isabelle. She agreed that the man who'd accomplished that feat was certainly powerful. She warned me against future encounters with him.

The problem was—I had no choice. It was either that or let Joe run into him. I didn't think it was likely the police would find a strong witch like him, but anything was possible. At least Elsie, Dorothy and I could handle basic defense.

"What did he look like?" Joe asked. "The man who might have been dating Olivia."

"I thought we were being interviewed after lunch?" I smiled at him and separated my silverware from my napkin.

"This isn't an interview. This is your husband and Elsie's friend asking what you remember of the encounter. Did he rush at you? Did he have a weapon?"

Elsie excused herself to go to the ladies' room. I glared at Joe after she was gone.

"It may not be an interview, but it feels like more than friendly questions from my husband."

"I'm sorry, sweetie. I was discussing this with Lisbet. It's hard to believe that *none* of you screamed. How did he push you off the boat?"

Lisbet. I knew they were going to talk about us. It was a little annoying but not unexpected.

"It's difficult to describe." I frantically tried to come up with a reasonable explanation. "For one thing, we were afraid of him. We're convinced that he killed Olivia."

He nodded. "But not afraid enough to call me when you saw him? I was standing right here by the dock. You have a cell phone. I'm pretty sure all of you have cell phones. One call, Molly. That's all it would've taken."

"I didn't think of it." That was the truth too. I *did* think about staying out of Joe's radar. Not that I would've called and endangered his life.

"Do you know this man? How long do you think he was dating Olivia? Were the three of you friends with him? Is that why you don't want to tell me who he is?"

I realized that he sincerely wanted to understand what had happened. I wanted to help him, but I could only mislead.

"None of us had ever seen him before. He strolled into the shop one day, and Olivia helped him look for what he wanted. They took a fancy to each other and left together. Does that sum it up for you, Detective Renard?"

He sat back in his chair and frowned. "You make me feel like you're hiding something. I've known you a long time, Molly. You're not a good liar."

It was all I could do not to laugh. *Not a good liar?* He had no idea.

I wasn't proud of the fact that I had lied to him since the day we'd met. It wasn't my wish to keep him in the dark about my activities as a witch. But it was necessary, and I'd become very adept at it.

I glanced down at my plate, the sun reflecting off the white china. What was I missing that Joe was picking up on? I knew he was good at his job, but this was surprising. We'd never had a clash of this type before. Was I handling it wrong?

Elsie returned as lunch was served. She ordered another glass of wine and shrugged as I wordlessly questioned her intentions. Was she trying to get tipsy? Wasn't that going to make talking to Joe more difficult?

"Do you think the two of you could help a sketch artist with a drawing of this man?"

"Of course." Elsie dug into her chicken salad as though it were the most important thing in the world. "I got a good look at him."

Elsie winked at me, and I shook my head. She obviously didn't understand the plan. What was she saying? We couldn't sketch Brian for the police and help them find him.

CHAPTER 9

Despite the dark, despite the night.
I seek the truth, to bring the light.
I see through lies, I see through pain,
The truth shall rise, reveal the way.

Elsie drank more wine and polished off her chicken salad. She kept making observations about people walking by on the street and boats moving back and forth on the river. What Joe had said seemed to have no effect at all on her.

But then he wasn't *her* husband.

It was a different story for me. I had never been so angry with Joe. He'd treated us like we were suspects in Olivia's murder. I saw no sign of him backing down from it either. Between him and Elsie—we'd be ruined.

After our regrettable attempt at a pleasant lunch together, Elsie and I drove to the police station in front of Joe's car, as though he were escorting us. I had to go along with his suggestion that we might be able to identify a photo of the mystery man Olivia might have been dating or help draw a sketch of him. Not to do so would've meant yet another accusatory conversation.

Besides, there was still a possibility of finding the man who'd heard Olivia scream in the alley. We had a better shot at it being at the police department—if I could keep Elsie from spilling the beans about *everything*. I was a little angry at her too.

"What was that all about?" Elsie's words were a little slurred.

"I don't know. I don't like it." I realized I was gripping the wheel so hard that my knuckles were white. "I know he's upset about the case, but I didn't like being interrogated—especially not by my own husband."

Elsie squeezed my hand. "Molly, we want the same thing—Olivia's killer. We've never faced a threat like this before. Maybe we should let Joe help us."

That made me laugh. "We've never faced *any* threat before."

"That's true." She giggled in her high-pitched schoolgirl voice. "I think the only threat we've ever had as witches was keeping those terrible big rats out of the cave. We came up with a permanent spell to take care of it, as long as we leave the cauldron down there."

I took a deep breath and tried to calm down. Hyperventilating wouldn't help. "I know you're right. I know we're not experienced in dealing with this kind of thing and Joe is, but we can't involve him. I don't want Cassandra paying him a visit and wiping away all of his memories to be sure he doesn't know anything about magic."

"You're right. I don't know if we could get those memories back." Elsie gazed out the window.

"I remember that time Cassandra wiped away poor Walter Slabs's memory. His wife was a witch too. What was her name?"

"Sylvia."

"Yes, Sylvia." I glanced in the rearview mirror at Joe. "The four of us managed to retrieve most of his memories after the council took them away. I don't know of a fourth witch we could work with again."

"True. I think Sylvia moved to Jamaica with Walter."

"I'd like Joe and me to make it to Boca while he still has all his memories."

"I know you would, dear. But we're never leaving Wilmington if we can't find our spell book."

"And we can't find our spell book unless we figure out who killed Olivia and took it."

"That's right. Eyes on the prize, my husband used to say. Sometimes I miss him saying that ridiculous stuff. I always miss him sleeping next to me at night, even though I had to wear earplugs so I wouldn't hear his snoring."

"I can't tell Joe that Olivia was a witch and was killed by another witch. I also don't want him and Lisbet to somehow get lucky and find Brian. They wouldn't stand a chance against him. We have to get a case together that we can present to the council. They could handle him."

Elsie rolled her eyes. "I'm not sure we could've handled Brian, even when the three of us were young. He was very strong. I've never felt so much strength. And why didn't he kill us? He could have."

"I think he was giving us a warning," I whispered back. "He knew we couldn't hurt him. He was mocking us."

"I wish I understood any of this, Molly. I'd like to know why Olivia called out Dorothy's name as she was dying too. I know she really liked the girl and wanted her to take one of our places, but surely her dying thoughts wouldn't have been of her."

"I know what you mean. There are too many things that don't make sense." I parked the car outside the police station. Joe was waiting on the sidewalk for us.

I felt the faintest prickle of distrust in his attitude, as though he had waited because he was afraid that we wouldn't come inside. *Where did that come from?*

It unsettled me and made me wonder exactly what was wrong. It felt like something more than him just being angry because we were trying to find Olivia's killer without his help.

Joe led us into the conference room rather than an interrogation room. That was sweet of him. I wouldn't say it changed my feelings about the way lunch had gone, but being guilty of not being able to tell him the truth had put me in a forgiving mood.

"Can I get you some coffee or soda?" His tone was pleasant.

Elsie nodded as she sat down. "I'd like a coffee, please. A double espresso would be nice. Do you have any aspirin? My head is starting to hurt."

"I'll see what I can find," he promised. "Molly?"

"Nothing, thanks."

He left us, closing the door behind him. The bigger room, where I'd attended birthday and retirement parties in the past, didn't put me more at ease.

Especially when Lisbet came in to question us.

"Ladies." She tossed a thin file on the table and adjusted her duty belt that held her gun, badge, handcuffs and pepper spray as she sat down. "I only have a few questions for you about the death of your friend. I'm sorry for your loss. I'm sure we all want to find her killer."

Lisbet's long black hair was held back in a ponytail holder, the only way I had ever seen her wear it. She was totally dressed in black—the good black that hasn't been washed too much and become gray. She wore knee-high boots with at least three-inch heels all year long, regardless of the hot summer weather. She was thin and short, even shorter than Elsie's five feet, but she was tough.

"We'll do what we can to help," I assured her.

She opened the file and rifled through the papers in it. "Olivia had no family, is that right? No one to inherit her property."

"That's right." I wondered where Joe was. Maybe he'd sent Lisbet in because of our argument during lunch.

"What about an ex-husband or a live-in lover?"

"No. She always lived alone." I glanced up when Joe returned with Elsie's plain coffee and aspirin.

"Sorry." He apologized as he set down the paper cup. "We were fresh out of espresso."

"Oh, that's fine." Elsie smiled at him. "Thank you so much, Joe."

He took a seat at the far end of the table beside Lisbet. Elsie and I were together at the other end.

No doubt this was their normal procedure when they worked together, I assured myself. It wasn't a personal slight.

"What about the two of you?" Lisbet continued her questioning. "Has Olivia left her property to one, or both, of you?"

What is she getting at? "The only thing she left us was her part of our shop, Smuggler's Arcane. I don't know who she would've left her personal possessions to."

Lisbet nodded and continued to peruse the files. "Joe tells me she'd gone out on a date with someone before she died."

"We don't know that for certain," Elsie corrected her. "All we said was that she may have been dating someone. It may not have been that night."

I knew she was trying to throw off the questions to protect Joe and Lisbet. I didn't think it was going to work.

"And you said his name is?"

"We don't know," I quickly answered. "She never introduced us."

"Thanks." She smiled at me.

Elsie glanced at me, frowned and took her aspirin.

"And you encountered this same man again on the riverboat today." Lisbet looked at me and Elsie. "Tell us *exactly* what happened."

Two hours later, Elsie and I swept out of the police station, thoroughly disgusted. We'd been mentally poked and prodded by Joe and Lisbet. We'd looked through books containing pictures of felons—of course Brian wasn't in them. And we'd helped draw a sketch of Brian that looked nothing at all like him.

But we'd also managed to learn the name of the man at the dock the night Olivia was killed, the one who'd heard her scream. His name was Colt Manning. He was a commercial fisherman.

"I am not happy about this, Molly." Elsie clutched her green bag to her.

"I'm not either. I'm sorry I said anything to Joe. If I weren't so worried about him going after Brian, I wouldn't have."

But we didn't know the half of it yet.

Aleese was waiting outside by my car. As soon as she saw us, she ran to her mother's side. "What in the world were you two thinking? First you get attacked on the riverboat, and then the police bring you here for questioning. What have you been doing?"

"The police didn't arrest us, dear," Elsie assured her. "No need for any drama."

"No need to worry about my seventy-year-old mother falling into the river and coming home soaking wet? You could have died. This has got to stop. It's bad enough the three of you sit around that depressing, dusty old shop all the time. No telling how many viruses are spread in there."

"*Sat* around," I corrected. "Olivia is dead."

"Did you tell her about Joe catching us at the crime scene?" Elsie ignored her daughter's tirade.

"No. Did you?"

"No way. You see how hysterical she gets over the least *little* thing." Elsie fumed. "Joe probably called her for my own good."

"I'm talking to *both* of you." Aleese focused on us. "Neither one of you should be at the shop anymore, like Joe said. You should sell it and move on."

That made me furious again. Joe had not only called her about us being in the police station, he'd said something to her about us selling the shop. I couldn't imagine what was wrong with him.

"I'm taking you home, Mom." Aleese grabbed her mother's arm and started pulling her toward her car. "I'm beginning to think Molly is a bad influence on you."

"I'll talk to you later, after we've settled this." Elsie went along with her daughter.

"All right. I'm going to see Dorothy at the library. I hope she isn't completely put off by everything that's happened."

"Give her my best." Elsie waved as Aleese closed the car door.

"Okay."

Aleese's eyes were riveted on me as she went around to the driver's side. She seemed genuinely afraid I might snatch Elsie out of the car before she could spirit her away.

I got in my car after Aleese and Elsie were gone and drove to the downtown branch of the library. I pulled into the parking deck, grabbed my bag, and locked the car doors.

"There you are, Molly." Cassandra appeared on the hood of my car, lying across it like a fashion model. "I've been looking for you."

CHAPTER 10

This circle I draw.
Evil dismayed.
Light the way.
Heed my call.

"The leopard skin suits you." I remarked on her outfit. It was skintight from neck to feet. I felt sure it was *faux* skin, but it didn't really matter.

"Thanks." She slid from the car, her long black hair swishing as she moved. "You seem to be having a few problems. I'll be glad to help."

In my experience, Cassandra, and the Grand Council in general, were never much help. I had known of cases where'd they made things much worse.

The problem with Sylvia and her husband, for instance. Cassandra had recommended Walter's memory wipe to the council. She was relentless in persecuting them. Once it was over, we were able to help Sylvia some small amount. We hadn't dared before because we didn't want to face the council.

"I'm fine, thanks. Just going into the library to speak with our new witch."

"What about the witch on the boat? It looked like you could've used a hand with that."

I faced her curiously. I was at a disadvantage in stature, magic and fashion.

"What do you know about that witch?" I asked her with the strict, no-nonsense tones of the schoolteacher I'd been for thirty years.

She shrugged. "Nothing much—except that you should be careful if you plan on retiring someday. Word on the ether is that there's a witch killing other witches and stealing magical items of power."

"And who is that?"

"We aren't sure yet."

"Why isn't the council doing something about it?"

"We're working on it. We don't want to persecute one of our own without being *sure* the witch is doing something wrong. It's not against the rules to 'inherit' another witch's spell book."

"But it is against the rules to kill another witch and *steal* her spell book, isn't it? We believe Olivia is dead by Brian Fuller's hand. She went out with him right before she died. We traced him back to his room at the community college. It shouldn't be that hard for you to do the same."

"You have no real proof that Brian Fuller killed Olivia, just like your husband isn't sure what's going on. You haven't told him about being a witch, have you?"

"No. I made up a story after we fell in the river. He's nowhere near thinking that magic exists or that I could be involved with it."

"That's good. What about your spell book? Is that still safe?"

"Yes." I lied with a straight face. Joe didn't realize just how *good* I was at lying.

"Well, keep your wits about you. You and Elsie aren't

strong enough to handle whatever is going on. I'm going to give you something to summon me if you get backed into a corner. I can't keep my eye on you all the time, you know."

In an instant, she was gone. In her place, rolling on the concrete, was a ring. I put it on my finger. It sized itself perfectly to fit me.

I wished that it made me feel better. I knew I wouldn't use it unless I was truly afraid this rogue witch was going to kill me. I didn't need the council's help that badly.

Thinking about everything Cassandra had told me—and *not* told me—I went into the library. Was it just my imagination or was there a touch of fear in her voice when she spoke of the rogue witch? She also wasn't in any hurry to help us find him either.

I found Dorothy sitting on the floor stacking books in the children's section of the library. I could tell she wasn't happy to see me.

"Hi, Molly."

"Hello, Dorothy." I sat on one of the small wood chairs. "I see you decided to work today after all."

She smiled at the books that surrounded us. "You know, my whole life, every time things happened that didn't make sense to me, I could come here and bury my nose in a book, and it was better. I still feel like that. I feel like nothing can hurt me here. None of it is real."

"Unlike finding out that there are witches and magic in the world, right?"

"Yes. I thought it was bad finding out that I'd been adopted when I was a kid. Finding out that I was a witch was much worse. I could always imagine that my parents were killed trying to save me from something terrible. How do I explain witchcraft? I don't know how we made those flowers grow today. I thought that thing on the boat was going to kill me. I'm not ready to die. Magic isn't fun like I thought it would be."

I looked at all the decorative items in the children's section and remembered all the times that Mike and I had come here to read books on rainy days when we couldn't play outside.

Dorothy was a little older than my son, but she still felt like a child to me. She was a child who'd been abandoned, a witch left on her own to figure out the mystery of who she was and what she could do.

I was glad Olivia had found her so we had a chance to correct that slight in her childhood. Being a witch meant being unique and seeing the world in a different way than most people. It didn't matter if Dorothy knew she was a witch or not, that feeling was still there.

"I'm not going to lie to you and tell you this is an easy road to follow," I finally said. "But being a witch with no idea of who you are and what you can do is even worse. Magic, *earth magic*, courses through you like your life's blood. You can't stop it, and it will be hard now to ignore it. You need me and Elsie as much we need you."

Tears welled in her eyes. Her smile faltered when she looked back at me. "I don't think I can do this, Molly. I'm scared. This is too weird, you know? I don't think I'm cut out to be a witch. Is that okay?"

I patted her hand. "It's your choice. You have to do what's right for you. You know where we are if you change your mind."

"Thanks, but I don't think I will."

On the verge of crying myself, I walked out of the library with my back straight and my head high. Though it had been a difficult day and everything seemed to be falling apart, I had to believe things would get better.

If Dorothy wasn't the right witch for us, there would be another. Elsie and I would find Olivia's killer and our spell book. Joe would get back to normal.

I'd always been a bit of an optimist. Olivia had teased

me about it. She didn't have my sense of the world mostly being in balance.

Her view was darker and sometimes scarier. That was why she'd never committed to another person and had refused to bear a child to take her place. She believed the world was essentially bad. I could never agree with her, even though it would've been impossible for two women to be any closer than we were.

I went home and dropped down into a chair, leaning my head back as Isabelle came to sit on my lap. My hand stroked her without thinking, her soft fur and calming presence making me feel a little better.

I closed my eyes and thought about Olivia. There was no time to mourn her properly, not right now. Too much was going on that threatened the foundation of my entire life. I had to focus on moving forward, working my plan as I saw it.

Isabelle's hiss alerted me to something in the house that wasn't right. I opened my eyes, and there was the ghost ball I had followed before finding out about Olivia's death.

I stared at the glowing presence right in front of my face. I knew this was Olivia. Ghosts weren't my specialty, but I could *feel* her presence—I could almost smell her perfume.

She'd wanted to let me know what had happened to her in the alley, and she had something she wanted to tell me.

Isabelle jumped down with another hiss at the ghost ball. She didn't care if it was Olivia or not, ghosts didn't belong in *her* house.

"Olivia? Is that you?" I stuck my hand forward with the intention of touching the ball of energy.

The front door opened quickly and slammed shut. "Mom? Are you here?"

It was Mike, home unexpectedly, probably with six loads of dirty clothes.

I glanced away for an instant, and when I looked back,

the ghost ball was gone. I was disappointed. I guess I'd hoped Olivia had some answers for me. Instead, I was left with the same bitter feeling of frustration. This day just needed to end.

"Michael!" I rushed to his side, almost tripping over his duffel bags. "I'm so glad to see you."

I hugged him. He *let* me hug him, with a small pat on the back. It used to be much better when he was ten. Those years were long gone. I was looking forward to grandchildren who wouldn't mind being cuddled.

"This is a surprise," I told him. "You're home a few weeks early."

My son looked more like his father—tall and lanky but with my blue eyes. He had a quick sense of humor and more curiosity than most people about how things worked. That was why he'd decided to become an engineer.

I'd long ago released any lingering disappointment that he hadn't inherited my abilities. I didn't love him any less for it. It was my choice to marry someone with no magic. I knew it was a good chance that my children wouldn't have magic either.

"I know!" He didn't seem happy to be there. "I left school. I'm done, Mom. I don't need it anymore. I hope you and Dad aren't too disappointed."

"Has the whole world gone insane?" Joe asked that night as we were getting dressed to take our son out for dinner at his favorite restaurant. "Are we supposed to be *happy* that Mike isn't going to be an engineer after that's all he wanted to be from the time he was five years old?"

I was looking in the mirror, trying to make my fine brown hair do something besides lie there limply. "I don't know what to tell you. He's an adult. There's not much we can do about it."

Joe's frown in the mirror behind me was like a thundercloud. "There's plenty we can do about it. Instead, we're going out to celebrate this stupid idea. We should tell him to go back to school right now!"

"Don't you think we should hear him out before we pass judgment? He's dealing with some problem, Joe. We can still talk him around once we understand what's wrong."

"It doesn't matter what's wrong, Molly. Whatever made him drop out of college is a bad idea."

I got up and put my arms around his neck, looking deep into his troubled eyes. "He's here. Let's have dinner and find out what's going on. Let's not alienate him when he needs us."

He kissed me quickly and turned away. "I guess we don't have any choice."

Where was my wildly romantic husband who would never have kissed my cheek and left me in the bedroom by myself? Maybe he was right and the world had gone insane. It certainly felt that way.

One bit of good news shortly after Mike got home—Elsie had told her daughter that she would move out if Aleese didn't leave her alone. It didn't make much sense to me since the house belonged to Elsie. But whatever worked to keep us together was what mattered.

"That's one piece of the puzzle back where it belongs," I told Isabelle. "We have to hold on to what we have right now. We can always add the other pieces as we go along."

She agreed and rubbed her head against my leg, requesting salmon for dinner instead of tuna. I laughed and fed her before we left. It was an easy thing to do that didn't make my brain ache like so many other things I'd been thinking about.

We left the house in Joe's SUV and drove to Flaming Amy's Burrito Barn on Oleander. This was Mike's favorite place to eat.

"I'm starving!" he told us as we walked into the restaurant. "I'm glad we could come here."

Joe kind of grunted at his words. The waiter, who knew us well, found us a quiet table in the back so we could talk. The restaurant was packed, as always.

"We'd like to talk about why you left school," I said as we sat down.

"Does there have to be a reason?" Mike picked up a menu. "I'm old enough to know what I want."

"And that is?" Joe's eyes narrowed.

"I want to be free to start my life," Mike said in a belligerent tone. "I've spent years in college. I don't want to be an engineer anymore."

Mike didn't seem to notice how angry his father was. We ordered dinner and got our drinks as Mike went on and on about how excited he was and what a good thing this was going to be.

I kept listening to him, hoping he'd give away what was *really* happening in his life. There hadn't been anything in his texts or phone calls that had made me think something was wrong. Whatever had happened was sudden, which probably meant he hadn't had a chance to think it over.

Our dinner had arrived, thankfully. Mike was finally out of words as he started eating. Joe was too angry to speak by this time. I knew it was a slow simmer that would erupt if he didn't understand the problem Mike was facing. I wanted to prevent that—I had enough unhappy things going on right now without dealing with something between them.

As I gazed around the crowded restaurant, I caught sight of Brian Fuller. He was sitting at a table only a few yards away with a pretty blonde as his companion. They were smiling and enjoying their meal.

Joe got a call from Lisbet and went outside to answer it. Mike went to the restroom.

It was crazy, I know, to approach Brian after his reception on the boat. What can I say? I felt desperate to find closure and put an end to whatever the disagreement was between us. At that moment, I even considered that Brian might *not* have killed Olivia. Maybe he just needed someone to listen to his story. Besides, this was a public place. He wouldn't dare use magic here.

I got up from my table and crossed the restaurant to him.

CHAPTER 11

Courage take and courage keep,
Bravery in my heart doth leap,
Faith and patience cover me,
Now until the end I seek.

"Molly, isn't it?" Brian put out a hand and shook mine. "Would you like to join us?"

"No, thank you." I glanced at the pretty blonde. She wasn't a witch. "You might want to ask your friend to powder her nose while we talk."

"Is there a problem?" He actually appeared surprised to see me and not a bit reticent to talk.

"I'm here about *Olivia*."

Brian took the hint and asked the blonde to give us a few minutes. She sulked, prettily, but left the table. "I don't know what Olivia told you, but we aren't only seeing each other. She doesn't want that kind of relationship any more than I do."

What was he saying? "Olivia is *dead*. Murdered. She died after the two of you left the shop together. Don't tell me you didn't know."

He glanced around the room. "I had no idea. I'm so sorry. She was a wonderful woman."

"You tossed me and my friends into the river. Why was

that, if you weren't trying to protect yourself from our accusations?"

"Molly, I didn't hurt Olivia. I don't know what you're talking about us being on a boat. I just got back from Charleston with Stephanie." He nodded toward the bathroom.

I let myself take a deep breath so I could feel his magic. He didn't *feel* like the witch we'd faced on the boat, but if he was powerful enough, he could mask his strength too.

"I think we should talk to the Grand Council about what happened."

His eyes darkened. "I don't like what you're saying. I'm not going before the council because you think I did something wrong. I didn't hurt Olivia, and that's that."

I studied him as I twisted Cassandra's ring on my finger. Would she come? The council was used to dealing with problems like this—I wasn't. I knew there wasn't much proof against him. I just wanted them to handle the situation so I could get my family back on track and mourn my friend.

"I think you should go, Molly." He was drawing magic to him for protection.

I put my hand on my cauldron I wore. Was there enough strength in it to help me?

I could feel the physical walls of the room melting away. There was a windstorm in Brian's eyes. *An air witch.* He could be as powerful as any water witch, definitely more powerful than me.

"Molly?" Joe was standing beside the table. His frown was as dark as the river during a storm. "Is this a new friend of yours?"

"Just an acquaintance," I told him, stumbling to my feet. What had I been thinking coming over here? I took Joe's hand and pulled him away.

"Who was that?" He glanced back at Brian.

"Someone I know from Smuggler's Arcane," I lied. "I was telling him about Olivia. That's all."

I'd been so close to ruining years of effort to protect Joe and Mike from magic. I couldn't let Brian draw me out into the open just to prove that he killed Olivia. I needed proof—hard proof. I couldn't let my emotions get carried away.

Mike was back too when we reached the table. "I thought you two had left without me."

"Your mother was explaining to a friend that Olivia was dead," Joe said.

Mike was horrified. "I'm sorry, Mom. I didn't know. What happened?"

I gave him a cursory explanation.

"I'm so sorry, Mom." Mike reached out his hand to me. "I know they'll find her killer."

"I'm sure you're right." I smiled at him. "Excuse me. I'm going to the ladies' room."

I walked away on unsteady legs. The whole incident had scared me more than being dunked in the river. I hadn't proven anything about Brian. I was going to have to be more careful in the future. I realized that I'd revealed my weakness to him—he knew about Joe and Mike.

In the ladies' room, I looked at my face in the big mirror. Fear fairly seeped from every pore. I was going to have to do a better job of disguising my feelings. I might not be able to match Brian's magic, but I could certainly hold my own in keeping up a good poker face.

I splashed a little water on my face and blotted it with a paper towel. My hands were shaky and cold. This wasn't the Molly Addison Renard I wanted to show when I walked out of the bathroom.

I glanced around and knew I was alone. I filled one of the sinks with water and plunged my hands into it, muttering a spell for courage as I did so. The water would enhance my magic. I closed my eyes and felt warm belief and steadiness flow into me.

By the time I left a few minutes later, the spell had taken effect. My cheeks were slightly pink, and my gait was confident. I picked up my bag with a sure hand and smiled at my reflection in the mirror. That was better. Maybe my magic was waning, but I didn't have to look like it.

There was a small alcove leading away from the bathrooms, separating the diners from that area. As I left the ladies' room, I noticed Brian waiting for me there, leaning negligently against the wall with a frown on his handsome young face.

"I could feel the magic from here." He slid his hands into his pockets. "It wasn't very strong, but when you know what you're looking for, it's obvious."

I couldn't walk away from this direct challenge. "I'm just looking for the truth about what happened to Olivia. If you aren't guilty of killing her and stealing our spell book, you have nothing to fear from the council."

"I didn't kill Olivia or steal anything from her. Leave me alone, Molly. I don't want any trouble, but now that I know about your family—"

He walked away, his threat lingering behind him like strong perfume. I wanted to reach out and drag him before the council. I twisted Cassandra's ring until it burned my finger. I couldn't stop him.

I almost couldn't believe what he was saying. He might not have killed Olivia, but he was breaking every sacred oath any witch had ever taken by threatening me. Maybe it would be enough to get Cassandra to take me seriously— when I saw her again.

I tried to find that courage I'd built up in the ladies' room. Maybe I'd done too good a job coming right out and confronting Brian. My hands were shaking again when I got back to our table. It wasn't from fear this time though; it was outrage.

"Are you okay?" Joe asked.

"I'm fine." I looked at Mike. "I think we should go."

He got up and pushed his chair under the table. "I'll wait for you outside."

Joe didn't seem like he was in any rush to leave. He sipped his coffee and stared at the people around us. "Did Mike say anything that gave you a hint what his problem is?"

"No. I'm afraid not. But we have time, Joe. We can figure it out and influence Mike into going back to East Carolina."

He squeezed my hand. "At least we agree about *that*, Molly."

I knew he was referring to his idea that I should give up Smuggler's Arcane and what he probably thought of as my crazy idea to find Olivia's killer. I couldn't figure out why he was suddenly so unhappy about me running the shop. We paid the bill for dinner and left the restaurant.

Mike was sullen and angry when we got outside. It was an unpleasant trip back to the house. No one spoke, and the drive seemed to take forever.

Joe pulled the car into the garage and turned off the engine. "Son, we have to talk about you leaving school."

"There's nothing to talk about," Mike informed him. He got out of the SUV and slammed the door closed.

"Okay. Any other ideas?" Joe asked me.

"We have to keep talking to him. Whatever is wrong must be important to him. Maybe there's a girl."

"A girl?" Joe shook his head, as though trying to clear his thoughts. "I didn't even think about that! Maybe you'd make a good detective after all."

"No." I wished more than anything that I could confide in him. Joe and I had always been a good team. Together, we might have been able to figure out what had happened to Olivia. But it was too risky.

"Look, Molly." He turned to me. "I know this has been really hard on you. You and Olivia were friends since you were kids. You have to believe that Lisbet and I can find the killer. Let us do our job. You concentrate on thinking of some way to keep Mike in school. Okay?"

"I'll do what I can." I couldn't promise to let Olivia's death go. Joe didn't know what was going on behind the scenes. It was better that way, but I could see it was going to be a struggle to keep him out of it.

"Why do you want me to close Smuggler's Arcane?" This seemed like a good time to ask. "You've never said that before."

He shrugged. "I guess I was thinking about retirement. I'm hoping we can do some traveling—see the world! We can't go anywhere with you tied to that shop."

"I see." My heart was lighter knowing his reasoning. He had no idea about my plan to retire in Boca where so many other witches lived. "You don't have to worry. When the time is right, I'll give it up. I'm hoping Dorothy—the young woman you met—is going to buy it."

"Great!" He gave me a lingering kiss. "I love you, Molly. Don't ever forget that."

"I won't, if you won't. I love you too, Joe."

We opened our doors to get out, and there was Lisbet, standing outside the garage. Her car was in the drive.

"Sorry to interrupt. I'm sorry, Molly, we've had a break in your friend's murder case. I have to steal Joe away."

CHAPTER 12

Calm of the winter night, come to me.
Calm of the summer sky, come to me.
Calm of the spring rain, come to me.
Calm of the autumn mist, come to me.
Come to me.

I went inside. Mike was already closed up in his bedroom.
Maybe it was just as well. I didn't know if I could talk a bee
out of buzzing around a stone flower that night.

I was exhausted and dispirited. I didn't know which way
to turn. Olivia had been murdered. Brian had issued a
not-so-veiled threat against my family. Coming at a time
when our coven was falling apart and my magic was going
away, it was too much to bear. I wished I could hide my head
under a pillow.

Isabelle reminded me that it wouldn't help. She told me,
as she always had since I'd found her twenty years ago, that
I was a powerful witch and that anything was possible. Her
purr was meant to set my heart and mind at ease.

While I appreciated her support, I knew her allegiance
was blind. It didn't matter what the circumstance—she always felt that I could overcome it. She was my one-cat cheer-
leading squad.

I thanked her and went into the bedroom to put on my pajamas.

I opened my jewelry box to put my pearl earrings away. I can't explain why I did it, but I opened the secret compartment under the box.

The compartment was made for only one thing—my mother's amulet. I picked it up and felt its cool weight in my hand.

The silver filigree was heavy and ornate around the single blue stone. The color inside the stone seemed to move, just like the sea, creating shadows and currents. It was a one-of-a-kind piece that had been spelled by a woman so far back in my family line, no one was sure who she was.

It was an incredible piece of jewelry, but I'd never worn it. My mother had given it to me when I turned eighteen. Every witch in my family had worn the amulet. I could feel the magic imbued within it.

My mother had told me that the amulet was a gift from a lesser sea god; I couldn't even remember what she'd said his name was—I'd never heard of him. I couldn't imagine what I would do with it since it was elaborate, and I'm not a chunky-jewelry person.

When she'd given it to me, I didn't feel like my magic needed a crutch.

I did now.

I closed the door to my bedroom and turned off the light. I held the amulet close to me and concentrated on it. The moon was shining through the windows. A single shaft of light fell on the stone and seemed to waken something inside it.

Iridescent lights emerged inside the stone in response to the moonlight. They danced in the blue depths, like fairies on midsummer. I watched them in amazement. Outside the occasional glance at the amulet, I'd never taken it out of the jewelry box since I'd received it.

I'd shown it to Olivia, of course. We showed each other everything. She couldn't believe that I didn't want to wear it. "Oh, wear it, Molly," she'd urged. "Maybe the lesser sea god is young and handsome!"

"Is this what you want?" I asked the amulet.

In response, there were more glowing lights in the stone.

It was chilly outside, but I stepped into the garden. It was heavy with the woody scents of fall—mums, dahlias and the last roses of summer.

In the center of the garden was a small stone altar Olivia, Elsie and I had used a few times for solstice celebrations. I put the amulet on the moonlight-bathed stone.

The blue stone took on a life of its own. The iridescent lights slowly emerged from it and moved in the moonlight as though they were alive.

I watched in fascination as they flowed into the night around me, leaving traces of blue energy behind them.

Why hadn't my mother told me about this? She hadn't said anything other than that the stone had been passed down for generations.

I could feel its magic in the moonlight. It reached out to me. The same feeling I'd had in the river that day encompassed me. I felt as though I could live in its light forever.

The door to the house opened and closed. The lights went away. I was left with the same amulet I'd always had. I picked it up and put it in my pocket.

"Mom, is there anything to eat? I'm starving."

The amulet felt cool in my pocket. It was hard to break away from its spell. "There are waffles in the freezer and some frozen French fries."

"What about pizza?" Mike asked.

"The number for delivery is on the refrigerator, just like always."

"My cell phone is dead. Can you call?"

I sighed. Maybe this interruption was for the best. I

needed some time to understand what I'd had for so many years—and to talk to my son.

"All right. I'm coming."

It was ten thirty before the pizza delivery driver got there. They had my credit card on file so all I had to do was give him a tip and take the box.

Joe had come home while Mike was watching basketball on TV. I put the pizza out on the table and got something to drink.

I knew there wouldn't be a better time for the three of us to discuss Mike's decision to leave college. I sat with them while they ate pizza and drank soda.

When the game was over—Mike's favorite team had won—I brought up the subject of him leaving school.

"There's nothing to discuss." Mike put an end to the conversation before it had even started. "I've made my decision. I need to try new things. Maybe do some traveling while I'm still young."

"Have you thought about what will happen when you're done seeing the world?" Joe asked him. "You won't be able to get a job."

Mike shrugged and stared at the floor. "I don't know. I can always go back to school after that. Or I could join the military."

I looked into his troubled eyes. "What happened, Mike? Whatever it is, you can tell us."

"There's nothing wrong." He shut down right away.

"Son," Joe began, but stopped when Mike got up and walked into his bedroom, closing the door behind him.

I turned off the lights in the rest of the house as we got ready for bed. Joe locked the doors. "Now what?"

"I don't know yet. This could take some time," I warned.

We went into the bedroom together. I was worried about

the growing gulf between us. I couldn't believe that I wasn't able to reach him after being married for thirty years. There had to be a way.

I put the amulet around my neck. It felt cool against my skin. I didn't know why I'd suddenly decided to wear it, but it felt *right*.

"Can you talk about the new evidence you found in Olivia's death?" I asked him.

"It wasn't much." He took off his T-shirt. "There was some blood at the house. It matched a sample we found at the crime scene that didn't belong to Olivia. Forensics will try to match it."

"So that might connect her killer to the house break-in."

"Maybe. We've combed through the house. I think the mess that was left behind was intentional. The killer probably took something and this is his or her way to throw us off the trail. We found an opening in the wall behind the washing machine that looked like something had been stored there. We don't know what yet. Any ideas?"

CHAPTER 13

Whispers hidden here forever,
Hide what I demand.
Invisible until I tell thee,
Found by no human hand.

"I'm sure Olivia had her secrets that even I wasn't privy to."
I got into bed and hugged the blanket tightly to me. "I didn't
tell her everything either."

Joe pulled on a pair of shorts and got into bed. "I've
known you most of my life, Molly. I know something's up
with you. I wish you'd tell me so I don't have to go around
worrying about it all the time."

"I'm completely blown away by Olivia's death." No truer
words were ever spoken. "I can't shake the feeling that I
could've done something to prevent it."

He put his strong arms around me. "I'm sorry, sweetie.
I wish I could change all that for you, but her death had
nothing to do with you. Olivia was always . . . a free spirit.
You have to make peace with that."

"I'm trying." Tears spilled down my cheeks.

"You'd tell me if there was anything else I should know,
right? You're not holding back on me, are you?"

"No." I sniffed and wiped away the tears.

He kissed me and turned off the bedside lamp. "Good night, Molly. Don't worry. Lisbet and I will find whoever did this to Olivia. Try to get some sleep." I turned off my light too and lay in bed for a long time, staring at the dark ceiling.

I hated that Joe and I were butting heads, especially now. He'd never come so close to learning about magic. Nothing we'd been through had prepared me to deal with this problem.

I thought I must be naïve not to have ever confronted this situation that so many families had faced with magic and non-magic members of their family. Somehow, I'd always managed to lead a quiet life as a witch. The Grand Council mostly left me alone, and I had led my life in a peaceful bubble.

Suddenly, I was thrust into the political deep waters of being a witch. I didn't like it, but what choice did I have but to fight back?

The next morning Joe grabbed a cup of coffee in a travel mug and headed out the door.

Mike was sullen and angry. He grabbed an energy drink and said he was going to play basketball with some friends.

I was left alone at the house with Isabelle, who cuddled and purred on my lap. She loved my mother's amulet and couldn't believe I hadn't worn it before. I had to admit that it made me feel stronger in this turbulent time.

It didn't help me decide what I should do about the problems that faced me—finding Olivia's killer, dealing with Brian Fuller—not to mention my waning abilities. But there wasn't an amulet capable of that kind of power. I was going to have to struggle through what was happening and hope the answers were going to come to me.

Elsie called to ask if I was going to the shop that morning. I realized it would be good to talk this over with her. I agreed to meet her there and got dressed.

It was good to be at the shop an hour later. Elsie was already there. Her daughter had dropped her off on the way to work.

She met me at the door with a deep frown between her green eyes. She was holding Barnabas, her large orange tabby, in her arms. Harper was meowing at her feet.

"What's wrong with the cats?" I closed the door behind me.

"I'm not sure. Barnabas acted strange all night. I got here, and Harper is just as crazy. I keep asking them what's wrong. They say they don't know."

I was surprised that Isabelle hadn't mentioned anything to me before I'd left. The cats were usually in sync, as were Elsie, Olivia and I.

We sat at the table together, and Elsie was able to put Barnabas on the floor.

"What do you think it is?" she asked. "I've never known him to act this way."

I told her about meeting Brian at the restaurant and his veiled threat against Mike and Joe. "But Isabelle wasn't acting odd at all. I don't know what to think."

Elsie pursed her lips. Her lipstick was slightly smeared— it was hard for her to find her lips sometimes. "What are you going to do about it?"

"I don't know yet. He said he didn't kill Olivia or steal the spell book. I tried to call Cassandra, but she didn't answer. The key has got to be getting this to the council. Brian can answer *their* questions. I don't think he'll answer ours."

"Maybe we should bolster our protection spells here, Molly. Then we could go to each of our houses together and do the same. These are dangerous times."

I agreed. At least it was something we could do to feel safer. I was tired of doing nothing—or the wrong thing—as we had on the tourist boat yesterday and in the restaurant last night. Maybe we weren't powerful witches, but we still had *some* magic.

We opened the trapdoor to the cave, and both cats ran down the stairs. Harper was obviously starting to get over

Olivia's loss. He would never be another witch's familiar, but he could enjoy his life here, surrounded by magic.

As I closed my eyes, Elsie and I did what we could to bolster the spells we'd put on the cave for secrecy and protection. I could still feel Olivia's magic. It was fading but still wrapped up with ours.

We would have been much stronger if Dorothy had been there too, but there was no point in going there. When all of this was settled, we'd have to look for another witch.

We went back upstairs. Elsie was quickly ready to go, a green fascinator with a big pink flower on her head.

"Should we bring Olivia's staff?" she asked. "I have my sword with me. I think it has more magic now than I do. I went to whip up a little breakfast this morning and started my dishwasher instead. It's ridiculous, really."

I smiled at her outraged tone. I put my hand on the tiny cauldron around my neck. I could feel the magic stored there from years of wearing it, but it wasn't as strong as the magic in my mother's amulet.

"We can't use Olivia's staff since we're not air witches or blood relatives. The power was only there for her. Let's get this over with. The sooner we update our protection, the better."

We drove back to my house and got out, looking around carefully. Elsie drew her sword, and I smiled at the picture she made with it.

"What is it?" she hissed. "Do you see *someone*?"

"I hope I wouldn't be smiling if I had. I was thinking how unique you look wearing that hat and carrying a sword."

"Now is not the time for fantasy," she informed me in sharp tones. "We must look to our safety. I wish you were a fire witch too. I'd feel a lot more secure if you had a sword in your hand instead of that tiny cauldron and an amulet around your neck."

I agreed with her. I would've felt a lot safer with a sword

too. Even Olivia's staff would've been enough to hit someone if my magic failed.

We walked up to the house and stood outside the front door. Both of us shut our eyes to better experience the emanations coming from inside.

"I don't feel anything different, do you?" Elsie asked.

"No. Let's go in and work the protection spell so we can go to your house. All of this is making me nervous."

I opened the door, and we crept inside.

The living room and kitchen were a complete mess. Pots and pans were thrown everywhere. Cushions on the sofa were ripped apart. Flour and sugar were spread all over both rooms.

"I guess the cats were right." Elsie held her sword out before her. "I'm sorry, Molly."

"I hope he didn't hurt Isabelle." I started calling for her, trying to feel her presence in the house. There was nothing. Elsie roamed the house, calling for Isabelle too. "Where would she be likely to hide?"

"I don't know. I've never seen her hide from anything." I wanted to drop to the floor and cry. "We're out of our league. We have to agree to some kind of truce with Brian."

Cassandra appeared in the middle of the mess. "Wow. Someone tore *this* place apart."

"We can do without you stating the obvious," I snapped at her.

"Sorry. Who did this?"

"We think it was Brian Fuller, the witch who may have killed Olivia and stolen our spell book." Elsie put a hand up to cover her mouth, but it was too late.

Cassandra's eyes narrowed on my face. "You told me you still *had* your spell book."

"Well, I lied." I was tired of playing whatever game this was. "I think this man killed Olivia and took our spell book.

Now he's threatening my family. If the council is *ever* going to help with *anything*, now would be the time!"

"I don't think Brian Fuller did this, ladies," Cassandra said. "I can't tell you any more than that, not until we can completely assess the situation."

"Great!" Elsie stared her down. "What are we supposed to do?"

"Don't get involved. There is a rogue witch who could be a serious threat to the council. We can't involve ourselves in petty feuds between witches."

I laughed as I picked up a broken vase that Joe had given me for my birthday. I'd seen it at an antique show in Charleston while we were on vacation. He'd secretly gone back and contacted the owner to have it sent to me.

"A serious threat to the *council*?" I asked. "This is a serious threat to *us* right now. The council has a lot of power. We need you to determine who killed Olivia. We aren't equipped to take care of this. Forgive me if I think our need is greater than yours."

Cassandra apologized and smiled. "That was insensitive of me. Of course what you're going through right now is very bad. But imagine if there were no council of witches. That would be far worse."

Elsie used the tip of her sword to push her fascinator back on her head. "Really? Because I've never known the council to do anything worthwhile. Maybe I'm mistaken."

"The Grand Council of Witches protects us all from threats we wouldn't be able to handle individually." Cassandra's tone was icy.

"What is the council going to do to protect us from *this* threat?" I demanded.

"They sent me. And I have a message. No way, no how, are you to try and stop this witch by yourselves. The council will deal with the problem, when the time is right."

"And we're talking about the rogue witch, not the man who killed our friend, right?" If I sounded snarky, it was because I was scared. I was more afraid of Brian than I was of the council.

"Is there anything you came to tell us that will actually *help*?" Elsie asked.

"Yes." Cassandra smiled. "Keep your wits about you, and be patient. You'll be able to persevere—with *our* help."

"Is that it?" I was wondering when she'd run out of trite phrases.

Cassandra studied her cuticles. "I think so."

Elsie and I exchanged angry glances across the room.

"We need something more." I wasn't sure what I was asking for, but my anger and fear demanded something else from the council.

"Oh. Isabelle is fine. She's in the garage. She was a smart lady to hide there before the rogue witch came to look around."

"What was he or she looking for here?" I asked Cassandra.

"The rogue witch is after objects of power—like your spell book. The objects don't have to be *very* powerful, but enough of them will build up the witch's strength."

Elsie shook her head. "Would you please make sense, dear? What does this rogue witch want to do? Challenge the council?"

Cassandra's smile faded. "She wants to live forever." She started to say something else and glanced at the door. "I have to go. I'll keep in touch."

Before we could say anything else, Joe and Lisbet burst into the house.

"What happened here?" Joe took in the scene of our ransacked home with disbelief.

Elsie used her sword to spear an apple that had been thrown onto a chair from the fruit bowl on the counter. "It's a long story."

CHAPTER 14

Heart of my heart,
I call to thee.
Come to me in the night,
And set me free.

Of course, Joe *had* to call the police. A special unit of investigators who were assigned to breaking-and-entering cases was brought in. They started going through the house as I went to get Isabelle out of the garage.

According to Isabelle, Cassandra had it all wrong. She'd woken up in the garage after I was gone. She felt sure she'd been drugged or spelled while the witch paid us a visit.

I sat and held her, stroking her soft fur as she complained about the state of the garage and how cats weren't meant to live outside homes. She didn't think her fur was ever going to be clean again.

I promised her a bath and all the salmon she could eat. I felt her pain since she was my familiar. We were sharing the anxiety and fear we both felt.

Elsie sat beside me, holding my hand. She'd put her sword away, though it was too late for it not to become a topic of conversation between me and Joe.

He didn't say anything to me for at least half an hour. He stayed huddled with police officers in one corner as they'd waited for the investigators. After they arrived, he'd gone over the house with them. Lisbet had also stayed, leaning against a wall, talking on her cell phone.

Joe came over to me then and introduced an investigator. "This is Lieutenant Matt Smith. He's the head of the Breaking and Entering squad. Matt, this is my wife, Molly, and her friend Elsie."

Lieutenant Smith shook hands with both of us and sat down on the sofa.

"So you two were the first on the scene. Did you see anyone leaving?"

"No," I answered, a little harshly. I was so tired of people asking me questions and not giving me answers. "We weren't expecting to find the house this way so we probably didn't pay enough attention."

"I didn't see anyone either," Elsie said.

Lieutenant Smith smiled. "I'm sorry this happened to you, Mrs. Renard. I understand you had a friend who was murdered recently."

"Yes."

"Do you think this break-in could have anything to do with your friend's house being broken into?" His inquisitive blue eyes watched me closely.

"I don't know. I don't see why it would." I sneaked a peek at Joe. What was he thinking?

"It seems as though someone was looking for something here, just as they were at Olivia Dunst's home. Any thoughts on what that was?"

"No. I don't know what someone would be looking for here, or at my friend's house."

"You were attacked yesterday by a man on the riverboat that you thought had dated your deceased friend." Lieutenant Smith read from his notes. "Do you think *those* events could be intertwined?"

"Not as far as I know." *How much longer is this going to continue?*

He closed his notebook and smiled again. "I'm sorry to have to ask you these questions, Mrs. Renard. We think there may be a pattern developing. We don't want anyone else to get hurt, do we?"

He was talking to me like I was a simpleton. I couldn't defend myself without giving something away.

I looked at Joe for help. He turned his head away. What did he think was going on? "No, of course not. If that's all, I'd like to call our insurance agent."

"That's it. Thanks for your time." He handed me his card. "If anything else comes to mind, please give me a call. I'd be happy to talk with you about *any* of it."

The emphasis on the word *any* made me uncomfortable. What else did he think I had to say? Maybe I was just being paranoid.

Mike came home at that moment, and a whole other round of questions and answers ensued. It was all I could do to keep my equilibrium and not scream at all of them.

Perhaps Cassandra was right, and this was the rogue witch, looking for items of power to use against the council. Items had been disappearing in the community. The bulletin board at Smuggler's Arcane was full of them.

Or this was another warning from Brian. Cassandra hadn't seemed interested in Brian at all—only her problem.

Joe was getting ready to walk out the door. I stopped him, putting my hand on his arm. "I wish you'd stay." Tears gathered in my eyes. "Maybe you could take a half day."

"I wish I could." He put his arms around me. "But I think we're getting close to figuring out what happened to Olivia. If I drop the ball now, I might not be able to pick it back up."

"I understand."

"Go out for a while, Molly. You can't do anything until the insurance agent sees this. Get out of the house. I'll help clean up tonight." He kissed me and left with Lisbet.

Elsie was standing beside me at the door as he walked out. She put her arm around me. "I'm so sorry. I'm sure he means well."

"It's the whole situation," I said. "I think he knows I'm lying to him."

"Ironic, isn't it?"

"Yes." I could appreciate her words. "I think the police are trying to tie Olivia's break-in to mine now. I know that happens sometimes. Maybe they think we both had something valuable from the shop. Who knows? That could mean you and I are involved in her death, in a roundabout way."

"It's a good thing we don't have to work with them," she said. "They sound even daffier than the council!"

I wiped away my tears and straightened my shoulders. I had to pick a focus and stay there. "We should go to your house and make sure nothing is wrong there. There's no point in putting up new protection spells here yet."

She agreed. "Let's do that. I think Joe is right about getting out of here. Besides, if the council is afraid of this rogue witch, so am I. Do you think the rogue witch could be Brian? He was very strong on the boat."

"I don't know. It's possible, I suppose. I don't think Cassandra really knows one way or the other."

I called our insurance agent and told him the door would be open. Elsie and I were on our way out when Dorothy walked up.

"Sorry for showing up without calling. And for looking you up in the phone book to find your address. And for deciding I couldn't be a witch. May I come in?"

Her plain face was appealing in its sincerity. I wondered what had happened that had changed her mind.

"Hi." Mike smiled at her. "Do I know you?"

"No, you don't." I introduced them. "Dorothy works at the downtown library."

"Wow. I love the library." He grinned, his gaze pinned on her. "Maybe you could help me pick out a few good books. Now that I'm not going to college anymore, I might have some time to read on my own."

"I'd be glad to do that, Mike." She smiled back at him. "Why did you decide to drop out of college? Your mom told me you're going to East Carolina. That's where I went to school too."

"Really?" He looked surprised and then frowned when he realized I was listening. "I'm just ready to move on now. Not everyone needs college."

"I see." Dorothy smiled at him before she looked at my living room. "What happened to your house?"

"Excuse us, Mike. Maybe you should go out for a while too. I'll text and let you know when I think it's safe for you to come home."

He shrugged. "I'm out of money, Mom. Could you loan me some for lunch?"

I gave him a twenty. "I'll see you later. Plan on helping with cleanup when you get back."

"Yeah. Whatever."

We went out into the garden to the same spot I'd brought the amulet last night. There were two benches and three chairs for our summer solstice events. I didn't think it was surprising that Dorothy sat in the same chair Olivia had always claimed as her own.

"So what brings you by?" I asked after relating my story about the break-in.

"I'm sorry," she said. "Maybe this isn't a good time."

"It's not going to get any better today." I pulled a few dead roses off the bush beside me.

"I've been having these really weird dreams. They're

about my mother. I used to have them all the time when I was a child. They stopped for years. Since I met the two of you, they've come back again. I was wondering what they mean."

Elsie snorted. She was a little allergic in the fall. "Dreams can mean anything. You might be better off consulting a dream specialist. I saw this wonderful movie once—I believe Dennis Quaid was in it. It was all about going into people's dreams."

"Thank you so much." Dorothy smiled at her. "I don't know anyone who specializes in dreams. Maybe you do?"

Elsie shrugged.

"What kind of dreams are you having?" I asked. "Witches frequently have prophetic dreams. It's possible that bringing you to an awareness of your abilities could have triggered them."

Dorothy sat forward, her brown hair swinging into her face. Her eyes were intense. "I think my mother may still be alive. I think she may be trying to reach out to me."

"What makes you think so?" Elsie asked.

"It's in the dreams. She's doing things—like spells and potions. She doesn't look anything like me. Of course, this would have been many years ago."

"No witch would simply abandon her offspring, especially offspring with magic," Elsie said. "She must have died."

"Maybe so. No one could ever tell me anything about her when I looked up my adoption records. She could be anyone."

"In time, if you don't continue to awaken your abilities, the dreams will fade again."

"No. You misunderstand me, Molly. I *want* to keep having those dreams. I'd like to find out who my mother was. Maybe the council of witches could help."

"I doubt that," Elsie said.

"So you're saying that now you *want* to be a witch again?" I was a little confused by her off-again, on-again attitude.

"Yes. I have to know more. I hope you'll take me back. I'd like to apprentice, or whatever you call it, with the two of you."

I couldn't say no. I knew Elsie felt the same. I believed Dorothy was sincere. We'd all liked her and wanted her to be the one we could leave our spell book with when the time came. That hadn't changed.

She'd had some doubts, but that seemed natural for someone who had never realized there was magic in the world around her. I was willing to give her some leeway. I knew Elsie was too.

"Thank you so much." She hugged both of us. "You won't regret this. I'll be the best witch in the world."

Elsie chuckled. "Our standards are not that high, I'm afraid. We aren't powerful witches who go around fending off evil or anything. Still, let's celebrate our reunion. A little tea and sparklers, I think."

Elsie muttered a spell, and we were immediately soaked by a tea rain that came down only where we were seated. Her wish for sparklers came out as dozens of fireflies that covered us from head to toe.

Naturally, we ran into the house.

Most of the fireflies were gone, but we were still saturated with sweet, warm tea.

Dorothy started laughing and danced around the room. "I *love* it."

"I *used* to love it," Elsie remarked. "I've ruined my fascinator."

"Maybe I can fix it," Dorothy volunteered.

"*No!*" Elsie and I both yelled at the same time. There was nothing worse than an untrained witch attempting magic without supervision—unless it was a witch whose magic was fading.

"Just a little tea storm." Elsie giggled. "Nothing to worry about. Can you lend me something, Molly? I don't want to get in your car this way."

We all changed clothes—I barely had something large enough for Elsie and small enough for Dorothy. When we were dry and didn't smell like tea, we went to the car.

"We'll go to Elsie's first to strengthen the protection spells there," I told Dorothy. "And then we'll go to the shop and try to figure out what to do about Brian."

I gathered Isabelle in my arms. I wouldn't take a chance on losing her again. The three cats would be fine at Smuggler's Arcane. Our protection was strongest there.

Mike was still outside, talking on his cell phone. He asked if he could go with us, obviously attracted to Dorothy. I had to tell him no. He had an expression of pathetic rejection on his face as we pulled out of the drive.

"Oh, he looks so sad," Dorothy mourned.

"Because your magic must remain a secret from those who don't have magic, there will be many times you have to keep your loved ones away from what you have to do," I explained as we drove away.

"Why doesn't Mike have magic?" Dorothy waved to him. "How did I get magic from my mother, but he didn't get it from you?"

"That's a good question." Elsie fussed with my old red beret that she'd insisted on wearing. "There's no real answer for that, although the council has tried to figure it out many times. It makes them nervous that the number of witches being born continues to decline."

I laughed. "Remember that time a few years back when the council was offering a bonus to every witch who married another witch? I don't think anyone took them up on it."

"And it doesn't always work," Elsie said. "You remember Reuben and Julie? They were both witches, but neither one of their children had magic."

"That's right. Magic is as elusive as any other force of nature," I added. "It can come from two witches, or only one witch. There are even cases where neither of the parents have magic."

"What about finding my mother?" Dorothy asked. "Is there a spell or something you can teach me that could help find her, if she's still alive?"

"That will be the first spell we teach you," I promised. "Aren't you also curious about your father?"

"I suppose I am. I haven't had any dreams about him." Dorothy gazed out the car window in the backseat. "Maybe both of my parents had magic."

We stopped at Elsie's house. Everything was fine there, thank goodness. I didn't think I could handle anything else being wrong. We worked together on a protection spell that felt good and strong. Lucky for us that Aleese wasn't there to see us do it.

We finally reached Front Street and the old Cotton Exchange. I was glad to see our shop and looking forward to a few minutes of peace after everything that had happened.

But we were immediately swamped with customers. Each of them had different stories to tell about the loss of some treasured magic item, most which had been passed down through their families for generations.

There were some whispered questions about missing witches. I realized that Olivia might not have been the only witch that had been killed. Everyone was afraid.

"Brian—or whoever is doing these things—has been very busy," Elsie said. "The council can't continue to ignore what's going on here. This witch must have half the magic items in Wilmington by now!"

I watched our last customer leave the shop. "The question is—what is he doing with all of them?"

CHAPTER 15

Open, portal closed to me.
Lift my spirit, set me free.
Let all that hinders be removed.
One. Two. Three. So mote it be!

"Lock the door," I told Dorothy as Elsie settled into a chair. "We need a few minutes alone to cast a new protection spell."

"We need a good spell," Elsie said. "Something simple. We're already protected, but let's not take any chances. With Olivia's magic fading, we need to build a better wall."

I was a little uneasy about the idea of another protection spell. It had worked at Elsie's house, but what if it backfired here and blew all the doors and windows out? Anything could happen—as I could see from Elsie's "tea" party.

I hoped we'd be okay with Dorothy's earth magic balancing us.

"It looks like your first spell is going to be a protection spell." I held the amulet and the cauldron around my neck. "Repeat what we're saying, and imagine something like a big earth mound protecting the shop."

"Or trees standing in front of it." Elsie took my hand. "Something to do with the earth. Not daffodils though. Anyone could come right through those."

The three of us joined hands and chanted together, each of us focusing on something that enhanced our native power. I kept the river in mind, feeling its strength and depth surrounding us like an impenetrable shield.

I could feel our magic melding. Dorothy was going to be a powerful witch. I was glad she had such a sweet disposition. Maybe it was good that she wasn't raised by her witch mother. She might've turned out differently.

Smuggler's Arcane began shifting and shaking as though an earthquake were trying to bring it down.

"Don't lose focus," I told Dorothy when I intuitively felt her open her eyes.

"Yeah, but—"

"It doesn't matter. Don't lose focus."

I knew when she'd stopped thinking about the shop shaking and was focused again on the protection spell. I could feel the three cats focusing their energies on the shop too.

I half expected to open my eyes and find the shop in ruins around us. I was surprised and pleased to find that we had created a new protection layer for the shop without destroying it.

"Is everyone all right?" I asked.

"I'm fine," Elsie said. "That was some *powerful* magic."

Dorothy looked around her. "Wow! That was awesome!"

"I think now we should look for the man who heard Olivia's last scream." I was trying to be single-minded, one thing at a time. "It should be safe since the police already questioned him."

We gathered our possessions and told Barnabas, Isabelle and Harper good-bye. They were still a little nervous, but they said they could see that everything was going to work out soon.

Elsie put away her sword and went to the front door. It wouldn't open. "That's odd."

"What's wrong?" I gave the door a try. It wouldn't budge.

"I think we may have protected the shop *too* well," Elsie muttered, glancing back at Dorothy.

"We'll have to open it." I bent my head and whispered a small spell to open the door.

It didn't work.

"Will we be able to leave the shop at all?" Dorothy peeked over our shoulders. "I only have the morning off."

"I think we might have to go into the cave and try to open it from there." I smiled at Dorothy, feeling a little foolish. How was she going to believe we could teach her anything if we couldn't do a simple protection spell?

Dorothy's eyes got wide. "You have a *cave* in your basement? Can I see it?"

I'd forgotten that everything impressed Dorothy. She didn't know the difference yet between a good spell and a bad one.

"If we can open the trapdoor." Elsie didn't sound sure of that at all.

I kicked aside the rug and pulled up the trapdoor. "It must only affect going in and out of the shop the conventional way."

"Well, that's good!" Elsie followed me down the stairs. "Come on, dear."

"Cool!" Dorothy smiled. "I've heard about the smugglers' caves under some of the waterfront buildings, but I've never seen one."

"Well, you're in for a treat," Elsie said. "If you like sand, rocks, moss and dampness—it's heaven."

We walked slowly down the old stairs. They were in worse shape now than they had been before Elsie had "fixed" them. If we couldn't use magic to repair them soon, we were going to have to hire a carpenter. Of course, that would mean erasing his memory of the cave. It was our most guarded secret—after the spell book.

Dorothy investigated every part of the cave like a kitten.

No nooks or crannies were ignored. She talked about pirates and smugglers the whole time she snooped around.

Elsie and I sat around the cauldron. We'd had about as much excitement as we could handle for one day.

"And this is where you do your magic." Dorothy grinned as she sat in the third chair. "This is really exciting."

"First, let's unlock the door upstairs. Then we'll move forward." It might take a few tries to get everything right with Dorothy's magic added to ours.

We were used to Olivia's magic. Every witch's magic vibrated at a different frequency. It was one way we could feel another witch, even with our eyes closed.

I repeated the opening spell for Dorothy—and Elsie, since she couldn't remember it. Witches learned and wrote hundreds of spells in a lifetime, which was why we kept spell books. Losing ours might seem like a terrible thing to Cassandra, but to us it was a catastrophe.

Together, we repeated the spell until we heard a popping noise upstairs. Isabelle told me the front door was unlocked. We sat back in our chairs with a sigh of relief.

"This stuff is hard." Dorothy twisted her neck from side to side to ease the tension. "I didn't realize it would be this difficult."

Elsie frowned.

"Not that I'm giving up again," Dorothy rushed to re-assure her. "I just meant—it seemed as though it would be easier, you know? Like you just snap your fingers or twitch your nose."

"That's TV magic!" Elsie took out her sword and pointed it at the small fire that always burned under the cauldron. "This is *real* magic, my girl. Magic of nature and the elements. Calling upon the *real* power of the universe."

The fire shot up into the cave, sparkles of light flying everywhere, illuminating the dark places.

Dorothy gulped. "While we're down here chanting and stuff, can we find my mother? Then we could find the man you're looking for? Please. It would mean so much to me."

"So let's find Dorothy's mother, shall we?" Elsie chuckled. "Then we can find Olivia's killer."

"We'll do a spell to find a missing loved one," I said. "That will probably work."

I *hoped* it would work anyway.

We set up the cauldron on the stones I'd culled from the river twenty years ago. Elsie danced around the fire with her sword, chanting and laughing. It made me think of happier times when Olivia and I had watched her gyrating movements.

Elsie's steps weren't as graceful as they once were, but she was still light on her feet. She loved to dance, and the fire came up hot, ready to do her bidding.

"Whew!" She fanned herself with her hand. "That took a lot out of me, but at least I can still make a fire."

"Now for the ingredients we need for the spell." I sent Dorothy up to lock the shop door (the non-magic way) and find what we needed among the bottles and tins of herbs and tinctures.

"Good idea to familiarize her with what we have in stock," Elsie commended. "I think she's going to make a great witch. I wish Olivia hadn't died. I was supposed to be the first one to retire."

"I know. We'll find another witch soon, don't worry."

"And not an evil witch like Brian."

"He's probably not really evil—just misguided."

"Rubbish!"

Dorothy eagerly found everything we needed and traipsed down the stairs. "I never realized how much stuff is up there. Am I going to have to learn what all of it does?"

"Absolutely." Elsie adjusted my red beret on her head. "No witch worth her salt would do anything less. Do you want to root around in front of a customer like someone who just walked in through the door?"

"I suppose not." Dorothy put the supplies on the stone table. "What now?"

"Now you brew up a potion that we'll use for the spell." I swept the area around the fire, muttering a cleansing spell as I went.

"Okay. What's first?"

"You need a hair from your head," Elsie told her. "Mind you keep the root on it."

Dorothy did as she was told and threw the hair into the cauldron.

Next came the herbs.

"Ground allspice berries for luck." Elsie added the berries. "And bloodroot to strengthen family ties."

"Fennel seeds for courage to face whatever you find out about your mother." I threw the seeds into the cauldron. "And goldenseal threads for wisdom.

"Now spit into the pot and stir it all together." I handed the large wood paddle to Dorothy.

"Are you sure?" She peered into the cauldron. "That seems a little unsanitary. I don't have to drink it, do I?"

Elsie giggled. "We didn't ask you to put any *real* bodily fluids into it. I remember that time with the love potion Olivia brewed. Now *that* took some bodily fluids."

"*Shh*," I cautioned. "Concentrate. We need to find Dorothy's mother."

We joined hands around the steaming cauldron, the smell of smoke and the river dominating the cave. Elsie and I began the chant. Dorothy joined in.

I could feel our strength together. We were going to make a great team. I almost felt guilty thinking that with Olivia gone. We'd made a great threesome. I missed her and the energy she'd brought to us.

We all heard a clunk upstairs.

"Is that the door opening again?" Dorothy opened one eye.

Isabelle alerted me that something was wrong. "Something fell—probably from Dorothy moving things around upstairs," I translated. "We're a little strapped for space here."

"Would you two *please* concentrate?" Elsie hissed.

There was a louder clunk from upstairs. Isabelle, Harper and Barnabas ran down into the cave.

"What's wrong?" Elsie asked Barnabas.

Before she had her answer, Olivia's staff came flying down the stairs at us.

CHAPTER 16

Spirits of the dead, depart.
Find thy everlasting light.
Your place is here, inside my heart.
Spirits of the dead, depart.

The three of us—and the cats—stared at the staff without moving.

"Well!" Elsie glanced up the stairs. "That's a fine how-do-you-do."

Dorothy whispered, "What does that *mean*?"

"I hope it doesn't mean what I think it means." I picked up the staff. "This belonged to our dead friend, Olivia Dunst."

Elsie's green eyes narrowed as she considered the possibilities. "You don't think?"

"What else could it be?"

"Stop talking like that," Dorothy protested. "What does it mean?"

"We'll have to do some tests," Elsie answered. "We can't speculate on something so important."

"There's only one perfect test to show us what's going on."

"Olivia was an air witch," Elsie reminded me.

I shrugged. "It shouldn't matter."

Dorothy stamped her foot. "Will you *please* tell me what's going on?"

"I'm not going to explain," I told her. "Instead, we'll let nature take its course."

"I'm telling you, Molly, it won't work." Elsie sighed as she sat in a chair.

"We'll see." I stared at Dorothy. "Take the staff."

She took a step back. "Why?"

"Just take it, and we'll see what happens. It may not mean anything."

Elsie laughed. "And the sun isn't going to rise."

Dorothy was clearly frightened by the idea of holding the staff. "I really don't want to do this. Do I have to? Is some kind of witch hazing?"

"Just take the staff." I held it out to her.

She started to reach for it and then drew back. "It's not going to kill me or turn me into a toad or something, right?"

"Goodness gracious!" Elsie shook her head. "A toad? Of course not. I can't even remember the last time I turned someone into a toad—although there was that witch from New Jersey who settled here that—"

"Elsie!"

"Okay." Dorothy wiped her trembling hands on her jeans. "I hope this isn't a bad idea."

In a fit of pique, I removed my hand from the staff and used magic to propel it at her. Lucky for me, it worked. You should never use magic when you're angry or impatient.

She put up her hands defensively to protect herself and caught Olivia's staff. It was in her grasp for only a moment before the runes on it began to glow.

"Molly? What should I do?" Dorothy shrieked.

"I'd say you're doing it." I smiled, tears starting to my eyes.

When all the runes were glowing, another change came over the staff. A white mist formed around it until it had enveloped the wood. The mist began to change and became a shape—the rough outline of a woman.

Elsie shot to her feet, her hand on the red beret. "Oh my stars! I can't believe it."

The figure continued to swirl and form into a definite, and recognizable, shape.

"Olivia!" I could hardly believe my eyes.

"Of course. Who else did you expect?" Olivia focused on Dorothy.

Most witches die at times they've expected their entire lives. Because of that, they die in peace and would never consider coming back to this plane.

I could only speculate that because Olivia had been murdered in such a brutal and untimely way, her spirit had returned to finish what needed to be done.

"Cassandra isn't going to like this." Elsie's voice made a little song out of her words, and then she giggled. "Welcome back, Olivia! I'd hug you, but there's nothing there. I suppose I could hug the staff."

Olivia patted her blond hair and peeked down at the red dress she was wearing. "Do I look all right? I'm not all grotesque and disgusting, am I?"

"No." I wiped tears from my eyes. "Not at all. That's your favorite dress."

"And thank goodness, my favorite shoes. If I have to spend a hundred years in them, at least they're comfortable. Stylish too."

Dorothy still held the staff, her mouth hanging open a little, her eyes glued on Olivia. Suddenly she dropped the staff and ran upstairs, slamming the trapdoor behind her.

"Could you please lock the shop door?" Olivia asked. "I didn't come all this way for her to run away from me."

Elsie and I exchanged uncertain glances.

"That might not be the best idea," I told her. "We had a little trouble with a protection spell earlier. She'll be fine."

I sat down in my usual chair, completely amazed to see her. "Why in the world didn't you tell us that you had a daughter?"

Olivia hovered over her chair in the cave, her pretty features distressed. "Oh girls, you don't know how many times I wanted to tell you. I had to keep it secret because her father is an ancient—slightly evil—witch."

"But Olivia—"

"I know." She wrung her opaque hands together. "Please hear me out."

"You've got our attention," I said.

"It turned out that he wasn't the *nice* witch that I thought he was to begin with. I found out I was pregnant after our tryst in Venice. It was such a wonderful affair! We had champagne and strawberries every day!"

"Coming to the part about Dorothy soon?" Elsie broke in.

"I'm getting there! I was afraid he might take her away from me and raise her to be like him. I couldn't have stopped him. So I gave her up for adoption. I hoped he'd never know she was born."

"Wow!" Elsie rocked back in her chair. The fire under the cauldron spit up into the air again. "I didn't see *that* coming."

"I know." Olivia wiped invisible tears from her eyes. "Maybe it was a bad decision. I knew she had magic when she was born. You wouldn't believe the trouble I had to go through to hide her birth. When I saw her at the library, I knew she had to be the one to take my place. I'd always planned to tell you all when I could. I'm so sorry."

"When did you have her?" I knew the answer to that, obviously. "I mean, where were you? Why didn't we even know you were pregnant?"

"Remember that year I took the sabbatical in Paris?" Olivia smiled and batted her long eyelashes. "I was really hiding in smelly catacombs under Paris where an ancient group of witches sheltered me. They didn't tell me where they took her. I couldn't ask. That was the deal. Imagine how I felt when I saw that she was right here in Wilmington!"

"That was an excellent plan," Elsie commended. "It had to be hard to give her up."

"Oh, you'll never know, and I'm glad you won't. There were nights I just ached to hold her in my arms. The only thing that kept me going was knowing I would see her again someday and that she was safe. The witches had promised me that."

It was hard to take it all in. I would never have believed my old friend could keep such a big secret from me. Even knowing she'd done it to save Dorothy's life—it was still hard to believe.

"And now what?" I asked her. "I think I understand why you came back."

"And why she called my name when she was dying." Dorothy had crept back down the stairs as we were talking. She was crying, wiping *real* tears from her face. "You're my *mother*?"

"That's right, baby." Olivia held out her arms. "Believe me, I never wanted to hurt you with any of this. We should've had plenty of time to get to know each other before you had to learn the truth."

Dorothy ran to hug her mother before Elsie and I could warn her. She ran right through Olivia, tripped in the sand behind her and fell flat on her face.

"Oh dear." Olivia frowned. "I'm so sorry. This ghost business is a nuisance, but I'm glad I transferred some of my magic to the staff. Otherwise, I wouldn't be here."

"Just no hugging." Elsie groaned as she got out of the chair. "I need some tea. Also one of those little chocolate cream cakes we keep upstairs for emergencies."

I agreed as I helped Dorothy off the ground.

Olivia's ghost followed us upstairs. The cats followed her. Harper was ecstatic to see his mistress back again.

"Have they caught my killer yet?" she asked as we made tea.

"No. Olivia, Brian is too strong. He stole our spell book after he killed you. He's been stealing magic tools from all across the area." I filled her in on what had happened since her death.

She laughed. "Don't be absurd. Brian would never hurt me. Yes, he's very capable—in more ways than *one*! But he didn't kill me."

Elsie covered her ears with her hands. "That's all I need to hear, thanks."

"Well, if Brian didn't kill you and steal the spell book, who did?" I asked her.

"I don't know, but I am mad as a hornet about it. And I wish I could eat one of those chocolate cream cakes. Wouldn't you know I'm finally at a place that I don't have to worry about my figure, and I can't eat anything?"

"How can you *not* know who killed you?" Dorothy was skeptical.

"Whoever did it came up behind me. Imagine the indignity of having your throat cut in a dirty old alley."

As we sat at the table to drink the tea, Elsie passed out the chocolate cream cakes.

I thought about everything that had happened. "Are you sure, Olivia? If you didn't see the killer, how do you know it *wasn't* Brian?"

"I would've known the feeling of him against me." She smiled dreamily. "I would definitely have known *that*!"

"But that *was* Brian on the riverboat. He threw us overboard. He warned me to stay away from him."

"It was absolutely *not* Brian who killed me, Molly. I don't know why you think it was."

Elsie unwrapped the cake. "Maybe because we saw him leave the shop with you before you died?"

"You're just mistaken," Olivia said. "Trust me, Brian is going to be *very* angry when he finds out I was killed."

"He already knows." I bit into the cake. "I accused him."

"Although I think Cassandra agrees with Olivia about Brian," Elsie reminded me between bites of cake.

"So my mother is a witch who has been around me all of my life." Dorothy took a bite of chocolate cake.

"*Was* a witch," Elsie corrected.

"And my father is an evil witch, so she had to hide me." Dorothy wasn't deterred by Elsie's assessment. "That is amazing! Does that mean I'll be evil one day?"

"That kind of ability isn't inherited," I told her. "It's your mind-set. No doubt your father has been alive for centuries. Some people continue to develop their powers as they grow older, and they become jaded."

"Actually," Olivia explained, "he's been alive for *thousands* of years. You are his *only* offspring, Dorothy. You are heir to his magic abilities."

"Unlike Molly and me, whose magic is fading." Elsie dusted cake crumbs from her hands. "This is a depressing conversation, even with the chocolate cake."

"You have a little chocolate mustache just there." Olivia started to touch the spot under Elsie's nose.

"Don't touch me!" Elsie leaned back in her chair. "It's unlucky to be touched by a spirit."

"What?" Olivia asked. "That's crazy. One of my favorite lovers of all time was a ghost. He was *so* special. The things he could do! It was a pity that they exorcised him from that bed-and-breakfast over on Fifth Street."

"If a ghost can touch someone," Dorothy asked, "why did I run right through you?"

"Because you have to know how to adjust your magic frequency so you can touch a spiritual being." Olivia smiled at her. "We have so much to teach you. I'm glad you decided to join us."

"Not *us*." Elsie snorted. "Me and Molly."

"You don't have to be so mean about it," Olivia charged. "Can't you see I'm cut up about the whole thing?"

Elsie chuckled. "No. I won't go there. It would be wrong to remind you that you are indeed cut up."

"Elsie!" Olivia said sharply. "That was uncalled for."

"Like you wouldn't have said it if our positions were reversed."

"Ladies." I pulled the conversation back from the pit it was falling into. "Let's not forget what's important. We have to find Olivia's killer and then our spell book. Now that we aren't sure if Brian killed her, we have to ask ourselves who else could have done it."

"I don't know," Elsie replied sullenly. "I had all my money on Brian."

"Elsie's right," Dorothy said. "We've been so sure it was him. How are we going to figure out who it is?"

"What about the rogue witch Cassandra was talking about?" I suggested. "I thought maybe that was Brian, but what if it wasn't?"

"I need another chocolate cake," Elsie complained.

"I think we should start by going along with Joe's wishes and visiting Olivia's house to see if we can determine anything else that might have been stolen." I shrugged and glanced at Elsie to see what she thought of the plan.

"We were already there," she reminded me. "It was such a mess, we couldn't tell anything—except that our spell book was definitely gone."

"A mess?" Olivia's form fluctuated in her distress. "What happened?"

"Let's talk about it on the way over there. Dorothy—bring the staff."

"What about the man who heard the scream?" Elsie asked with a significant glance at Olivia.

"We'll get to him too."

Olivia flew out to the car like a red comet.

"Show-off," Elsie muttered.

"Can't witches *fly*?" Dorothy's eyes were excited by the idea.

"We can," I explained. "But we need a conveyance."

"Like a broom?" she asked.

"It could be a broom. Mostly they show witches on brooms in old texts because women always had a broom with them. It could be anything that has been spelled to take us where we need to go."

"But it takes a lot out of you," Elsie added. "I haven't flown in years."

"Anyway, a novice can't do it. You have to build up your magic," I finished. "I think we should take the car today."

"Couldn't the car be spelled to fly?" Dorothy wondered.

Elsie shrugged. I shook my head. It was much easier teaching a child as they grew into their magic.

Cautiously, we left the shop after locking and spelling the door behind us.

I glanced nervously around the parking lot. There was no one around. I unlocked the car and we all quickly climbed inside. Even Olivia flew in through a window, as though someone were chasing her.

Elsie laughed at her. "I don't think anyone can hurt you now, dear."

"You don't know that." Olivia hovered in the backseat with Dorothy. "Ghosts can be exorcised or spelled. We know that."

Not seeing anyone around us made me feel safer, but I went ahead and started the engine so we could get away. Who knew how long the calm would last?

As I prepared to back up, the car suddenly shut down and all the doors locked at once.

"This can't be good," Elsie muttered.

CHAPTER 17

Be gone irritating pest.
Your presence affronts me.
I cast you away—north, south, east and west.
Leave me be.

"What's happening?" Dorothy glanced around. "Did you do that, Molly?"

"I didn't do anything." I *hoped* I hadn't done anything. I could never be completely sure.

"I didn't do anything either," Elsie said.

"Me either," Olivia agreed.

"Of course not," Elsie added. "You're dead."

"Oh! I see. That's why you said she wasn't a witch anymore." Dorothy nodded. "You lose your power when you die."

"Which is normally not a problem because witches don't come back." I scanned the parking lot as we sat, but there was still only us. I tried to start the car again, but nothing happened.

"Were you ladies going somewhere?" Cassandra appeared in the narrow gap between me and Elsie in the front seat. Only magic could have put her there, even as thin as she was. "You should think about staying somewhere safe."

"Hello, Cassandra." Olivia grinned and waved.

"I don't speak with ghosts." Cassandra shuddered. "They

are the *lowest* life forms. Not even a life form, really. A shadow. What is *she* doing here?"

I opened my mouth to explain and thought better of it. Cassandra was the one who needed to explain. "Why have you locked us in here?"

"Because people have been trying to kill you." She waved to Dorothy. "Hi, newbie!"

"We can't stay here," I argued. "We have other things to do besides keeping safe. We're going to take another look at Olivia's house where our book was stolen."

"The council will deal with that when they deem it appropriate. Go on. Get out. Go back inside."

"When did it become your job to protect us?" Elsie wondered.

"Yes," Olivia added. "Since when does the council care what we do?"

"Don't be stubborn, ladies." Cassandra turned on the charm. "This is bigger than you can handle. Let the council do its job."

"Is that what the council does?" Dorothy chipped in. "I was wondering."

"We're going to Olivia's house." I'd made my decision. Elsie nodded in agreement.

Cassandra shrugged. "I can't protect you if you leave the shop."

"You're not offering us any answers. We have to do what we think is right." My heart was racing. I had never spoken to Cassandra or any member of the council this way.

I knew their magic was strong—a lot more so than mine, Elsie's or Dorothy's. I didn't know what I was doing. I was only a witch from Wilmington, nothing special.

But I felt like I had to stand up for what I believed. I hoped that wouldn't cause me to end up spending the rest of my life in some unfocused netherworld.

"All right," Cassandra agreed. "The council needs you to stay out of the way and not make the problem any worse."

"So they admit there *is* a problem." Elsie straightened her beret. "That's nice."

"Is this about the witch that you said killed Olivia?" I asked her.

"Not Brian." Olivia made sure her opinion was heard.

"I never said it was Brian." Cassandra heaved a bored sigh and made a few sunbeams dance around her. "I can't tell you what's going on. Just stay out of it."

"I guess we'll have to do it without you," Elsie muttered. "Like we have all of our lives."

Dorothy frowned at the council's herald. She had no idea what was going on. If she had, she would've run out of the car screaming. At least Elsie and I were at the end of our magic. She would have the rest of her life to deal with the council.

Cassandra didn't say another word. I blinked, and she was gone.

"Look at that." Dorothy pointed at Smuggler's Arcane. "It kind of glows."

There *was* a charmed glow about the shop. Only those with magic could see it. I was impressed and confused. "Why is she doing this?"

Elsie said, "Maybe it will scare away Olivia's killer."

"It's not Brian," Olivia insisted again.

"Well, whoever it was." I started the car. Cassandra's magic was gone. "Let's see what we can find out. Without promises of protection for Joe and Mike, I'm still going to look for the killer."

"And our spells!" Olivia called out as though she were at a football game.

We explained everything to Olivia on the way. She cried about the loss of her valued possessions, although technically, they were already lost to her.

When we reached her house, the drive was empty. No

doubt the police had towed Olivia's car away for further inspection. There was still crime scene tape across the doors. Joe had said he wanted us to look around. I was taking him at his word.

I scanned the yard carefully before I got out of the car, even though I realized that Brian might be able to appear as suddenly as Cassandra had.

Oh, to have that kind of power. Not that I ever had.

"Looks clear to me," Elsie said. "I didn't expect anyone to be here. With our book gone, there's probably nothing of any real value inside."

Olivia took offense to that. "I beg your pardon. I spent my entire life collecting exactly the right items to add to what my mother and grandmother had brought into the house. There are antiques in there worth hundreds of thousands of dollars."

"That will go to the council now because you have no heir," Elsie reminded her.

"I have Dorothy. Did you think I didn't provide for her?"

"You *did*?" Dorothy stared at her. "You mean this house is *mine* now?"

"The council will demand proof of lineage," I said. "But that shouldn't be a problem."

"That's right. All this is yours, Dorothy. It's your birthright. I even made out a will so it would be all nice and legal for you."

"I'm a witch, and I own one of these cool old houses." Dorothy leaned her head to the side to take a better look at her inheritance. "I hope I can afford the taxes."

"I'm afraid I didn't include my Mercedes," Olivia said. "I made out the will a few years back, and I'd been thinking about trading it. I'm so sorry."

"I think a lawyer can take care of that." I still felt uncomfortable outside, as though someone were watching us. "Let's go in."

The protection spells were broken for good on the doors. The front door was locked, but the back door, where someone had broken in, was still wide open.

Olivia complained about the sloppy work the crime scene techs had done, leaving the door open. "I don't understand why a witch would have kicked in the door—unless he or she was having trouble with their magic too."

I agreed with her. "Once you were dead, the spells that remained were weak. If those could be bypassed, a witch would have used a spell to walk in, without breaking anything."

"Maybe it wasn't only a witch," Elsie suggested. "Maybe it was a witch—and an impatient person without magic."

Dorothy brought the staff and we went inside.

"Why would anyone want to destroy these beautiful antiques?" Olivia mourned her loss.

Elsie agreed for once. "Why do any of this if you're a witch? I would have used a search spell to find what I was looking for. It confirms my theory."

"So it *wasn't* a witch?" Dorothy put a broken Tiffany lamp back on an antique table. "Could a non-witch have killed Olivia?"

Elsie and I mulled it over.

"It's possible. But sneaking up on a witch isn't easy to do." I thought about Olivia's diminished magic, but even drained as we were, it would be difficult.

"Especially sneaking up with malevolent intent," Olivia said. "I would have felt that a mile away. That's why most witches aren't murdered."

"Why were you out in the alley?" I asked her.

She rubbed her forehead. "I don't really know. It's kind of fuzzy right now."

"It's probably one of the drawbacks to being dead." Elsie nodded sagely.

We tried to do a spell that would show us what had

happened in the house after Olivia's death. It was a simple spell, but it completely fizzled out.

"Maybe someone made this mess so no one could tell what was missing, like Joe said, in a nonmagic way," Elsie said. "Another thing a witch wouldn't have done to hide her tracks."

"Are we saying a witch killed Olivia, then broke through the spells here for a person with no magic to come in and steal the book?" I shrugged. "It doesn't make any sense."

Olivia flitted around the open area in the foyer near the stairs. The antique chandelier above us made a crystal tinkling sound as she moved.

"Why would someone do that?" Dorothy asked.

"Maybe if you wanted to mask your movements," I considered.

"So the council wouldn't know *exactly* what you were doing!" Olivia swooped down to say.

"Maybe that's why Cassandra wasn't quite sure what was going on." Elsie inspected a broken figurine of a Springer spaniel. "Either a witch is using a person without magic to shield her movements, or vice versa."

"Why would a witch help someone *without* magic?" Dorothy tried to have some input.

"Maybe Brian has a girlfriend who likes magic tools." Elsie was happy with her idea.

"Not *Brian*!" Olivia defended her former lover.

"I think we should see what else we can dig up about Brian. I know you don't think he's guilty, Olivia, but he's the best suspect we have right now." I opened the front door, and there were Joe, Lisbet and Lieutenant Matt Smith.

"Hi, Joe." I tried to act like everything was normal. I was only doing what he'd asked to help the case. "We looked through the house again. Nothing is missing, as far as we can tell. I'm sorry we couldn't be more help."

I'd hoped to get away quickly so we could follow up on the idea we were nurturing.

"Molly, is there something you need to tell me?" Joe's eyes were sad and confused.

Olivia's ghost was hovering beside me. Dorothy was holding the staff as though she might be about to attack someone with it. Elsie still had her sword under her coat.

"No." I could feel my pulse flutter a little as I lied to him. It certainly wasn't guilt. I didn't feel guilty about trying to protect him from the witch who'd killed Olivia. "Is something wrong?"

Lieutenant Smith, the officer in charge of the Breaking and Entering division, stepped forward. "I'm sorry, Mrs. Renard, about the loss of your friend and all. But we found this brooch hidden in the flour canister at your house after the break-in."

"My diamond brooch?" Olivia peered close enough at it that I could see Matt's hand behind her face.

"I didn't even think about it until I had a look at Olivia Dunst's list of insured valuables," Lieutenant Smith continued. "She had it listed for two hundred fifty thousand dollars. Care to explain how it came to be in your possession?"

CHAPTER 18

That which was liquid, turn to solid.
As water becomes ice, so shall it be.

There was a reasonable explanation for how the brooch got to be in the flour canister. Joe, Lisbet and Lieutenant Smith wouldn't understand it. I knew whoever had broken into the house must have left it there to make me look even worse, if that was possible.

It was probably the sole purpose for breaking into my house. The brooch had been taken from Olivia's house and hidden at mine.

I couldn't explain that to Joe because it would imply that I had some idea of who'd done it. The risk to Joe and Mike was greater than ever. I couldn't let them get involved, even if it meant becoming a real suspect in Olivia's murder.

I sat at the police station *again*, waiting for them to talk to me. This time I was actually in an interrogation room. It was very small and a terrible shade of brown. There was a table and three chairs. That was about it.

"This whole thing is crazy." Olivia fluttered around me.

Elsie and Dorothy were waiting outside. I'd tried to get

Dorothy to drive Elsie home and then go to work in my car.
There was no telling how long this would take.

Instead, Olivia had persuaded Dorothy to stay at the station with the staff so she could hear everything that was
said.

"You'll just have to tell them that I lent you the brooch
but insisted that you keep it in the flour canister for insurance purposes. That should do the trick," Olivia said. "They
can't prove a thing, Molly. I have the name of a good lawyer,
too, if you need it. He's handling my estate. Very discreet—
and fluent in both the magic and the mundane world."

I couldn't answer her. There were cameras in the room.
I didn't want Joe to think I was crazy too.

I wish I could have told her that this was so much worse
than them finding her brooch in my house. It was all I could
do not to cry at the way Joe had looked at me. It all seemed
to fit together, and yet it was all a terrible mistake.

One that I couldn't explain.

Joe had barely spared me a glance when we'd left the
house. Lisbet had apologized for taking me to the station in
the police car. Joe hadn't said a word.

"I overestimated how much that old brooch was worth
for the insurance company anyway." Olivia laughed. "It's
better to get too much than not enough, right?"

I closed my eyes and tried to find my center. It wasn't
easy. There was too much noise going on in my mind. I
needed some calm. I whispered a little spell for calm and
quiet while I held my mother's amulet.

The door opened and Lisbet came in. "I'm so sorry about
this, Molly."

"So am I." I opened my eyes and faced her. "Does Joe
really think I'm capable of doing something like this?"

"It's out of his hands right now." She shrugged. "Lieutenant Smith is only letting us sit in as a courtesy."

Lieutenant Smith joined us. He put a file on the table and sat down. "Everything okay in here?"

"I'm not sure what your definition of 'okay' is," I snipped. "But this probably isn't it, at least not for me."

Joe came in, nodded at Lieutenant Smith and sat down. His handsome face that I loved so well was set in grim lines.

"Mrs. Renard." Lieutenant Smith smiled at me. "May I call you Molly? We should've known each other better by now. I apologize for that. I'm new in town."

"Yes, I know." I didn't respond to his request. Let him say what he wanted. That was what he was going to do anyway.

Joe reached across the table and held my hand. "Just answer the questions, Molly. Everything will be fine."

Lieutenant Smith shrugged and opened the file, starting again. "There have been some odd circumstances surrounding your friend's death. Detectives Renard and Hernandez have had no luck with anything involving this case. The Dunst home was broken into after the murder, and then *your* home was broken into. I'm wondering what the key is to all of this."

"I have no idea."

"I think it might be *you*, Molly."

"And you think the brooch you found at my house ties it all together. Is that right?"

He nodded. "Do you have another explanation for it?"

I was really good and mad by this time. My husband was sitting across the table from me, his eyes beseeching me to tell the truth. Lisbet looked like she was going to cry. I'd had enough.

I looked up at the camera that was in front of me. "I have a very good explanation for it. My friend lent me that brooch. I'm sure if you look carefully enough through the rest of my things, you'll find other items that belonged to her too. In fact, you can probably find some of *my* belongings at *her* house as well. And don't forget my fingerprints—they're everywhere at her place. But then hers are everywhere at my house too!"

"Molly." Joe frowned and shook his head.

"No. Let me finish. You're blaming *me* because your efforts haven't worked out yet. May I suggest, Lieutenant, that you try to find someone who *is* guilty?"

"You go, girl!" Olivia was laughing. "Give it to 'em."

I got to my feet. "Unless you plan to arrest me for something, I'm leaving. I'll see you later, Joe."

With as much dignity as I could muster, I walked out of the room and closed the door behind me. Dorothy and Elsie jumped to their feet and started asking questions.

"I'll fill you in on the way to Smuggler's Arcane."

"Oh no. I get to give them the lowdown. You've never been very good at driving and talking at the same time, Molly," Olivia said. "I don't want the three of you joining me over here. There's not much to do."

Until we actually got out of the police station, I thought someone might stop me. My heart was pounding. I could barely breathe. I really hoped it wouldn't be Joe.

I had to find some way to get through to him. I didn't want to endanger him, but we couldn't go on this way.

But no one tried to stop me. We got out to the car and I looked back at the police station. I realized I might have no choice but to go it on my own.

I sat behind the steering wheel for a long time, trying not to fall apart. My hands were shaking as Olivia regaled Elsie and Dorothy with our "success."

It didn't feel much like success. I was pretty sure Joe suspected me of terrible things. Lieutenant Smith thought I'd somehow been part of Olivia's murder. What was I going to do?

We got back to the shop in record time. Dorothy sprinted up the stairs while Elsie and I came slower.

Cassandra was lounging on the counter. She'd eaten our entire stash of chocolate cream cakes. The floor was littered with wrappers where she'd dropped them.

"Good news." She sat up. "Nothing happened. The bad news is that I'm bored. I'm glad you finally got back."

"Don't leave!" Dorothy grabbed her arm. "You have to help us find my mother's killer before the police arrest Molly."

"Why is she touching me?" Cassandra asked. "You should teach her the rules, Molly. I'd hate to do something that she'd regret."

"Just let go of her, Dorothy," Olivia coaxed. "She could hurt you."

Dorothy let go and took a step back.

"Smart girl," Cassandra purred. "Wait! The newbie is the ghost's daughter? How is that possible?"

"We're more interested in what you know about the witch that killed Olivia. We know that witch is working with someone who has no magic." I put my hands on my hips. "Tell us what you know, Cassandra."

"I've told you what I can," she insisted. "You people can't know *everything*!"

"I know what to do." Elsie put down her bag.

"No, don't do it!" I didn't know what she had in mind, but I knew anything she tried might turn out badly.

It took only a moment. Cassandra didn't even react, as though she were smugly sure Elsie's spell wouldn't work.

"Too late." Dorothy went over and poked Cassandra. "I guess the spell worked. She's not moving."

"Of course it worked." Elsie sat down at the table. "But I'm exhausted now. Has anyone thought about lunch?"

Cassandra was a statue on our counter, right beside the cash register.

I knew the spell Elsie had used. It was strong enough to keep a herald of the Grand Council of Witches here for as long as we needed.

But there would be a hefty price to pay afterward.

"Now what are we going to do?" Dorothy stared at Cassandra's face. "She's gonna be angry."

"That's for sure." I took a deep breath. "What's done is done. Maybe we can get some straight answers this way."

"How?" Dorothy knocked on Cassandra's solid form.

Elsie nodded. "We'll have to get the seer. She should be able to tell us what Cassandra knows about Brian—and the rest of it. She might even be able to tell us where we can find our book."

"We've talked to her before." Olivia scrunched up her face. "I didn't like her. She was kind of scary. I don't know if my daughter should be exposed to her."

"I'll be fine." Dorothy smiled at her. "May I call you Mom? I know Mama or Mommy is out of the question. I'm not a little kid."

Olivia wasn't sure. "You know, I was only your mother for a few minutes, actually, although I have kept tabs on you since you were born. I suppose Mother would be okay."

"Thanks, Mother. This is really awesome that I still get to know you, even though you're dead. I really like being a witch."

"Do we have anything to pay the seer if we can get her to come?" I asked.

"We could have that very nice silver teapot from Olivia's house," Elsie offered. "You know she only takes the old silver. The new stuff isn't pure."

"Now wait a minute," Olivia protested. "You can't give away my belongings because I'm dead. That tea service belonged to Maria Theresa of Austria. It's worth a lot of money."

"Which doesn't mean anything to you anymore," Elsie reminded her. "How do you feel about it, Dorothy?"

"I guess it's okay, if we can figure out what's going on." Dorothy shrugged. "There are lots of nice things in the house, Mother."

"Only because I *put* them there," Olivia whined. "If you give everything away, there won't *be* any nice stuff."

"It's only this one time," Elsie said. "It's been at least twenty years since we had to get something from you to pay the seer. I can't even recall why we had to have her here."

"It was that stupid box we found by the ocean when we went on vacation in Greece together," Olivia remembered. 'It wasn't worth anything, but it cost me one of Queen Victoria's silver goblets."

"Well, let's get this done." I tried to end the debate. "I don't know any other way to pay the seer. Do you, Olivia?"

"No," she admitted. "But I wish the two of you would start collecting some antique silver so we wouldn't always have to raid *my* things."

"You mean *Dorothy's* things, right?" Elsie giggled.

Olivia didn't reply.

"While we're at the house, maybe we should try to do a spell to repair the damage that was done," Elsie suggested. 'We've done that before. I think it was after that last hurricane came through town."

"We can't do that, at least not yet," I disagreed. "There are already crime scene photos from the house. We could do it later after the investigation is over."

"I'm staying here with Cassandra." Elsie waved her hand in the air. "Bring back a pizza, please. I'm famished."

"I'm staying with you." Olivia hovered above the table. "I can't bear to look at my things again unless we can repair them."

"You two take care of Cassandra until we get back. For goodness' sake, don't let anything happen to her until the seer gets here."

"Don't worry," Elsie promised. "I won't let *anything* happen to her."

CHAPTER 19

The gift of sight, a precious thing,
Open my eyes, show me the way.
Light of moon. Water and wing.
Let me see, clear as day.

"How do you find a seer?" Dorothy asked as we drove
toward Olivia's house.

I was going to have to start thinking of it as *Dorothy's*
house. "You have to call a seer. Not on the phone. You have
to do a spell to reach out to her. I hope that's possible."

"What exactly does the seer do?"

"She's able to see through deception of any kind. There
is no spell or magic that she can't see. She sees the truth of
everything.

"So then what?"

"I suppose it all depends what we learn from her. We
could try to summon the council." I turned the car in to the
drive. "I've never done that. It might be worth the risk of
calling them to be done with this."

"Are they evil?" Dorothy's voice was filled with excitement. "Are they like Darth Vader evil?"

I turned off the car and rubbed my eyes. I was tired and
frustrated. Explaining every little detail of a witch's life to

Dorothy was taxing. I was trying to be patient. We needed each other. But this was why girls were raised by their mothers to be witches.

"No. They aren't evil. They're more like uncaring bureaucrats. They want everything to run smoothly, no bumps in the road. Unfortunately, life isn't like that."

"And part of their responsibilities is making sure people without magic don't know about magic, right?" Dorothy got out of the car. "Because really, I didn't have a clue. I thought it was all fairy tales and poison apples. My eyes have really been opened."

"How do you feel about that?" I asked before we went in.

"I'm charged up about it. I can't wait to do something amazing with my magic."

"I don't know if I've ever done something I'd consider to be amazing." I walked inside to the kitchen to find the silver teapot. "I guess I've always been happy that I was a witch, but my spells have been mediocre. I haven't needed anything more."

"Do you think that's why your magic is fading?"

It was an honest question, and one I'd asked myself. "I've known witches who were much older, even older than Elsie, and their magic was still strong. Not using magic to its full potential might be what causes it to go away. I don't know. Maybe it's like everything else that falls apart while you age. Maybe it's genetic."

She shrugged. "You know how they say if you don't use it, you lose it? That's what I was thinking."

"If we have to summon the council, you could ask them." I spied the silver teapot in the cupboard and took it down.

"I don't think so." She backed away from the idea. "They don't sound like witches I'd like to learn from."

"That's probably wise."

I repeated the spell for summoning a seer to us. It required both of us to put our hands into the teapot so she would know we had the silver. I added water to the silver to help things along.

We said the spell several times. I reminded Dorothy that concentration was everything. "If you lose focus in the middle of a spell, even for a moment, there could be disastrous results."

"I'll try to stay focused, Molly."

"I think that's done it," I told her finally. "She'll go to the shop. We should go there too. The seer doesn't like waiting."

"How can you tell when you've done the spell right?"

"You can't always." I gazed around the kitchen. Almost everything was on the floor, including food from the cabinets and the refrigerator. "You do the best you can with your choice of spell and your mental focus. Most of the time, it works."

As we walked out of the house, Dorothy asked, "Do you think we can put everything back the way it was?"

"I don't know. If we can find the right spell and get the focus correct, we should be able to do some of it. It could take a while. There are no guarantees."

She wrinkled her nose. "I can see that already. I think it's worth a shot though, don't you? I know it would make my mother happy."

"I'm sure you're right. I wish we could simply take it out of our book. Personalized spells that you've already done once or twice are the strongest."

"Thanks, Molly—for that—and for your patience with me. I know I must sound like a baby to you. It would've been great knowing all of this when I was growing up."

I hugged her briefly. "I was a schoolteacher for many years. Your questions don't bother me. Let's go get that pizza."

I called in the order at a small restaurant close by the Cotton Exchange. My plan was to pick up the pizza and take it with us. Usually we had it delivered to Smuggler's Arcane.

Today I was afraid of who might deliver it and accidentally become involved.

Dorothy went in for the pie, and we drove to the shop with the wonderful aromas of herbs, cheese and crust filling the car.

"There seem to be a lot of cars, considering the shop is closed." I had to hunt for a parking space. At least twenty cars were parked outside.

"I hope it's safe," Dorothy said. "I don't have the staff to hit anyone."

I laughed. "You'd better not let Olivia hear you say you're going to hit anyone with her staff. We need to find the right tool for you, being an earth witch. Probably your best bet would be a good, solid rock."

"A rock? You have a cauldron. Elsie has that cool sword. My mother has a runed staff. I get a *rock*?"

"Each according to their own," I told her. "It won't be just any rock. It will be something special."

"You mean like a big diamond?"

"Maybe. Or a flat, brown river rock. You'll know when you find it."

We took the pizza inside. I could see through the windows that a large group of people was jammed into the shop. What was going on?

As Dorothy and I entered Smuggler's Arcane, I realized that all the people were witches. I didn't recognize all of them, but I felt their magic. Music was blaring and the smell of incense filled the air.

I looked for Elsie in the crowd—it was easy to see Cassandra. As I watched, I saw a witch named Phoebe, who lived out at Atlantic Beach, give Elsie a dollar bill. Elsie stowed it in a pouch we kept for change and then moved aside to allow Phoebe access to Cassandra.

"*No!*" I called out as Phoebe poked Cassandra in the ribs several times. "What in the world are you doing? When she comes out of this spell, she'll know everything that happened to her."

Phoebe had a big grin on her swarthy face. "Yeah, well, at least we had this chance to get back at her. She's such a *princess*. Do you know what she did to my turtles last year? She deserves a lot more than a poke."

I pulled Elsie away from the crowd. Olivia, who'd been hovering around Cassandra, joined us in the supply room.

"What are you doing?"

"I'm making some money because we have to stay closed. I don't think that's a crime," Elsie said. "Where's the pizza?"

"Dorothy's got it. You'd better hope Cassandra can't remember this. She'll have your head."

"Oh, she's a lot of hot air." Elsie ignored my warning. "Where did you say the pizza was?"

"No pizza until we clear this crowd out," I told her. "If the seer shows up with the shop looking like there's a party going on, she'll leave."

Reluctantly, Elsie told everyone they had to go. She managed to make a couple more dollars from last-minute witches who poked Cassandra a few more times.

"I wish I'd known this was going on earlier." Kay lived in Wrightsville Beach and was a water witch like me. "She caused my marriage to break up. I would've brought something a lot stronger than a *poke*."

I nodded and smiled, escorted her to the door and locked it behind her. "I hope everyone who was here realizes that we probably can't do a spell strong enough to wipe Cassandra's memory of this."

I glanced into the parking lot. The last car had gone. I pulled down the shade.

"Oh, you're taking it too seriously, Molly." Elsie slid a piece of pizza out of the box.

Dorothy was already working on her second slice.

"That smells heavenly." Olivia inhaled slowly, closing

her eyes. "It's not much fun being a ghost. Why am I here anyway?"

"Unfinished business," Elsie said around the pizza in her mouth. "You were always good at starting projects and not finishing them."

"That's not fair. I didn't *ask* to be murdered. It ruined my whole life."

Dorothy laughed as she took a big gulp of soda. It came out of her nose before she could hold a napkin to it. "Sorry. It was just—you know—the whole murder-ruining-her-life thing."

"My own daughter, turned against me," Olivia said dramatically.

"If it would help, Mother, you don't have to stay for me." Dorothy smiled at her. "I release you from my training as a witch. Is that better?"

Olivia raised her brows. "We have to get this girl *trained*. She thinks everything is a spell."

A gray haze slowly fell over the shop. The lights were still on. The sun was still shining through the windows, but it was as though a shadow had darkened everything.

The shade was not only something that could be seen. It was also something that could be felt—like a terrible sadness or loss.

"She's here," I said unnecessarily. "Don't say anything, Dorothy. Let us do the talking."

She nodded, her eyes large and frightened in her face.

The door to the shop squeaked open slowly, but the chime didn't ring. The seer was suddenly there with us, the door closing behind her.

"You have summoned me."

It's difficult to describe the seer's voice. It was like a dry wind blowing through fall leaves in the trees. It's something you hear and feel in your soul. Even the most uninitiated know that they are standing in the presence of vast knowledge.

The seer, according to legends, had once been a Greek pythoness, one of the divine priestesses who sat at Delphi and interpreted the will of the gods for travelers who went there seeking answers.

Since that was thousands of years ago, most witches assumed she was immortal. No one had ever seen her face. She always appeared in a gray hooded robe that obscured everything about her but her stature. She was tall, and one of her hands was a skeletal claw that held a staff.

"Yes, seer." I bowed my head to show respect. "We have need of your service."

"And you have payment?"

"Yes." I brought out the old teapot. "We hope it pleases you."

She nodded and put the teapot inside her robe. "What is it you want of me?"

I turned to face Cassandra. "We need to know if the herald Cassandra has the answers we seek."

The seer didn't move. "I am curious what you seek."

"We seek to know who killed our friend." Elsie curtsied. She'd always been terrified of the seer. She thought she seemed more like the angel of death. "And took our spell book."

"And you believe the herald knows these answers?" The seer seemed to be ruminating over the task. "Why would she keep them from you?"

"Because that's what she does," Olivia had to add. "You know Cassandra thinks she's better than any of the rest of us."

"*Silence!* I do not speak with the undead."

The seer tipped her staff toward where Olivia was hovering above the pizza. After that, I could see Olivia's mouth moving, but I couldn't hear her.

"Cassandra is not in the form you have captured," the seer said. "There is nothing there now." She pointed her staff at the herald, still on the counter. "But there *is* something of what you seek. The thief does the witch's bidding. The witch protects the thief. Both are obscure and dangerous. Beware. Hold tight that which is yours."

As I watched, Cassandra began to crumble. It took only a few moments for her to be nothing but powder that covered everything beneath her.

"Oh my," Elsie muttered. "We killed Cassandra. This is very bad."

CHAPTER 20

I seek to find what has been lost.
With wand and light, I seek the way.

I was so busy staring at what was happening to Cassandra that I didn't realize the seer was gone until the gray fog lifted. "I wish we could have asked her a few more questions."

"That's the way it always is." Elsie picked up another piece of pizza and sighed as she ate it. "So what do we do now?"

"I don't know." I couldn't think of eating pizza, but I had a cup of tea to settle my stomach.

"I can't believe she did that to me," Olivia complained. "What did I ever do to her? And why is everyone so prejudiced against ghosts?"

"We were right and there are two people." Dorothy wiped her hands and mouth with a napkin.

"Out of the mouths of babes." Elsie shook her head.

"But we're no closer to knowing *who* they are," I said. "Or why the witch wants the thief to steal things for her."

"Or *him*." Elsie cleared her throat.

"Girls, I'm telling you—Brian isn't the way you're portraying him at all!" Olivia passionately protested. "He's a wonderful young man. You don't understand."

"Forget her," Elsie said. "She's a ghost. What does she know?"

"I've had about enough of that kind of talk." Olivia zoomed down toward Elsie. "You don't want to make me *angry*."

"I'm *so* scared." Elsie managed a small spell that pushed Olivia toward the door. She clapped her hands. "It worked!"

"Molly!" Olivia stamped her foot in the air. Obviously, without much significance.

"Let's concentrate." I fed some plain pizza crusts to the cats and stroked each of them. "We know there are two people—probably a witch and someone with no magic. They're working together to collect magic artifacts and maybe killing other witches."

"Why would anyone do that?" Elsie wondered.

"Maybe as Cassandra said, the witch wants to live forever."

"That doesn't make any sense," Elsie scoffed. "No one lives forever."

"People get desperate," I said. "Anything could happen."

"And they killed Olivia!"

"Do we have to say it *quite* that way?" Olivia asked.

"It's no secret that we're witches—at least not to the witch community," I continued. "It would be easy for us to be targets."

"Where does Brian fit in?" Dorothy asked.

Olivia made a growling sound.

"We don't know yet," Elsie translated.

"Let's keep an open mind," I suggested. "Maybe Olivia is right about him. Let's try to talk to Colt Manning about what he heard that night. And there has to be someone else who knows Brian Fuller. We need more information about him."

"Do you want to stir up *that* hornet's nest?" Elsie asked. "He could go after Joe."

"We'll work around it. He won't know." I *hoped* he wouldn't know anyway.

"What about Cassandra?" Olivia's movements spread some of the gray dust that had been Cassandra on the floor. "Shouldn't you get in touch with the council and let them know what happened?"

"Do we *know* what happened?" Dorothy shrugged. "Just asking."

"I think we'll save that for later," I said. "I want to get in touch with the council about Cassandra as much as I want to fly across the moon on a broomstick."

Elsie giggled. "Good one, Molly."

We were all out of the shop and locking up when Mike drove up in his old Camaro.

"Hey, Mom. Elsie." He eyes focused on his real reason for visiting. "Hi, Dorothy."

"We're in a little bit of a hurry." I opened the car doors. "Can we talk about whatever it is later?"

"Actually, I was here to see if this was a good time for Dorothy to have coffee or whatever."

"Oh." Dorothy looked at me. "Is this a good time?"

"I don't think there could be a worse time."

"Come on, Mom. I could go with you and help out with . . . whatever you're doing."

"We have some things we have to do for Olivia, Mike. I'm sure you don't want to do that kind of boring stuff."

The expression on his face said otherwise. "Give me a chance. I feel bad about Olivia too. I can be a big help."

It was against my better judgment, but things had to get better between us if I ever hoped to know what was going on with him. It was the only way I might persuade him to go back to school. "All right." I gave in. "But you'll have to drive since we can't all fit in my car."

His gaze was excited. "Maybe Dorothy could ride with me."

It was a done deal. Dorothy got in the Camaro with Mike. Olivia played chaperone in their backseat.

"I'd hate to be Mike if he tries anything funny with Dorothy," Elsie said as we left the parking lot. "There's nothing worse than an angry, protective mom-ghost."

"You're right. I hope he'll tell Dorothy what's wrong at school. If it's a girl, she could take his mind off it."

Traffic was light going to the other end of Water Street. There were no guarantees that our only witness would be there, but if we were lucky, we'd find him.

There was a bar near the spot where the riverboats docked that was popular with fishermen. At least it would be a place to start asking around about him.

I parked in a public parking zone, and Mike parked next to me. He was still in the car talking to Dorothy when Olivia streamed out of the window like hot air on a cold day.

"You have managed to bring up your son without a bit of class or manners," Olivia accused when she reached me.

"I *told* you." Elsie smirked as she tried to keep from smacking the door into the car next to her.

"Olivia, leave them alone," I told her. "Nothing is going to happen."

"He was looking at her *chest*, Molly," Olivia complained. "She didn't see it, but I did."

Elsie laughed out loud. "If we're going into a bar, I want a Sex on the Beach drink. I had one last summer. It was really good."

"It's not that kind of bar—no cute drinks." I searched for a good place to set a spell for finding Colt Manning. "And we're here to work, not to drink."

I remembered a spell I'd used years ago to find Mike one rainy afternoon when he'd wandered off. He was only about eight years old. I hoped I remembered it correctly.

"Isn't Dorothy going to help?" Olivia asked. "Or are you just going to let her sit in the car so *your* son can ogle her?"

Dorothy waved as she got out of the car. Mike followed on her heels like a big, cute puppy.

"How are we gonna ditch him?" Elsie asked.

"We're going somewhere he can't follow." I smiled and waved back.

I pretended not to hear Mike try to order a beer at the counter inside. The bartender asked for ID. Mike shrugged and got a club soda instead.

He assumed a patient expression when I announced that we were going to the ladies' room.

"Are we really going to try to find this man with a spell in the ladies' room?" Dorothy tried not to touch anything in the less-than-sanitary room. "I've never even been in a bathroom at a bar. *Ugh!*"

"Never mind. Concentrate." I held out my hands to her and Elsie. I recited the spell for Dorothy so she could hear what it sounded like, and for Elsie because she couldn't remember it. I held the small cauldron and the amulet around my throat. Elsie took out her sword.

The bathroom door opened and a young woman entered. She took one look at Elsie's sword and headed back out the way she'd come. Two other women weren't so shy. They came in, lit cigarettes and then stood there, watching us.

"What now?" Dorothy didn't take her eyes off the other woman.

"Let's go into one of the stalls." I moved in that direction. *"Seriously?"*

"Yes. At least we'll be alone."

Once the three of us had squeezed into one stall and closed the door behind us, I repeated the spell again.

"Ready?"

"When do I get my rock?" Dorothy asked. "Should I go and look for it, or will it find me?"

"Shh." I closed my eyes. "Concentrate on what we're doing, or you might not like the results. It's all in the focus."

Dorothy was quiet then, her eyes closed and her hands clasped in ours. We recited the finding spell together several times.

"Is that it?" she whispered when we were finished.

"I don't know. We'll have to wait and give him a chance to get here."

"Not *here*, right?" Dorothy carefully opened the stall door. "In the bar?"

"Yes." I smiled at the women who were talking and smoking.

"I had a sword like that once," one of them said to Elsie. "Nice."

"Thanks."

I pulled Elsie away from discussing the merits of her sword with them, and we walked out of the bathroom.

"Dorothy, you aren't interested in that boy, are you?" Olivia was still worried about Mike. "He's so much younger than you, and a college dropout."

"That's my son you're talking about," I said as we found a table. "And since when do you care how old the man is, or if he went to college?"

Olivia frowned. "That was different, Molly. I want something better for my daughter."

"Relax," Dorothy said. "I'm not interested in him that way. But he's . . . nice."

"Well, he's gone now." Elsie looked around the bar. "Maybe you could call his cell phone or something."

"Of course. It's always in his pants."

Olivia folded her arms across her chest. "And he better keep it there *too*."

Elsie giggled. "Molly, please call the boy before we have a war."

That's when I remembered that I didn't have a working

cell phone, not after the dunk in the river. Elsie's and Dorothy's phones were also ruined. Magic and electronics weren't a good mix, at least not for me.

I was about to go outside and look for Mike when the door to the bar opened and Brian walked inside.

CHAPTER 21

A new bond of friendship and trust is made.
It prospers and grows.
Seal the bond and put trouble aside.
My word to yours.

"What do we do *now*?" Elsie muttered. "Weren't we hoping to avoid running into him?"

"Let's spend some time with him," Olivia suggested. "You'll see he's not the villain you think he is."

"Shouldn't we run away?" Dorothy asked. "There's no water here for him to throw us into, but he could find something else to hurt us."

At that moment, an older man wandered into the bar too. He was wearing jeans and a plaid flannel shirt. He glanced around and scratched his head as though he wasn't sure why he was there.

"That's Colt Manning." I tried to point to him without being obvious.

"How can you be sure?" Dorothy wondered.

"You can tell by the confused stare," Elsie replied. "I look the same way most mornings when I get up, and I'm not spelled."

"So what do we *do*?" Dorothy looked worried. "What do we say to him? What do we do about *Brian*?"

"What did you have in mind, pretty girl?" Brian was there beside us—with Mike in tow. "Hey, we thought we'd come in and join you, Molly. And you're Elsie, right?"

He and Mike pushed in with us at the table.

Mike had the same glazed-over expression in his eyes that I recognized from Colt Manning. He had no idea what was going on. Brian was directing his movements.

"Brian!" Olivia waved from above us. "It's *me*. That's my daughter you're flirting with."

"Awkward." Elsie looked away.

"Olivia." Brian smiled at her. "I'm glad you're here. Maybe you can tell these ladies that I didn't kill you."

"I've tried." She touched her hair, a familiar gesture she'd used when she was alive. "They won't listen."

"The truth is that she doesn't *know* who killed her," I explained. "We think it was a witch—"

"Or someone who isn't a witch working with someone who is," Dorothy added.

"So you're still coming after *me*?" His mouth was set in a dark line. "What can I do to convince you that it's not a good idea?"

I leaned across the table, not so afraid as angry. "You could release my son. He's not involved in this. You could tell us what you know about what happened to Olivia. That would be good for a start."

"Unless you *are* the one who killed her." Elsie peeked out from under her hat.

"It wasn't me," he proclaimed.

"See?" Olivia smiled and fluttered around. "I told you so."

"That doesn't prove anything," Dorothy said. "Anyone could say that."

"What do you want me to say?" Brian asked her.

"Our witness is leaving." Elsie nodded at Colt Manning.

"Oh my gosh!" Dorothy shot to her feet. "I'm sorry, but I have to go! I'm late for work. Can Mike take me?"

"Go on." Brian released Mike. "I'll catch up with you later."

Dorothy handed me the staff. "I probably shouldn't take this with me."

"That's fine." I laid it on the table. "We'll see you later."

"Are you *sure* you're okay here?" She glanced significantly at Brian.

He nodded. "I'm harmless."

"Falling off the riverboat wasn't harmless," she retorted.

"That wasn't me! Besides, you were with a water witch—nothing was going to happen to you."

"We're fine," I assured her. "Go on to work. We'll talk later."

"What about Colt Manning?" Elsie reminded me. "It's now or never."

I watched Mike and Dorothy leave the bar and then glanced at Brian. "You want to prove yourself? Come with us."

"Okay." He nodded. "After you."

We walked quickly outside and had to scan the street to find Colt Manning. He was walking away at a slow pace, going toward the river. I grabbed Elsie's hand and we went to talk to our witness. Brian followed us.

"Mr. Manning?" I called breathlessly. "Excuse me. Mr. Colt Manning?"

He turned and smiled. "Yes. Something I can do for you?"

"I'm Molly Renard and this is Elsie Langston. You spoke with police about the night our friend, Olivia Dunst, was killed in the alley back there."

"Oh yes." He nodded. "I'm sorry your friend died."

"We were wondering if you could tell us what you heard."

"Sure." He coughed. "I was sitting on a bench, waiting

for my head to clear. I'd had a few too many. But I wasn't driving, so I thought I'd just sit here and wait until I felt better."

"And you heard something?" Elsie prodded.

"Yeah. I heard some scuffling sounds, but there are some big rats down here by the river. Then I heard a woman scream. I stood up and started that way. Someone ran out of the alley. It was dark. I didn't get a good look at a face or anything."

"What *did* you see?" I asked him.

"Like I told the police, the person was dressed in black. Short too, maybe less than five feet. He ran up the street and disappeared."

"Disappeared?" Elsie questioned sharply.

"Well," Manning chuckled. "Not really *disappeared*. Just kind of blended into the dark, I guess. I took out my phone and called the police."

"Did you go into the alley to see what happened?" Brian asked him.

"No way! Things happen back there. I felt bad about it, but the cops said she was dead already anyway. I couldn't have saved her." He hung his head. "I'm sorry."

"That's okay." Elsie gave him a kiss on the cheek. "We appreciate you telling us what happened."

"Sure." He smiled at her. "Hey, you want to get a beer or something?"

Elsie was ready to go with him, but she bit her lip and demurred when I glared at her. "Maybe next time, thanks."

We thanked him again for his time and walked toward the car.

"You see," Brian said. "Not me. I couldn't be mistaken for being less than five feet—even if I were dressed in black and it was dark outside."

"Except that he was drunk," Elsie reminded him.

"Come on." He leaned on the hood of the car. "I did what you asked."

I wasn't impressed with Colt Manning's statement either. No wonder Joe and Lisbet were so frustrated. I wasn't certain that let Brian off the hook, but I had no proof that he was involved either.

Brian leaned close to me. "I didn't kill Olivia. Hunting me down is a waste of your time."

"We weren't hunting you down. We came here to see Mr. Manning."

He seemed surprised. "No? I came because I felt you pulling me here, like you did Manning. That's why I spelled your son—for protection."

Elsie shrugged, and I felt a shiver race up my spine. Was Olivia right, and Brian wasn't the rogue witch? Had someone compelled him to come here because it would set us against each other?

"That wasn't us," I replied. "But it could be whoever is responsible for all of this." I quickly explained about the disappearance of magic artifacts, fears that other witches might be dead and the council's dithering on the problem. "I think they're afraid of this witch too."

He glanced away, acting like it didn't matter, but his voice was worried. "Seriously? I don't remember why I came here at all. I feel like a zombie. That takes some power, in *my* case."

"Can we just smack him for being so obnoxious?" Elsie asked.

"So what are you doing about this? What's the council doing?"

"Nothing right now," I answered. "We're trying to see what we can find without them. We're hoping they'll take over once we have some answers. I don't think we can handle this witch by ourselves."

"Maybe with *your* help—" Olivia's tone was seductive. "I know how *strong* you are, Brian."

"And you owe us for throwing us in the water," I reminded him. "And threatening my family."

"I didn't throw any of you in the water," he argued. "That had to be this other witch."

"But you did threaten Molly's family," Elsie said.

"Let's take it out in trade, shall we?" He held out his hand. "I owe you a debt. You name it."

I put my hand in his. We both whispered a similar bonding spell. "Yes, you do. I'll let you know when we need you."

Elsie and I got in the car. Olivia darted in through an open window. I drove quickly to the downtown library and parked. I wanted to tell Dorothy that everything was all right. I knew she'd be worried. We were going to have to do something about getting new cell phones. This wasn't the Middle Ages!

"There she is!" Olivia pointed her out when we were inside the building.

"And there's Mike with her." I smiled at him.

"You know this is never going to work between my daughter and your son," Olivia told me.

"Why not?"

"Because I want her to marry another witch. Maybe someone strong, but not evil like her father."

"Why would you want that?" Elsie asked.

"I don't know." Olivia tried to toss her hair. Nothing moved. "I think it might be better. And then her children would probably have magic too."

"There are worse things than your children not having magic," I told her.

"I know. But I feel so *bad* for you and Elsie being married to people you can't talk to about magic, and now having children you can't talk to about it. I wish you could know the joys of being a witch's mother."

"Oh brother!" Elsie sat down at a book table. "You've been a witch's mother for all of a day!"

Dorothy and Mike looked surprised to see us.

"Hi, Mom. Find what you were looking for?" Mike quickly removed his arm from Dorothy's shoulders.

"We should separate them *now*!" Olivia tried to wedge herself between Dorothy and Mike.

"What did you find out?" Dorothy asked carefully. "Did you talk to you-know-who about you-know-what?"

I smiled at her expression. She was definitely the kind of person I wanted to play poker with. Everything was written on her face.

"I forgot my bag in the car." I tossed Mike my keys. "Would you mind getting it?"

He minded—*a lot*. But he did it.

When he was gone, Elsie, Olivia and I explained what Colt Manning had told us and what had happened with Brian.

"I'm so relieved!" She let out a long breath. "I was afraid he might do something terrible to you."

"I think we'll be okay with him, for now anyway," I assured her.

"What about the killer?" She glanced at her mother. "If we eliminate Brian, all we have is a short person who dresses in black and likes to steal magic items. That's not much."

"I know."

"Maybe you should just give up this quest for my killer, Molly." Olivia smiled and tried to act as though it didn't matter. "We need to concentrate on training Dorothy. That's more important. What's done is done, so to speak."

"Except that we still don't have our spell book." Elsie picked up a book and shuffled through it.

"And we can't give up on this." I reached out to Olivia's not-so-solid form. "You're our sister. We can't let this go. I don't want the police to find this witch, even if they find her accomplice. If the council is afraid, the witch could kill any police officer who comes knocking on her door. We *have* to do this."

Olivia made sobbing sounds, though her eyes were dry. "Oh, girls, I love you so much. I don't know how I would have lived my life without you."

"For better or for worse then." Elsie grinned. "Let's get some tea, shall we?"

Mike brought my bag up. We left right away. Dorothy was trying to work, after all.

I smiled at him as we were going back to the cars. "You like Dorothy, huh?"

"She's awesome. Who knew you'd be friends with someone like her?"

"I appreciate that."

"I don't mean because she's young and beautiful." He attempted to explain. "Well, not completely. I mean, she's really smart and knows a lot about the world."

I put my hand on his face. "I think you'd better stop before it gets any worse."

"Are you okay with me asking her out?"

"You already asked her out. I think the two of you make a nice couple."

He tilted his head back. "We're not a *couple*, Mom. We're just dating—if I get lucky. I can't be too serious about a woman right now since my whole future is ahead of me."

"Is that what happened that made you leave school? Did you and a girl get too serious?"

"No. What are you talking about?"

"Why did you leave school, Mike? I think your father and I deserve to know. It's not fair to play games with us."

"It's nothing." He stared straight through me. "I-I don't want to talk about it."

"All right. I'll see you at home later." At least he'd admitted that there *was* a problem. That was something. "I love you."

"Yeah." He ducked his head as he got in his Camaro. "See you later."

In the car, I turned to Elsie. "We have to try to contact Cassandra again. Failing that, we have to contact the council. I don't know what else to do."

Elsie agreed. "There will be hell to pay if we let the seer destroy what was left of Cassandra, but you're right, Molly."

"I hope we can do a decent summoning spell without Dorothy." I started the car.

We tentatively agreed on our course of action and headed for Smuggler's Arcane. It would be the best and safest place to consult the council, if that was what it took.

"Oh look!" Elsie said as we pulled into our parking place in front of the shop. "It's Larry. Is it Wednesday already? I've lost all track of time."

"Of course it's Wednesday," Olivia said. "I'm dead, and I know *that*."

Elsie glared at her and then got out of the car. She had a soft spot for Larry.

He was an older werewolf who lived on a boat. At the right time of the month, he anchored off the coast to make sure he didn't make any mistakes during his change. He'd been a vegetarian for the last twelve years. He always came in for his special tea and a new book before the moon got full.

"I was beginning to worry about you." Larry took in Olivia's present state, swiping his hand across his graying beard. "Geez, what happened to you? I'm gone a few weeks and everything changes."

We explained as we went inside. Elsie already had Larry's special herbal tea mixed. She even put a purple bow on top of the bag she gave him.

"Are you gonna stay a ghost?" Larry asked Olivia. "I mean, there's nothing wrong with that. It's just unusual to see a witch in ghost form."

Olivia smiled. "It's about time someone had something *good* to say about ghosts. I don't know how long I'm going to remain this way, but I'd like to think of it as time well spent."

"Yeah, sure." Larry took the bag of tea from Elsie with a wink and a smile at her. "Thanks, doll."

Elsie giggled. "I have the perfect book for you too." She searched the counter, but everything was such a mess, covered with bits of Cassandra. "I might have left it on the shelf."

Larry leaned down and sniffed the dust. "What is this stuff?"

"Just some remodeling." Elsie looked for the lost book.

"Remodeling with witch dust?" Larry shook his head. "What are you up to in here, ladies?"

"It might be best not to say anything to anyone about this," I added. "There are some things going on right now. Have you found that book yet, Elsie?"

She pulled a book off the shelf. "I guess I'm not going to be able to find the book I put aside for you, Larry. But this is a very good book too. I'll try to find the other one the next time you come in."

"You're the best, Elsie." He kissed her on the cheek and took the book. "I'll be out on the boat next few days. Full moon. I wouldn't want to be around here. I heard about that woman who was killed in the alley by the river. Werewolves are easy prey for accusations after something like that."

"That was *me*," Olivia said. "And I wasn't killed by a wolf. I think it was only a magic-hungry witch who cut my throat and left me to die."

That was more information than Larry wanted to hear. His face turned a pasty shade of green and he swallowed hard. He was squeamish for a werewolf. Not that I'd known many, but the ones I had known were a little more bloodthirsty. Witches and werewolves rarely mingled.

"I better get going." He tried to smile and finally gave up, leaving Smuggler's Arcane as quickly as he could.

"He's such a nice man." Elsie lifted Barnabas and stroked his soft fur. "I could imagine making tea for him in bed every morning." She sighed lustfully.

Olivia laughed, apparently still a little miffed by their earlier conversation. "Elsie, dear, I think those days might be over for you. No doubt Bill was your last love."

Even I was shocked at the level Olivia had sunk to with that jibe.

"You're right." Elsie sat down at the table and adjusted the red beret. Her eyes welled with tears. "I'm just a crazy old woman who no man will ever look at again."

I glared at Olivia. She bit her lip.

"I am so sorry, Elsie," she apologized. "I'm a wee bit frustrated right now with being dead and all."

"That's okay. I understand. At least I *had* a man for more than forty years. He lied and cheated almost every day we were together. But at least I had someone to wake up with each morning." Elsie slyly smiled. "And I'm not dead *yet*, which means I still have more game than *you*."

I laughed as I lifted the trapdoor into the cave. "All right, you two. Let's get this over with. Cassandra isn't going to come to us on her own. We have to call her."

The magic was there for us. It would've been stronger with Dorothy, but I could feel that the summoning spell had worked. There was still no answer from Cassandra.

"What do you think that means?" Elsie asked.

"It means that you killed Cassandra," Olivia said. "You put that spell on her, and it worked, for a change, but it killed her instead of suspending her. You should know better by now than to lose your temper and do something silly."

"Is that what you think, Molly?" Elsie asked me.

"I don't know what to think right now. I'm tired. It's been a long day. I think we should keep this to ourselves awhile longer. If we don't hear anything from Cassandra by tomorrow, we'll call the council."

"Good thinking," Olivia said. "Cassandra doesn't always answer right away anyhow. She could be in Venezuela right now. I'm sorry I said she was dead, Elsie. I don't think any of us have the magic for that. I spoke hastily. I guess I'm tired too."

"I don't know." Elsie put away her sword. "Maybe Aleese is right and I just need to go to a retirement home."

"Even if you did, you'd still be a witch." I put my arm around her shoulders. "You've always been a *very* good witch. Don't give up yet. We'll find someone to take your place."

"Promise not to die so I get the next witch?"

"I promise." I touched my mother's amulet. "Let's go home. We'll start again tomorrow."

We went upstairs and closed the trapdoor. We got our things together and were ready to go.

"Girls," Olivia called. "You're forgetting my staff. You know I can't leave here without my staff. Just take it home with you, Molly."

"Good night, Olivia." Elsie waved.

"See you tomorrow," I said.

"Come on. You can't just leave me here all night. I need a home too. Molly? Elsie?"

We walked outside and closed the door behind us, locking it securely.

"That was kind of mean," Elsie remarked.

"Yes, it was," I agreed. "Any problem with that?"

"No. I'm fine with it. I'm sure Dorothy will take her home later. For now, we'll let her stew."

I dropped Elsie off at her house and drove home from there. Mike's Camaro was in the drive next to Joe's SUV.

For a minute, I wished things were back the way they had been two or three years ago. I wished Joe weren't planning to retire and that Mike were still living at home.

But life had moved on, and I had to move with it. I went inside; the TV was on. The smell of pizza filled the house. I wished it had been anything but pizza. I'd had a little too much pizza the last couple of days.

"Hey, Mom," Mike greeted me from his spot on the sofa. "Dad brought pizza home to celebrate."

"Yes?" I smiled at him as Joe walked into the kitchen. "What are we celebrating?"

"We arrested Olivia's killer today, Molly. I thought that was cause to party."

CHAPTER 22

I call upon the ancient forest,
And the cold sea.
Keep my secrets safe from prying ears,
Keep them close to me.

I was hopeful. Joe was a hardworking and experienced detective. I knew he'd captured many bad guys in his years with the police.

The problem was, at least to my mind, that this was a unique situation. As far as I knew, Joe had never been involved with witches in any way. That made things more complicated, and the rules he usually followed didn't apply.

"Aren't you interested in who we arrested?" He took one of the pizzas out of a box.

"Sorry. Of course I am. I was caught up in thoughts about Olivia."

He slid his hand up and down my arm in a sympathetic manner. "I'm sorry. Maybe we shouldn't be celebrating. It reminds you of what happened."

I bowed my head. He was so sweet after our terrible discussion at the police station today. I knew he was as upset over Olivia's death as I was. He wanted to understand what was going on. So did I.

"No," I replied quietly. "Tell me."

"It was someone you know, as a matter of fact. His name is Larry Tyler. He lives on a houseboat. He actually gave you as a character reference when we picked him up. He said he was good friends with you and Elsie."

There it was again. I saw the suspicion in Joe's eyes. I loved him, but I wanted to hit him with a sledgehammer. How could he think I could be involved with Olivia's death? Now he thought Larry, Elsie and I were in on it together.

"Really?" I maintained my calm outer demeanor. "Yes, I know Larry. He's a regular at the shop."

"Killers are frequently people the victim knows and trusts." Joe quoted words I'd heard him say many times.

"What makes you think Larry killed Olivia?"

"We found his prints on the second exam of the crime scene. We also found some hair and blood samples that match his. He hasn't confessed, but we know it was him."

"Did those blood samples match the ones you found at Olivia's house?"

"No. That's something we haven't pieced together yet. Maybe he had an accomplice."

"Larry never seemed like a killer to me."

Joe rolled his eyes. "Do you know how many times I've heard that from people who know confessed killers? No one ever spots it—until it's too late."

"I suppose that's true. Still, hair and fingerprints in an alley frequently used between bars and restaurants seems a bit circumstantial."

"Circumstantial?" Joe glanced at Mike. "Look at your mom, Son. She's a regular Sherlock Holmes today."

I gritted my teeth. He was being *so* obnoxious. "What about the murder weapon? And don't blame me because I've been married to a cop for the last thirty years."

"As a matter of fact, we searched his houseboat today. We found the knife on board. Surprised?"

Not surprised. *Dumbfounded*. It was as though someone were watching the shop.

To make matters worse, Larry was on the verge of changing. The full moon was only a few nights away. I wasn't sure how shape-shifters had avoided police and government detection in the last hundred years or so. I knew it was vital for it to remain that way. The council certainly worked hard to keep witches under the radar.

I knew Larry wasn't guilty. I knew he was being set up by the rogue witch and her accomplice. Were we getting close? Did they throw Larry into the mix to make it harder for us to find out who they were—as they might have done with Brian that day?

It seemed laughable to me that a witch as powerful as the one we were talking about would be worried about me, Elsie, Dorothy or even Brian. He or she would know that we weren't exactly a force to be reckoned with.

I couldn't try to persuade Joe to investigate further without sounding as though I knew more than I was telling. The witch thought he had us right where he wanted us.

Maybe he did—but I had one more card to play. It was risky. I'd never contemplated it before. I had to do something. This seemed to be the only answer.

"Could I talk to you for a moment in the bedroom?" I began walking in that direction.

"You're in for it now, Dad." Mike laughed. "I know *that* voice. I think it was the same voice I heard when I got that C minus in chemistry last quarter."

Joe looked surprised as he finished eating the slice of pizza he'd started. "Sure, Molly."

My hands were shaking and cold. I fingered both amulets around my neck. If they had any magic to lend me, this would be a good time. I was terrified, not only of doing the wrong thing, but that I would screw it up.

"What's up?" He came into the bedroom and closed the

door. "If it's about what happened today at the police station—"

"It's something to do with that." I moved close to him and hoped that what I was about to do would work.

I muttered an enchantment that I'd learned when I was very young. It was very basic and simple. It was supposed to create a barrier between a witch and the world around her. Light, sound and other distractions were eliminated.

The witch could use this for meditation or for making a place where she couldn't be heard talking to another person. The spell was also to neutralize all other spells that might have been cast on the witch.

"What's going on, Molly? What are you doing?"

I heard fear in Joe's voice and slowly opened my eyes.

We were encased in a neutral space. Everything had become colorless around us. There was no sound except our voices. No witchcraft except my own.

I did it! The amulets felt warm against my skin.

"This is a safe place for us to talk," I explained. "We can't be overheard. How do you feel?"

He surveyed the small space around us. "I feel like I've been kicked in the head. What happened?"

"What's the last thing you remember?"

He thought back. "You told me you wanted to talk. What's going on?"

I studied his face. "There is no easy way to tell you this, but it's necessary."

"What? I've lost my mind? I've had a stroke? Whatever it is, I need to know."

I smiled, even though my stomach was in knots. "I'm a witch."

"In other words, I've lost my mind. I guess that explains it. You're not really here. Maybe I'm not here either."

"It's dangerous for me to tell you this, or I would've told you years ago. Witches are bound to serve the Grand

Council. The council has been known to wipe out entire lives full of memories from people like you who have no magic."

"Yeah. Can I just go back to sleep now? Maybe I'll survive and this will be a bad dream."

"I'm afraid it's not that easy. I wouldn't have done this if something terrible hadn't happened."

I explained everything—from Olivia and Elsie being witches to what had happened with Brian and Mike. I could see from his face how hard it was for him to take it all in. It would've been hard for anyone. But for a man who deals with facts and figures every day for a living, it was almost impossible.

"So this bad witch has threatened me and Mike. Someone killed Olivia for her magic and took your spell book for the same purpose."

"That's right."

"And then he went after Larry Tyler to throw someone else under the bus. Does that sum it up?"

"Yes. I know it's hard to believe."

"It's *impossible* to believe. There isn't any *real* magic in the world, Molly. This isn't *Bewitched*. Either you—or I—need a shrink."

"There might be a way I can convince you." I thought fast, feeling desperate for this to work. I was tired of being alone and worried about him. "I might be able to do one other spell."

I concentrated hard on doing one of the first spells I'd ever learned. I wasn't an air witch, like Olivia; it would've been easier on water.

"Hey!" Joe called out. "Molly, what's going on?"

I opened my eyes. Both of us were still inside the enchanted bubble, but I had also managed to displace enough air that we were floating about a foot off the bedroom carpet.

"It worked! I've been having a little trouble with my spells recently. But this one worked."

"I believe you. I believe you." He put his arms around me. "Now, please put us back down."

I shouldn't have said anything about the spell working. We were abruptly dropped back to the floor. The privacy bubble still maintained around us, but even that magic was starting to give me a headache.

"There are witches and shape-shifters, Joe. There are also werewolves, like Larry, who will go through the change in one of your jail cells if you don't find a way to release him."

"What can I do, Molly? We've got so much against him. I can't let him go."

"We'll have to think of something." The bubble around us was starting to deteriorate. The world was starting to push back. "When we get out of here, Joe, we can never speak of this again outside a neutral space like this."

"But what if something comes up?"

"We need a code word."

"What about 'broccoli'? You know how much I hate broccoli. I'd never even say the word unless it was an emergency."

"'Broccoli' it is."

"I love you, Molly." He kissed me and held me tight. "In case I haven't said it since Olivia died."

"I was afraid you thought I'd killed Olivia," I said quickly.

"I didn't think that. I was just afraid that you might be involved in some other way. Everything has been so weird. I guess I know why now."

The enchanted bubble slowly melted away, like ice after a winter storm. We were back in the real world.

"I love you too." It was a terrible risk I'd taken telling him the truth. I'd known so many witches who'd regretted telling their spouses about magic. I could only hope I wouldn't be sorry.

There was a rap on the bedroom door before Mike opened it. "Hey! You guys aren't supposed to be in here doing this kind of thing. Dad, Lisbet is here to see you."

"Thanks," Joe said with a wink at me. "And we're married. We can do it whenever and wherever we want."

"You know, I just ate," Mike retorted and left the room.

"Right." Joe took a deep breath before he followed him.

Despite my fears, my heart felt light and free. Joe still loved me as I had always loved him. Thirty years hadn't diminished what I felt for him.

I went into the kitchen and grabbed a slice of pizza as Joe and Lisbet spoke together quietly by the door. "Hello, Lisbet," I said pleasantly.

"Oh, hey, Molly. Sorry if we gave you a rough time today. Just following the leads as they come up. I never thought you had anything to do with killing your friend."

"I understand. Don't worry about it. I'm glad you got Olivia's killer."

"Yeah. Me too."

Joe and Lisbet went out. They were starting another case that they had a lead on. Now that their part of the investigation into Olivia's murder was over, they were free to move on to something else.

It seemed to me that it was a good thing. Without all the attention focused on a case that involved me, there would be less pressure on Joe.

On the other hand, there was the matter of getting Larry out of jail. There was only one way I could think of to take care of that problem—we were going to have to speak to the local werewolf representative.

CHAPTER 23

The perfect love is here for me
The only one who is meant to be.
This spell guides us to unite,
Stay with me through this tonight.

I called Elsie first thing the next morning.

It had been such a pleasure to really *be* with Joe again. He'd come home late last night, and we'd talked in roundabout language to manage a few words about magic. We'd gotten up together and eaten breakfast. Mike had slept in, of course. It was nice to have the private time together.

"I'll see you later," Joe said when he'd kissed me good-bye.

It was a wonderful, lingering kiss. "Yes. I love you. Good luck today."

"You too." He glanced around the room. "You know, your *friend* has no attorney. He's supposed to be appointed one today at his bail hearing. They aren't always the best in the world."

I took the tip that he gave me. I didn't see where there was any harm in what he'd said. I could tell he was nervous saying it. I knew it would always have to be this way.

I couldn't tell Elsie about my big reveal to Joe. I knew she'd never told Bill. She didn't trust him not to make a mistake, despite their long relationship.

It was one of the perks of being married to another witch, as Olivia had said. You could share that deepest part of yourself with that person.

I picked Elsie up at her house. Aleese was surprisingly pleasant. She asked me if I wanted to come in for coffee. Elsie was putting the finishing touches on her purple ensemble, including purple hat and shoes.

"We don't have time for coffee," she told her daughter. "There are important matters afoot."

"Better grab an umbrella, Mom," Aleese said. "It's supposed to rain today. Good luck with your important matters."

Elsie grabbed a purple-flowered umbrella from the stand near the front door. "Love you, darling. Take care."

As we were walking out to the car, I commented on Elsie's rejuvenated relationship with her daughter. "The two of you were very nearly friendly today."

"She's seeing someone. It always puts her in a better mood. I think I may have done a love spell that worked for her. Now, tell me again why we're going to see the werewolf representative. You know they mostly don't like us."

"And we don't like them." I opened the car door for her and then went around to the driver's side. "It's the age-old feud between witches and everyone else."

"There's plenty of good reason for that," she reminded me, closing her door after I helped her buckle up.

"I'm sure there is, but there's even more good reason for us to try to address this issue with Larry. If he turns in jail, it could be disastrous."

"Let's break him out," Elsie suggested. "There's no reason to involve other werewolves. You know Larry is nothing like them."

"I don't think we should try to do this by ourselves."

We had never been to Dorothy's apartment. It was on Market Street, within walking distance of the library. The building had once been an old hospital during the Civil War. Now it was four apartments.

Dorothy came out with a cat carrier. She and Elsie exchanged compliments on each other's choice of purple garments. She was wearing a white top with a purple and pink plaid skirt. Her black boots went slightly below her knee.

"I thought I'd bring my cat with me today. It might be good for him to hang out with your cats. You seem to be able to communicate with Harper, Isabelle and Barnabas. Scooter doesn't communicate with me."

"Scooter?" Elsie's tone made it clear what she thought of the cat's name. "You'll have to come up with something better than that. A witch's cat needs a classic name."

"Oh. Is that the problem?" Dorothy glanced around in the car. "Where's my mother? Did she decide to stay home?"

Elsie and I exchanged guilty smiles.

"Olivia doesn't really have a home anymore," I explained. "She lives wherever her staff is."

"Where's that?" Dorothy played with her cat through the mesh in the carrier.

"Last night, it was Smuggler's Arcane," Elsie said. "Tonight, it could be wherever *you* choose to take her."

"Was I supposed to be responsible for that?" Dorothy's face was shocked. "I didn't know. Of course I'll start taking her home with me."

"I think that's a good idea." I smiled at her in the rearview mirror.

"Have you heard anything from the council of witches?" Dorothy asked.

"Not yet." I pulled the car into the parking lot in front of the shop. "Let's pick up the staff and drop off your cat. We need to speak with the werewolf representative right away. The sooner we get Larry out of jail, the better."

"Don't the werewolves keep track of each other like the council of witches seems to keep track of you—I mean *us*?"

I turned off the engine. "They're a little more *loosely* organized. I'm hoping they'll do something about Larry. No one is going to like it if we step in."

"If they won't do anything," Elsie said, "I'll be glad to put up my house as collateral for a bail bondsman for him."

"Really?" I asked as I got out of the car. "He has a boat. He could be gone right after we get him out."

"He's a dear friend." Elsie eased out of the car. "I don't want to leave him there. Besides, if people find out werewolves exist, witches could be next."

I hadn't even noticed a small man by the shop door until we were already halfway up the stairs. Elsie immediately drew her sword.

"Wait!" He held up his hand. "I'm an attorney hired by Olivia Dunst to make sure her will is honored following her recent demise."

"He's a witch." Elsie sniffed, not standing down with her sword. "How can we trust him? He might be the rogue witch."

Dorothy agreed. "We can't invite him in. He could kill us too."

I considered the problem. "I guess we'll have to talk to him out here. Sorry, Mr.—?"

"Brannigan. Richard Brannigan, madam." He held out a business card. He was barely three feet tall and wore his glasses perched on the end of his large nose. His suit was impeccably tailored. He *looked* like a lawyer.

"This is Dorothy Lane. I believe she's the beneficiary of Olivia's will." I opened the shop door and grabbed the staff. "Olivia, can you come out here, please?"

She appeared on the old concrete landing outside the door. It was cracked and had plants growing in it.

"I can't believe you girls left me behind last night. You

knew I couldn't go anywhere unless one of you took the staff. I had to spend the night with those three cats. And I think the shop has *mice*."

Richard Brannigan's eyebrows went up. "Am I to understand that Miss Dunst is now a *ghost*?"

Olivia noticed him for the first time. "That's right. I was murdered before my time. You must be Mr. Brannigan. I'm Olivia Dunst. This is my daughter and sole heir, Dorothy."

"We're doing this out here because of you-know-who," Elsie told her. "We don't want to invite someone we don't know into the shop."

"I assure you, madam, that I have the highest references and credentials you could hope to find." Mr. Brannigan's voice was high-pitched and nasal.

"Yes—but can you assure us that you're *not* an evil witch who's stealing artifacts of magic and killing other witches?" Elsie squinted into his eyes.

"Probably not."

"I'll get a few chairs," Dorothy volunteered.

"I'll make tea." Elsie went inside.

Dorothy released Scooter into the shop. There was immediately a chorus of howls, hisses and meows. "I don't think the other cats are going to play nice with Scooter."

"Well, no wonder. What kind of name is that for a cat?" Olivia asked.

"He scooted across the floor on his butt a lot when he was a kitten." Dorothy shrugged. "It seemed like an appropriate name."

"Let's deal with this later," I suggested, lifting the table. "Our time is valuable, and so is Mr. Brannigan's."

We brought the table and chairs out of the shop and sat on the landing within the sights and sounds of the river. There were hundreds of yachts, commercial vessels and small pleasure boats out on the water that morning. The sun poured down on the city and warmed the cool air around us.

As we drank tea, Mr. Brannigan went over all the important details in Olivia's will. The house, money—everything she'd ever owned except the Mercedes—went to Dorothy. The ownership of the Mercedes might be up for approval by the council of witches.

Dorothy looked stunned as the change that was coming to her life began to sink in. She took the file that contained the deed to the house.

"Now, because Miss Dunst was killed prematurely, there will be a small fee for my firm to file something that will allow the mundane courts to process this claim."

"Surely that must be only a *tiny* spell to alter what the records will say," Olivia said.

"That's true," he admitted. "And my fee is *tiny* too." He named a price.

"Wow!" Elsie's mouth dropped open. "That's *tiny*?"

"These things must be handled delicately." He kept pulling papers from his satchel. "The Grand Council frowns on anything heavy-handed that might stand out and be noticed. There must be no clue left behind as to our manipulation."

Olivia's ghostly face puckered up like a pickle. "What? That's outrageous! I won't pay it. You've already charged me enough to give Dorothy these documents."

"No, madam." He handed the papers to Dorothy. "This bill is for your *daughter.*"

Dorothy took the papers from him with a smile. "It's fine, Mother. I don't mind. I never expected in my life to own a house. Not to mention all the valuable art and antiques you've collected. Thank you for leaving it to me."

"In case you consider selling off any of those antiques or works of art." Brannigan handed Dorothy another card. "My firm takes care of *those* delicate matters as well."

"Why, you little buzzard!" Olivia shot straight up like an angry plume of smoke. "She is *not* interested in selling

anything. You should take your cards and leave now. I'm
not sure what a ghost is capable of, but I may be angry
enough to find out."

"A thousand apologies." Mr. Brannigan picked up his
briefcase. "I'll be leaving now."

We watched him walk down the stairs and into the parking lot before he completely disappeared.

"I'd like to learn to do *that*," Dorothy said.

"We *all* would, dear." Olivia went inside.

"Does that mean it's time to give Dorothy's cat a new
name?" Elsie asked when Mr. Brannigan was gone.

"No. It means we have to pay a visit to the werewolves
and try to get Larry out of jail," I reminded her.

"Why are *we* responsible for what happens to Larry?"
Olivia wanted to know. "We're witches. As long as we're
doing what we're supposed to do, the werewolves should
take care of themselves."

"We could at least give them a heads-up for Larry's sake,"
I told her. "You don't have to come if you don't want to."

"Well I certainly don't want to be trapped here at the
shop again. Those three cats never shut up last night. I could
barely sleep."

"Considering that you're dead," Elsie said, "I don't think
you're supposed to worry about sleeping anymore."

Olivia pouted as we put the chairs and table back in the
shop, locked up and got in the car.

Dorothy brought the staff with her. "Maybe my mother
is right. Do wolves and witches mingle much?"

Elsie got in the car and adjusted her purple hat. "Not
usually. Larry is a special case. If we don't act and he
changes while in police custody, it will be a *very* big deal
for him. And it will be proof that werewolves exist."

I nodded and adjusted my rearview mirror when I sat
down. "The last werewolf that changed in front of the

unsuspecting public was found torn to bits the next day. The police said it was a reaction from the public. I think we all know better."

Olivia and Elsie nodded.

"What makes you think it was something else?" Dorothy tried to find room in the backseat for the staff without setting it on top of her mother. She finally placed it on the floor.

"Because that's the way the wolves deal with that kind of thing." Olivia said what we were all thinking. "The witches make people who find out about them disappear, or they wipe their memories clean."

"It's much more humane." Elsie put on her seatbelt.

"We all know what's at stake." I tried to get my troops ready for battle. "I like Larry. He's always been a good customer."

"And a good friend," Elsie chimed in.

"Please!" Olivia rolled her eyes, which was quite unpleasant in her current state. "We all know why *you* want to save him!"

"Nothing wrong with a little romance, right, Dorothy?" Elsie winked at her.

Dorothy blushed.

I drove down Water Street past the ships and boats on the river. Some of the old structures had been renovated down through the years. They had a mellow kind of charm about them. Other structures looked neglected, barely standing after the hundred years or so since they'd been built.

The werewolves gathered at an old tavern that had once been owned by a heroic blockade runner during the Civil War. He'd retired here, so the legend said. Late one night, he was called from his sleep by a knock on the door.

It was a werewolf that had changed during the full moon. He'd come into Wilmington on board a ship from Greece and had killed everyone on that lost ship.

He asked the tavern owner for sanctuary. Of course it

was a mistake for the gallant hero to let the wolf in. By the next full moon, he too had become a werewolf.

The tavern was renamed Wolf's Head, and werewolves had come to hang out there ever since.

"You'd think they could keep the place up a bit," Olivia observed as we found a spot in the parking lot between potholes.

"Are you sure we should go in there?" Dorothy asked. "My mother—my *adopted* mother—told me never to come into this part of town."

Elsie smiled. "We're witches, dear. We have nothing to fear from these wolves, especially since it isn't time for them to change for a few days. Nothing to worry about."

"Can you recall what the name of the new werewolf representative is?" I asked after I'd locked the car. "I know they got someone to take Harold's place. I can't think of his name."

"Wasn't it Jerry something?" Elsie asked.

"No." Olivia shook her head. "It was John something, wasn't it? I kind of remember because he was really good-looking—for a wolf anyway."

"If you're talking about me"—a man's deep voice startled us—"I'm John Mayhew. We don't get many witches visiting us here. Why don't you come inside for a drink?"

CHAPTER 24

From ghoulies and ghosties, and long leggedy
beasties, and things that go bump in the night,
good Lord protect us!

John Mayhew was tall, dark and handsome, wolf or not. He stood at least a head above all of us. His broad chest was covered by a white T-shirt that said "Wolves Do It in the Full Moon." He wore his tight jeans low on his narrow hips.

"Oh, what a *wonderful* idea." Olivia giggled. "I'm Olivia Dunst, and these are my friends, Elsie and Molly."

John, it seemed, only had dark eyes for Dorothy. "And what's your name, little one?"

"Oh. That's Olivia's daughter, Dorothy," Elsie introduced them.

"Hush," Olivia muttered. "I'm too young to have a daughter."

"Nice to meet you." Dorothy shook hands eagerly with John. "I'm a witch-in-training. I work at the downtown library. I've never met a werewolf before."

John kissed her hand but observed the parking lot a little furtively. "Such matters are better discussed inside. Come with me, Dorothy, witch-in-training. I think you'll be surprised how *charming* werewolves can be."

"He's making a play for my daughter." Olivia shook her head. "I can't believe it."

"Quiet," Elsie said. "Maybe she can keep us from getting in trouble here."

We went into the old tavern with John. The heavy door was made of large pieces of oak that had been spliced together. The floors were black with age and spilled beer. The seats were rough and crudely made, as was the huge bar.

The door closed behind us, and we were enveloped by the dark. There were no windows, and the light from the ceiling was dim.

"What will you have, ladies?" John got behind the bar. "I think we have a little wine. It's red, of course. We like to *pretend* sometimes."

"You don't kill people when you turn?" Dorothy hopped up on a bar stool.

"Not anymore, little girl. That's a thing of the past. Too much bad publicity can ruin a haven."

"We're not really here to drink," I told him. "We're here to talk to you about Larry Tyler. He's been arrested for murder. The chances are pretty good that he'll still be in custody when the moon rises."

Several other werewolves joined us at the bar. They weren't handsome or charismatic. They looked tough and a little on the mean side. They might *not* have been thinking about killing us, but they were definitely sniffing around on us, like nice steaks.

"That's Larry's problem." One man had a huge scar that ran from chin to hairline. "Why should we care?"

"Because if he turns in jail, everyone in Wilmington will know that there are werewolves here," Elsie said in a clear, concise voice. "I'm sure you don't want *that* to happen."

"You're right, of course," John agreed. "I don't know what we can do about it. None of us have money or property to use as bail. I'm afraid Larry will have to stay where he is."

I started to offer to help with the problem, but before I could speak, Elsie added her own take on it.

"What about a jailbreak?" She grinned. "We're witches. We have magic."

Olivia peered around at the growing number of werewolves in the tavern. "Elsie, maybe that's not the *best* way to handle this."

"That's true," John said. "But why would a few witches and their pet ghost want to help us?"

Elsie adjusted her hat. "Because Larry is a *personal* friend. We know what happens to werewolves who turn publicly."

The werewolves exchanged glances. Olivia and Dorothy huddled as close to me as they could. One or both of them were standing on my foot. I was too scared to move and find out. I didn't know one could "feel" the weight of a ghost. Maybe it was because she was so frightened.

"You know, I think there's a better answer," I said. "A jailbreak isn't as easy as it sounds. There are high-tech surveillance devices. You can't simply waltz in there and take Larry out."

"It sounds like it's either that or we shred old Larry," a third wolf growled.

This was getting out of hand. There had to be some way to talk some sense into everyone there. I didn't want to come right out and tell them that our magic didn't always work. That could be another road to disaster.

"Couldn't Joe help us?" Elsie smiled at me. "Her husband is a police detective. In fact, he's the one who arrested Larry. He was misguided."

"This keeps getting better and better," Olivia whispered. "*Do* something, Molly."

"I'm trying." The werewolves were staring at me. I could see they weren't happy about what Joe had done. Not that I was involved with it, but that thought might not have crossed their minds.

"Is that true?" John asked.

"My husband did his job. We think Larry was set up by another witch who actually committed the murder," I explained. "Larry was an innocent bystander."

"Who is Larry supposed to have murdered?" the werewolf with the scar asked.

I swallowed hard. "He's charged with killing a friend of ours."

"For goodness' sake, Molly, just come out with it," Olivia added. "He's accused of killing *me*. I don't know who did it, but I feel sure it wasn't Larry."

Elsie nodded. "Werewolves don't *need* knives to rip out a throat."

The group of werewolves jostled each other, as though a silent communication had passed between them. And then they looked at us like we were lunch.

"Why don't *you* clean this up?" John asked. "It seems that you ladies are at the heart of it. Find the killer for the police, and they'll release Larry before the full moon."

"It's not that easy," I started to explain.

"You're witches," the scarred werewolf pointed out. "Do a spell or something."

"Yeah," another werewolf agreed. "Larry's a good friend of mine. I'd hate for *anything* to happen to him."

The implied threat made Elsie nervously giggle. I knew we had to find a way to get out the door. I didn't have a clue what to say or how to explain our position without making the situation worse.

I glanced at the door, wishing our powers were strong enough to spirit us away. "I think we should go."

Dorothy smiled. "I haven't been a witch for very long. I'm not sure how to find the killer yet. But we're working on it. I'm sure we'll figure something out. You'll be the *first* to know."

John smiled at her. The other werewolves did the same.

It was as though her innocence made it safe for the rest of us. At least I hoped it was going to work that way.

The heavy door to the tavern squeaked open, and Richard Brannigan stood there for a moment, framed by the light. "Ladies. Pardon my interruption. I forgot to have you sign a document. Excuse us, gentlemen."

"Let us know how the magic goes," John said. "There are a few days before the moon comes up. We could still plan that jailbreak—with your husband's help."

"We'll do that." I smiled and put a hand on Dorothy's and Elsie's arms. "Thank you for hearing us out."

"Lovely to meet you," Elsie called out.

"Next time, leave the ghost at home," John responded. "Ghosts hanging around give a place a bad reputation."

"Will do." Dorothy smiled and fled quickly out the door and into the sunlight.

Once we were outside, there was a collective sigh of relief.

"That was *not* the best idea," Olivia said.

"I thought it was fun." Elsie giggled.

"I think I'd rather be a witch than a werewolf." Dorothy squinted at Mr. Brannigan. "What paper did you forget to have me sign?"

He cleared his throat and fidgeted a little. "Actually, the council of witches directed me here. They were a little worried that there might be an *incident*. Werewolves and witches have gotten along amicably for more than a hundred years. No one wants that to change."

"You mean you were lying?" Elsie asked.

His face turned red. "This is in *no* way indicative of my normal practice. But where the council sends me, I go."

Dorothy hugged him and planted a kiss on his cheek. "Thank you so much. I thought we were going to be eaten today."

"I was happy to be of assistance." He cleaned his glasses on a pristine white cloth he pulled from his pocket.

"But this still leaves us with the problem of Larry becoming a wolf in jail." I peeked back at the werewolf bar. "We won't get any help from them."

"Perhaps I could be of assistance in this matter as well," Mr. Brannigan offered. "I'm quite familiar with cases like this. I'm sure I could get Larry out of jail with very little fuss."

"Let's get *us* out of here first," Olivia said. "Those werewolves could change their minds."

We agreed with her and got in the car to drive back to the shop.

Before we could get there, Elsie suggested that we still couldn't trust Mr. Brannigan. "We don't know who he is."

"We won't ask him in," Dorothy said. "That worked last time, right?"

"Yes," Elsie agreed. "But do we want to trust him with our plan to free Larry?"

Dorothy and I stared at her.

"Is there a plan?" Dorothy asked.

"Of course," Elsie said.

"What is it?" I sided with Dorothy. "You aren't still talking about breaking Larry out of jail, are you?"

"We could do it—with Dorothy's magic. We could pretend we were visiting Joe and do the spell right there in the jailhouse. Come on, Molly. It would be fun."

It didn't sound like fun to me. The spell would be hard, and Dorothy's magic was unpredictable, as was our own. We could free Larry, or we might turn the jail—and everyone in it—inside out. I wasn't willing to take that chance.

"We need a better plan, girls," Olivia said. "I wish ghosts could do things. I could get in and out with Larry easy. And why did that sexy werewolf say that about me? I'm beginning to feel a little hurt by the attitudes toward ghosts in this city."

We met Mr. Brannigan back at the shop.

After a long discussion about whether we could trust him,

we decided to do a small binding spell on him that would keep him from using his magic while he was there. Our spells protecting the shop from outside magic were strong. There seemed to be no reason why we couldn't sit down, have tea and talk about our situation.

It was even possible that by listening to his ideas, we could understand what the council was thinking. We didn't have to trust him to spy on them.

Mr. Brannigan seemed pleased with the idea. He walked in carefully, sniffing the air as though he could smell everything in the shop. He had a little of the hobgoblin look about him. Maybe he could.

"This is very nice." He checked out some of the books on the shelves. "You have some very rare magic books."

Elsie was filling the teakettle. "We've been collecting them for fifty years ourselves."

"Not to mention our mothers' collections," Olivia added. "I wish I could have a cup of that lavender tea. It smells wonderful."

Mr. Brannigan studied her through his tiny spectacles. "Ghosts can't smell. They have no olfactory senses. You must be imagining it."

That riled Olivia. "I am *not* imagining it. I know what lavender tea smells like."

"I didn't tell her what kind I was making either," Elsie said.

"Never mind." He shrugged away the thought. "She probably glimpsed the tea or is simply used to what you make. Do you have any horehound? That's my favorite."

"That stuff is really *nasty*." Elsie shivered thinking about it. "But we have it, if you want some."

"If it's not too much trouble."

He boosted himself into one of the chairs. I brought out two extra chairs from the supply closet. It dawned on me that Olivia didn't need one anymore. I was glad that I'd made that mistake, however, when she thanked me, with tears in her eyes, for not forgetting her. It seemed old habits die hard.

We gathered around the small table when the tea was served. Mr. Brannigan opened his binder, casting uncomfortable glances at us, until we looked away. He shuffled his papers and cleared his throat when he felt his secrets were safe.

He studied his documents before looking up at us. "Larry Tyler will change into a wolf in a few days. We don't have time to allow the mundane courts to work on this. We don't want to take a chance that he could be denied bail either."

Elsie sipped her tea. "We *knew* that already."

"Yes." He straightened his shoulders beneath his expensive suit. "Because of the situation—and the fact that witches are involved in the problem—the witches' court has granted me the right to use a spell that will make sure Larry goes free. At least temporarily. He will have to prove that he wasn't involved with Olivia Dunst's death. Otherwise, *our* system will take care of him."

CHAPTER 25

Spirit haunting, leave this space.
Your life is done, give back your place.
Among the living, your time is gone.
I banish you, before the dawn.

That wasn't at all what we had in mind.

"Wouldn't that be bad for witch and werewolf relations?" Dorothy asked. "And isn't that what we're trying to avoid?"

"As far as the council is concerned, it's more worrisome to them that a witch has been killed, and the theft of the magic tools. They're concerned about the possibility that a werewolf could have killed a witch. They don't want that to get out in public, of course."

Elsie had also put a cup of lavender tea at Olivia's place. Olivia put her nose to it and inhaled. "Will you put a little extra sugar in that, Dorothy?"

"Sure." Dorothy ladled in a few extra sugar cubes. "How's that?"

"It had plenty in it already," Elsie protested. "Just the way you've always liked it, Olivia. Did you suddenly develop a sweet tooth?"

"Sometimes I like it a little sweeter than other times."

Mr. Brannigan cleared his throat again. "As to the matter

of a witch who now seems to be a ghost, the council is also concerned. It simply isn't done. There are spells to disperse this random energy."

Olivia shrieked. "You want to kill me—*again*? I have a second chance to know my daughter, and you want to *disperse* me?"

"No one is going to disperse you." I stared at Mr. Brannigan with cold eyes. "She may be a ghost, but if we're correct and she was murdered by this witch even the council is afraid of, I think that makes it their fault. They failed to protect us."

His beady eyes wandered the shop for a moment before returning to gaze sharply into mine. "Witches don't become ghosts unless their life plan is interrupted. We've learned throughout generations that this can lead to bothersome apparitions. Nipping it in the bud is best for all."

"We aren't *nipping* Olivia." Elsie's voice was firm and decisive on that issue.

"We believe the council should have informed us that there was a rogue witch who might want to kill one of us," I argued our case. "They were negligent. I think that means the normal rules don't apply to this situation."

He sipped his tea. "I'll let you take that up with the council. I'm stating their position. Right now, we're talking about rescuing the werewolf."

We agreed to that, after a brief discussion away from the table. Since the only plan we had was to break Larry out of jail, I was willing to hear what Mr. Brannigan had to offer. If we didn't like his idea, we didn't have to do it.

Olivia was in tears as she gave Dorothy, me and Elsie each a wispy hug. It felt more like a cold draft wrapping itself around me. Not a particularly pleasant sensation, but I knew Olivia was trying her best to thank us.

"What do you need us to do?" I asked him when we went back to the table.

"The spell is a difficult one," he said. "I'll need whatever magic you can spare to help me with it."

Elsie snorted. "You mean the council couldn't give you a little *extra* for the job?"

He glared at her, but continued. "I have a special apparatus in which I can collect your magic."

"I don't like the sound of that." I glanced at Elsie, who also looked uncomfortable with the idea. "We can come with you to do whatever it is that needs to be done. We're not putting our magic into a pot."

"You can trust me, ladies." He gave us a small smile. "I won't play you false. Of course I would return your magic when we're finished."

"I haven't been around that long," Dorothy said, "but even *I* don't like the sound of that."

"Fine," he huffed. "I suppose that means you'll have to come with me. Get your tools together, and let's go. The sooner we get this over, the sooner I can go home."

"What about me?" Dorothy was a little forlorn. "I don't have a magic tool yet."

He nodded to the staff. "What about that?"

"She's not an air witch," I told him. "She has earth magic. She needs something else, but we haven't had a chance to find it yet."

He glanced at his pocket watch. "I can give you an hour, no longer. It would be good to have her magic, beginner though she is. Without her magic tool, she's probably useless to us. I'll meet you at the jail."

Mr. Brannigan left the shop with the four of us staring at each other.

"It took me two years to find the right piece of wood for my staff," Olivia whispered.

Elsie nodded. "It was about the same for me finding the right sword."

I could see where this conversation was headed. I couldn't let it go there.

"I found my cauldron in about twenty minutes at a flea market in Charleston. It doesn't have to be a huge process."

Dorothy bit her lip. "I don't even know where to start to look for a stone. I mean, not a *magical* stone."

"The stone isn't magic, dear," Olivia explained. "It's a vessel for your magic—a tool you can use to focus your magic. Think of it like a diamond necklace. It won't help if you're not pretty and charming to begin with."

"That's the worst explanation I've ever heard," Elsie said. "We'd better get started if we're going to find a stone for Dorothy."

"Has anyone seen Scooter?" Dorothy glanced around the shop for her cat.

"I hope Barnabas didn't eat him," Elsie said.

"I haven't noticed him around," Olivia added. "I hope he didn't get out the door."

"We don't need to panic on that score," I said. "We would've seen a large tuxedo-colored cat running out the door. No one has been in here since we left."

"What about the cave?" Dorothy glanced at the carpet covering the trapdoor. "Maybe Scooter went down there."

Isabelle told me that she had seen Scooter in the cave. Harper agreed with her, though he made it clear he wasn't going into the cave again.

"He's probably down there." I went to uncover the trapdoor. Time was against us. If we were going to find a stone for Dorothy—and her cat—we needed to get a move on it.

"Oh my poor baby!" Dorothy rushed to precede me down the stairs.

Olivia went too, with Elsie coming behind me.

"You know, this damp chill isn't good for my arthritis," Elsie said. "Who came up with the idea to use the cave anyway?"

"I believe it was you," Olivia chided her. "If I remember correctly, you used it as a selling point for us to buy the shop together."

"That's right." Elsie reached the rocky bottom of the cave. "It wasn't one of my better ideas."

"It's served us well," I reminded her. "Our magic is strong here. Now let's find the cat."

The cave wasn't very big. With all of us searching, it only took a few minutes to determine that Scooter wasn't there.

Elsie put her hand to her hat. "You don't think he wandered down to the river, do you?"

Olivia looked that way. "We haven't been down there in years."

"There's nothing to stop him," I said. "We're going to have to search."

"I can fly down there," Olivia offered. "Wait a minute. Where's Dorothy? Is she missing too?"

I glanced toward the entrance from the river to the cave. I could barely make out Dorothy's form headed in that direction. "Let's go."

"The young are too fast for their own good." Elsie sighed before following us.

"Wait for me," Olivia commanded. "I really should've been the advance scout on this mission."

"The scouts always die," Elsie reminded her.

"Nothing to worry about then, I guess." Olivia was soon too far away for us to see.

"If my magic were better," Elsie huffed, "I'd make new legs."

"You know we don't do that."

"Maybe we should start."

The darkest part of the entrance to the cave took about five minutes to walk through. We'd explored it all the time right after we'd first moved into the shop.

Olivia had been worried that someone would find the entrance and come into the cave. We'd put a confusion spell at the opening near the water. It had kept anyone from accidentally wandering inside.

"I always forget how dark it gets walking through here," Elsie said. "We should have brought flashlights."

"I hope we can find Dorothy before she comes on the confusion spell. That could make things even more difficult. As it is, I don't see how we're going to meet Mr. Brannigan in an hour."

"I can take care of the dark anyway."

"No, Elsie. Don't do it." I urged her to restrain from a spell for light.

She snapped her fingers, and I knew I was too late.

Light flooded the tunnel leading to the river, but it was so bright that I couldn't see anything. It was as though the sun had come down into the darkness. I stopped walking and covered my eyes with my hands.

I knew this spell well. It wasn't friendly to those who used it. Witches long ago had created it to defend castles against invaders. The invaders fell from their ladders, blinded, as they tried to breach the castle walls.

"That didn't work exactly as I'd expected," Elsie said. "Are you still there, Molly?"

"I am. I'm not sure if my eyes are."

"I'm so sorry. I was working on a *little* light, like a candle or a flashlight."

I found her hand and held it in mine. "We'll be fine. Let's move on."

Both of us had been blinded by the spell. We walked together, my hand guiding us along the wall.

I could smell the river getting closer. I could feel its magic coursing through me as I moved toward it. The magic didn't help my vision, but it kept me going in the right direction.

"Hurry, girls!" Olivia came back to us. "I think Dorothy may have hit the confusion spell. I can't believe it's still so strong after all this time."

"Did you see Scooter?" I asked.

"Yes, he's down there. What's wrong with you? I know you're old, but you're usually not so slow."

"Did she just call us *old*?" Elsie asked.

"I think she did." I told Olivia about the light spell. "Neither one of us can see a thing."

"That's great. How can you save my daughter if you can't see?"

"We're working on it," I told her. "Won't she talk to you?"

"I don't think she can hear me. Please hurry. I'm afraid she might wander out into the water."

When we'd reached the end of the tunnel, my vision cleared a little. Everything was in shadow, but at least I could see forms.

"Is Dorothy here?" Elsie asked. "I still can't see. I'm so sorry, Molly."

I saw a large, flat rock and guided Elsie to sit there. "I'll look around. You wait here until you can see."

"She's over this way," Olivia said. "Hurry, Molly."

I followed the shadows along the edge of the river. Even after two hundred years, there were still rough outlines of the wooden docks that had once been used by the smugglers. A few posts still stuck out of the water.

I could see Dorothy on the rocky shore. She was lying prostrate on the ground.

Quickly, I took some of the river water into my hands. I blessed it and muttered a healing spell before I touched my face and closed my eyes with it. This close to the water, I knew the spell would work without backfiring.

A few minutes later, I could see clearly again. I went over to Dorothy, not sure how to remove the confusion spell. It shouldn't have worked on her—or anyone else coming *from* the cave. It wasn't set to be that way.

"Dorothy?" I leaned close to her. "Are you okay? Do you know who I am?"

She was covered in dirt but seemed all right. "Of course. I was trying to commune with the rocks. I know we don't have much time to look around. I figured down here was my best chance."

The confusion spell had obviously dissipated through the years. We'd have to tackle that problem·later unless we wanted visitors in the cave.

"Thank goodness. I was worried about you. Did you find your cat?"

"He's right over there. I told him how silly he was to run out this way. If he said anything in return, I didn't hear him."

"What's that in his mouth?" I went closer and peered into Scooter's face. "There's something green in there."

"I hope he didn't hurt himself." Dorothy got off the ground and stood beside me. She picked up her cat, and something fell into her hand. "What's this? It feels warm."

I looked at it without touching it. "I don't know. How do you feel holding it?"

Dorothy smiled. "Different. Strange. Can this be *my* stone?"

Olivia peered over her shoulder. "If it is, you are the luckiest witch in the world. That's an old emerald cull, probably dropped by some pirate two hundred years ago."

"Oh." Dorothy gazed at the dirt-encrusted stone. "That must mean I'm a *real* witch now."

CHAPTER 26

Clear my sight of cloudy lies.
Heal the darkness from my eyes.
Bright of day and dark of night
That which was wrong shall be made right.

"Seriously?" I gazed at the stone a little closer. "It doesn't look like an emerald to me."

"I guess my vision is much better from the spirit world."

"Let me see." Elsie took it from Dorothy, spit on it and then wiped it off on her top. "I guess it could be an emerald, at least a cull. It doesn't matter anyway. It's not like it has to be something valuable. It's how you *feel* about it."

"I feel great about it." Dorothy took the stone back and put it in her pocket. "Okay. Let's go save Larry."

She lifted Scooter and started walking into the tunnel that led to the cave. It was only a moment later that she screeched and dropped him.

"Oh my gosh, I think Scooter just talked to me. Or thought to me. Or whatever you call it. My cat *communicated* with me."

"I hope he has a better name," Elsie said.

"I don't know if I'd call it better or not. He says his name is Hemlock. Isn't that a poisonous plant?"

"Not only poisonous," I explained as we continued walking. "It's an ancient medicinal plant that has been used for all kinds of good too."

"I'm glad to hear it. I was afraid he was an evil cat." She whispered the "evil cat" part as though she were afraid of what he might do.

"There is no real evil," Elsie said. "There may be some mismanagement, but nothing is completely evil. There is good in the most deadly thing."

"Well said." Olivia applauded. "I'm so glad my daughter will have the three of us around to teach her."

"That's right. What are we going to do about the council wanting to get rid of Olivia's ghost?" Elsie asked me.

"We won't let them, right?" Dorothy asked.

It was hard to explain that we had no power to combat the council. They were very strong and could do what they liked.

"We'll do the best we can to protect her," I replied. "She may have to live in the cave, where our magic is the strongest."

"Live in the *cave*?" Olivia's tone was one of disbelief. "I hardly made it through the night in the *shop*. I can't imagine living—or I guess this would be ghosting—in the cave."

"Technically, I think that would be haunting, Mother," Dorothy corrected her.

"There has to be some quality and dignity to death," Olivia continued.

We reached the cave and carefully climbed the stairs to the shop. Olivia was still complaining about living in the cave, and Elsie was offering to keep a large fire burning for her there at all times.

I noticed the shop door was open again and took a quick survey of the interior. "I don't think we're alone."

Elsie kicked the trapdoor into place and slid the rug over it. "I don't *see* anyone else."

"I feel someone here too," Olivia added. "Why can't we see who it is?"

"Because all of you together have the magic of a flea."

The cloaked witch from the boat appeared to us, lounging in one of the chairs at the table. "What a lovely place this is. I can understand why you'd hate to lose it."

"Lose it?" Elsie frowned. "Who said anything about losing it?"

"I just did. All it would take is a snap of my fingers."

The figure snapped gloved fingers, and a row of books started to burn.

Dorothy put the fire out with her hands. "I can't believe you'd burn a book. What are you thinking?"

"Just a warning," the faceless figure said. "It could get much worse!"

"What do you want?" I demanded, almost too terrified to speak.

"The council can't help you. I do what I want. I think I'll use some of this nice, *young* magic myself. Say good-bye."

One minute, Dorothy was there beside me, glaring fiercely at our visitor. The next, they were both gone.

"What happened?" Elsie slowly spun around. "Where did they go?"

"I don't know. I've never seen a spell like that before." I looked toward the ceiling, wondering why Olivia had been so quiet. "Olivia is gone too."

"No." Elsie pointed. "Look. There she is. Or at least some part of her is there."

I searched the ceiling area. Something that looked like a mural of Olivia was embedded in the old tiles. Her mouth was open, and her hands were up in fright.

"He can't do that in *our* shop." Elsie took out her sword and muttered a spell to free her.

"Do you think that's a good idea?"

Too late.

"Girls?" Olivia was down from the ceiling, but she'd lost

dimension. She was completely flat, as though someone had peeled her away. "I feel so odd."

Elsie snorted. "You look pretty odd too."

"What happened?" Olivia tried to get her three-dimensional form back. She *was* only ectoplasm, after all. "I came up here, and then poof, nothing. Where's Dorothy?"

"The rogue witch took her. Dorothy's magic attracted him or her." I shook my head, hating the feeling of power-lessness that gripped me. There was nothing we could do to stop the witch from killing Dorothy to take her magic.

"The witch was here? That's who put that awful spell on me?" She popped her hand out and wriggled her body shape around. "Why kidnap Dorothy? She hardly knows what to do."

I stared at her before I sat down heavily at the table. Isabelle jumped into my lap. "I'm sorry, Olivia. I'm sure the witch means to steal her magic."

"You mean *kill* her?" Olivia jerked her form in agitation. "We can't let that happen, girls. We just can't."

"Whoever it is knows some great spells." Elsie stroked Barnabas. "I'd like to steal *their* spell book."

"Our top priority now has to be finding Dorothy."

"She's absolutely right," Olivia agreed.

"What about Larry?" Elsie asked. "We have to go to the jail if we're going to help Mr. Brannigan free him."

"What's to decide?" Olivia demanded. "Larry's a were-wolf. Dorothy is my daughter, and she's in danger."

"Do you have any idea how to find Dorothy?" I asked Olivia.

She kept working at regaining her form. As various parts of her body filled out, they made sounds like knuckles pop-ping. "I wish I did. She could be anywhere."

I drew in a deep breath. "I don't know how to find Dorothy."

"I think we should finish what we're doing." Elsie pushed

her purple hat down firmly on her head. "We have to meet Mr. Brannigan and free Larry. Then maybe he can help us talk to the council about Dorothy."

Olivia wasn't comfortable with that plan. "No. We can't let her stay with that creature a minute longer than absolutely necessary."

"We don't have a way to track them," I reminded her. "I think Elsie is right."

"Really?" Elsie grinned. "Wish I had a flag to wave."

Olivia finally agreed. Elsie and I got our things together, fed the cats and left the shop, with the staff in tow.

We got in the car and drove across town to the jail. Olivia was looking almost as good as new. Her face was a little flat, like a Persian cat. Otherwise, she had escaped the full brunt of it. I had no doubt that whatever spell or curse had been used against her would've been much worse if we hadn't been in our stronghold.

There were police officers everywhere outside the jail. I hoped we wouldn't run into Joe. That would take some explaining we couldn't do in public. It was imperative that we didn't speak of anything to do with magic outside the enchanted bubble.

While the bubble could be called on anywhere, I knew Olivia, Elsie and Mr. Brannigan would notice it right away. I couldn't answer their questions without putting Joe in danger. It was best only to employ that device in private.

Mr. Brannigan was waiting for us impatiently by the front door. He alternately tapped his foot on the sidewalk and glanced at his pocket watch.

"You're late," he accused when he saw us. "I have better things to do than hang around here all day waiting for you."

"I'm sorry." I was very conscious of the people who passed us going into the jail. I wished I could hide my face. "We've come up against another problem."

I explained to him about our visit from the rogue witch

and Dorothy's kidnapping. "Our protection spell wasn't strong enough to keep us safe. Now we're vulnerable. We don't have the background or experience to fight someone like this. We need help from the council. Where is Cassandra?"

"She's on vacation," he said. "I'm all the help you're going to get from the council."

"Can you help us find Dorothy?" Olivia asked him.

"I'll try." He sighed heavily. "But first, my instructions are to free the werewolf. After we do that, we can consider this new problem."

"This is a day I thought I'd never see." Olivia's voice was bitter. "A member of the council choosing to help a *werewolf* over a witch."

He shrugged. "Not my decision. The council wants to keep a good relationship with the werewolves. I'm sorry. I do what I'm told. That's my job."

"That's what I said!" Elsie clapped her hands.

"I'll need you to combine or share your magic, ladies." Mr. Brannigan bowed his head and laced his fingers together. "This is going to be harder without the new magic from Dorothy."

Elsie and I held hands and focused our magic on helping him. I could feel the energy building between us. It felt like a thunderstorm approaching from the Atlantic, threatening and overwhelming. The feeling moved up from my hands and into the rest of my body.

"That's it," he grunted. "You're doing fine. Keep going."

"I don't know how much more I have to give," Elsie whispered.

I held her hands more tightly. "We're together. We can do this."

It seemed as though we were covered in blue light. It filled the air around us and permeated our senses. My hands were trembling and cold. It was difficult to breathe. I kept my focus on freeing Larry, not sure what the outcome of that would be. Trusting our magic, as I always had, to do what was best.

"That's it!" Mr. Brannigan's voice made me open my eyes.

"What the—?" Larry was there on the sidewalk with us outside the jail.

"Let's get out of here." I was relieved that it had worked. "They'll notice that you're gone. It won't take long for them to search for you."

"But that's the beauty of the spell we cast," Mr. Brannigan gloated. "There's a doppelganger in Larry's place. No one will know the difference—until it evaporates. In the meantime, he's safe."

"Which gives us the opportunity to find the witch who killed Olivia and took Dorothy," Elsie said. "Coming, Mr. Brannigan?"

"That's not going to happen," he told her. "If there's some way to track and capture this witch, the council will take over. You won't be involved."

"So what are we supposed to do now?" I asked.

"The waters are a little *muddied* right now." He procrastinated, clearly having no real answer. "We have the wolf. I suggest we get out of here!"

CHAPTER 27

Water, air, earth and fire—help me find what I desire.
Cauldron, candle, wind and seed—help
me find what I need.

"Oh my goodness! Don't tell me you can't save my daughter."
Olivia was prone to panic attacks. "Someone get me a paper
bag to breathe into. I'm afraid I'm going to faint."

Elsie laughed at that. "How do you suggest we give you
a paper bag?"

"Good one, granny!" Mr. Brannigan laughed too.

"Granny?" Elsie was immediately offended. "Mind your
manners, *junior*, or I'll take my sword to you."

"Hey, all this is fun"—Larry glanced around us—"but
could we get a move on it? I'm a little paranoid standing out
here like this."

"He's right," I agreed. "Let's drop him off at his boat and
then go to Smuggler's Arcane. That's the safest place we
can be until we decide what to do next."

It was a tight squeeze in my car. Mr. Brannigan didn't
want to call another taxi. Olivia wanted to ride in the car
but didn't want anyone to sit on top of her.

"Man, the police still have my herb tea and my book."

Larry was disturbed by the loss. "They can't tell the difference between marijuana and any other plant, I guess. Maybe we should swing by the Arcane before you take me home."

"We could do that." Elsie was pleased with the idea.

"No. We can't. You need to get on your boat and sail away for a while until all of this blows over," I told him. "We can't take any chance that someone could see you there."

"But I'm not stocked for a long trip," he complained.

"Sail to the Outer Banks and pick up supplies," I suggested. "Do whatever you have to do—just don't do it *here*."

He grumbled but finally got the idea. I let him off by his boat at the marina, and he promised to leave Wilmington right away. "You'll let me know when I can come back, right?"

"I have your email address." Elsie smiled and waved. "I'll write every day, and save you some tea and a new book for when I see you again."

"You're the best." He leaned his head in the window and kissed her cheek. "I'll be counting the days."

That was enough to spin Elsie's head. She talked about Larry nonstop until we reached the shop. "He's such a handsome gentleman. I'm going to miss him. I feel like the ladies of yesteryear when their captains sailed off to sea."

"Oh, how romantic," Olivia gushed.

"Please." Mr. Brannigan rolled his eyes. "Can we talk about death or dismemberment rather than all this drivel?"

I smiled but didn't comment. Elsie's relationship with Larry the werewolf would probably never come to anything, but everyone needed a little romance in their lives.

It surprised me to see Joe waiting on the steps of Smuggler's Arcane when we got there. My pulse started racing, and my heart was pounding.

I had a terrible feeling that he needed to talk about what he was doing in regard to the investigation into Olivia's death. We couldn't do that here—not now. It would be bad enough in front of Elsie and Olivia. Mr. Brannigan would immediately report the violation to the council.

"Good morning!" Elsie greeted him as she got out of the car. "It's a grand and glorious morning, don't you think? Perhaps a little sad, but there are brighter days ahead."

Joe nodded, obviously not sure how to respond to what she'd said. "Good morning, Elsie. Hi, Molly. Could I talk to you a minute?"

"Richard Brannigan." He shook hands with Joe. "We'll wait inside. One romance is enough for the day."

Olivia laughed as she blew through the wall and into the shop. Elsie yelled for her to wait as she trudged up the stairs with the staff in her hands.

After they were inside, Joe put his arms around me and whispered, "Can we do the *thing*? I can't remember the code word, but I need to talk."

"This isn't the time," I hissed in his ear. "I'm sorry. It has to wait."

He took a step back, still holding my hand. "It's important, Molly. There may be a development in the case."

I couldn't take any chances. "We can't get sloppy with this. We'll have to talk later."

"Okay." He shrugged. "Then I have to get back to work. Be careful, sweetheart."

"You too." I sighed as he left. I knew it wouldn't be easy once he knew the truth. It would be simple for the council to pick up on anything we said about magic right now while we seemed to be front and center. Joe didn't realize that I was acting in his best interest. I hoped he never had to find out.

Still, I was curious about the new development. I wished we could have taken a moment to talk. He looked troubled and uncertain. His wish for me to *be careful* made me nervous.

Inside, Mr. Brannigan helped Elsie and me renew and strengthen our protection spells on the shop. It would make it harder for the rogue witch to get inside again but not impossible.

"Why is this happening?" I questioned him. "There are ancient magic tools being stolen, and a witch has been killed. Someone purposely tried to start a fight between witches and werewolves. Still the council does nothing."

"I don't know," he admitted. "The council can't see this witch. They can't find her magic."

"How is that possible?" Elsie asked. "I thought they could see all magic."

"Not *this* magic." He shuddered.

"How are we supposed to fight this witch?" I couldn't believe it. I knew the council was nosy and restrictive. I never realized they could be completely spineless.

"They don't want you to fight anything!" Mr. Brannigan reiterated.

"Of course not," Elsie said. "I don't even have enough magic to keep my hair from frizzing each day. A witch like that would make mincemeat of us."

Mr. Brannigan climbed on one of the chairs so he was close to the same height as us. "You ask too many questions. If the council wanted you to do *anything*, they'd tell you. Just stay out of it."

Olivia was raging. "If they don't want us to do anything, then *they'd* better do something! That's my daughter out there with that killer!"

"They can't. Not right now." He strained his neck to scan the shop. "You're in danger. Be smart and lay low for a while until *they* figure out what to do. And quit using that amulet!" He glared at me.

"Using it?" I put my hand to my throat, fingering my mother's amulet. "I haven't used it."

He closed his eyes and sniffed. "You're wearing it. When you're close to the water, the magic is amplified."

"I've had it my whole life, and it never amplified anything before. Why now?"

"I don't know. Maybe because you need it. Have you *worn* it your whole life?"

"No," I conceded. "Only since the day Olivia died."

"There you have it. Its magic becomes stronger as it's worn. There are many magical tools of that nature. Didn't Cassandra explain *any* of this to you?"

"Some," Olivia said. "That was before Elsie accidentally turned her into pottery."

"What are you talking about?" He glanced at me. "What is the ghost saying?"

I did my best. His face kept clouding over. I knew he didn't really understand.

"And you haven't seen Cassandra—alive—since then?"

"No." Elsie shook her head. "Not really. Although there's a bit of dust left from her on the counter. All of it wouldn't come up."

"I'm going to have to report this."

"Could you do it after you find Dorothy?" I asked.

He huffed and got to his feet. "How can you even suggest that an untrained witch is more important than finding Cassandra? Don't do anything until I get back."

We watched him stalk out of the shop and disappear in the middle of the parking lot again.

"Wasn't that what *we* said about the werewolf taking priority?" Olivia asked.

"I guess there are priorities and then there are priorities. I think we're on our own again." I found myself touching my mother's amulet and stopped. I sat at the table, tired and dispirited. "I'm open to suggestions on ways we can get Dorothy back, if either of you has one."

Elsie sat too. Barnabas purred loudly at her feet. "I wish we *could* wait for the council. I don't know where to start."

"The council?" Olivia tried to put her hands on her hips. They went right through her, and she was left looking a little ridiculous. "Since when do we ask them for help? We may not hear from Cassandra or Mr. Brannigan for weeks! Dorothy might not have that long."

"We can try a locator spell," I suggested. "If Mr. Brannigan is right about the amulet enhancing my magic, it could help us."

"Good idea, Molly!" Olivia came close to the table. "We'll need something of hers."

"We have her cat," I said. "Maybe we could use Scooter."

"Hemlock," Elsie corrected me.

"Right. Hemlock." I looked around for Isabelle and asked her if she'd seen Hemlock.

"Barnabas says he's back in the storage room," Elsie said.

"I miss being able to talk to Harper." Olivia pouted. "Who knew being a ghost wouldn't be any fun?"

I went back to the storage area and lifted Hemlock out of the mop bucket. He was slightly damp and smelled like Lysol. "Come on. You're going to help us find Dorothy."

He meowed at me and hid his face.

"There's no reason to be embarrassed. There was nothing you could do to help her. But you could be a strong anchor to help bring her home."

I put Hemlock on the table. Elsie and I sat close to him.

Elsie shook her head. "We could sure use our book right now. I can't remember a single word of any locator spells, can you, Molly?"

I was fine until she asked. Then the only locator spell fled my mind like the clouds after dawn. "I can't think of one either."

"Don't look at me," Olivia said. "Even if I could *think* of one, it might be the wrong one."

"Any locator spell would be better than none," I told her.

We all tried to think of a spell we could use. Most of the

spells we'd cataloged down through the years were spells we'd used only once or twice. Most witches knew their everyday spells by heart.

"This is crazy." Elsie got up and filled the teakettle. "It's bad enough when we can't do them, but when we can't even *remember* them? I need a nap."

Olivia yawned. "Me too. You wouldn't think I'd get tired floating around like this all day."

"All right. Let's concentrate. We need this spell if we're going to try to find Dorothy." I rubbed Hemlock's back to make him feel better.

"Maybe we could call someone and borrow their locator spell," Elsie suggested. "There's Phoebe. She's always been friendly."

"Or Kay," Olivia said. "I've always liked her, even though she has such bad taste in clothes."

"I don't know if they'd be willing to share a spell," I said. "But I'm willing to try anything."

We tried Phoebe. She'd gone out of town on a fishing trip. We called Kay. She had never used a locator spell and didn't know one.

"How can she *not* know a locator spell?" I asked after putting down the phone.

Elsie cleared her throat. "She's not exactly a sweet young thing. Maybe she can't remember either."

Olivia sighed and sank to the table beside Hemlock. "This is so depressing. My little girl is in trouble, and I don't even have any chocolate to eat."

"Wait!" Elsie jumped up suddenly. "I have an idea. Remember when we were much younger, and we used to hang out in the cave a lot. We'd scratch spells into the cave walls. Maybe we scratched at least part of a locator spell."

I nodded. "I remember that. I think I'd know the spell if I saw it."

"Me too," Olivia agreed. "Let's go down there and see what we can find."

It was true that the walls of the cave contained spells we'd played around with years ago. Some had worked, and we'd included them in our missing spell book. Others hadn't been so good.

Despite Elsie's large and illuminating fire, we couldn't find a decent locator spell. After an exhausting hour of climbing around, squinting at spells etched on the walls, we went back upstairs.

"You aren't giving up already, are you?" Olivia asked. "I don't think you looked at all the spells down there."

"I think we did." I dropped to the chair with a sigh.

"I can't believe we had so many dog grooming spells." Elsie sank down too. "What was that all about? None of us even have a dog."

"Don't you remember when we were thinking about opening a dog spa ten years ago," Olivia reminded her. "There was that spot where the old dog grooming place closed in the Cotton Exchange. We thought it might be a good way to make extra money."

"Oh yes." Elsie tapped her chin. "I remember that now. Joe had been furloughed for a few weeks during that city budget crunch, and Bill had lost his job at the car dealership."

"That's right." I sat back in my chair and stared at the ceiling. "Things were slow here at the shop too. We just never got into the idea of dog grooming."

"I could go down and search higher on the cave walls for the locator spell," Olivia offered.

"You know we didn't climb up there and put spells on the walls. Six feet is the most we could have managed," Elsie said.

I agreed with her. "Without the council's help, I don't see any way we can get Dorothy back."

Olivia cried.

I'd almost had it for the day. I was exhausted and disheartened enough to lie down and cry. I wanted to know what Joe had to tell me too. Maybe it was something that would make all of this okay—though I doubted that was possible.

Then I suddenly had the best idea ever. "Brian owes me a debt. He probably knows a locator spell!"

CHAPTER 28

Capture and hold, stay with me.
Capture and hold, your fate to be.

I called Brian with the shop phone. There was no response.
We had to get his attention. I tried to think what I would do
to get Mike's attention, since Brian was probably only a little
older than him. Nothing came to mind, except cutting off
his allowance. That wouldn't work with Brian.

"What about the clarion spell?" Olivia asked. "We could
lure him here. Once he's here, we could collect on the debt.
I've used the call plenty of times!"

Elsie rolled her eyes, but it was really a very good idea.

"What should we do?" I'd never done a clarion spell,
since it was mostly used to attract a mate. I felt fairly certain
that Elsie had never used it either.

"It's so simple," Olivia assured us. "It's the easiest summoning ever!"

The plan was simple. We each needed to be in our
element. We'd entice Brian to come to us and then talk him
into helping with a locator spell.

We set our spell for midnight. There was so much to do.

We had to rush home to bathe, according to ritual, and change clothes. A potent spell needed serious magic. Olivia stayed at the shop, complaining that there wasn't much *she* could do.

It was raining, a cold breeze blowing in from the Atlantic. I could feel the angry water around me. The rain was fierce, pelting the night, while black clouds moved quickly through the sky.

I stopped for Elsie. True to her word, she was wearing her full-length, hooded purple robe.

"I don't even remember when I wore this last. You should've seen Aleese's face when I came downstairs with it on."

"You still look lovely and mysterious in it."

"You're just saying that so I'll go to the shop with you." She giggled and made sure her sword was pulled all the way in before she closed the car door. "What's that you're wearing, Molly? I don't think I've seen it before."

"I've only worn it a few times." I looked down at my tight leather pants and matching vest. I'd paired them with a loose-fitting white blouse. My amulets settled well in the square neckline. "I wasn't even sure it would still fit me."

"I guess Joe didn't see you in that outfit. I can imagine the questions it would bring up."

In fact, it had raised Joe's dark brows. He didn't ask about it. It was hard to see the questions in his eyes and not be able to answer. One thing at a time, I reminded myself. *Don't get ahead of what you can do.*

We'd discussed his newest lead in Olivia's murder case. It didn't involve magic, so we sat and talked quietly in the bedroom while Mike watched an old movie on TV in the living room.

There wasn't much for him to tell me, after all my excitement. He was following a new development in the case that he wasn't happy about, but he didn't go into detail. He said he'd know more later. Our conversation was stilted—probably because both of our minds were elsewhere.

I started the car, and we headed back to Smuggler's Arcane.

Elsie turned to me at a red light on Market Street. "Do you think we could do a big love spell for Aleese before we retire? I know our best love spells were in the book, but maybe we could come up with something."

"I think we could do that. That way, you wouldn't have to leave her alone when we go to Boca."

"Why do you think witches have such a strong compulsion to retire there? It's a huge hotbed of old witches."

"I don't know." We'd reached the shop, and I parked beside Dorothy's car. It reminded me why we were putting so much extra effort into what we did tonight. "Maybe it's the weather. Every witch I've ever known has retired there."

"I wish I were as excited about it as you and Olivia are—*were*. I suppose it doesn't really matter to her where she lives now."

"Are you afraid?"

"I am. I've seen what life has been like with limited magic. Why would I want to live with *no* magic? That's what's kept me here. Well, that and you and Olivia. I wouldn't want to go anywhere without you."

We got out of the car as a mournful sea bird cried out in the darkness. The river was still alive with lights and traffic, despite the storm. The large structure that was the old Cotton Exchange was silent and empty before us.

"This is like the old days, huh, Molly?" Elsie nudged me with her elbow. "It's great to be back in the saddle again."

Olivia met us at the door. "I'm glad you're back. Let's get this over with. I'm tired of being stuck here alone."

"You might have to get used to it," Elsie remarked.

Olivia ignored her. "This is so exciting, isn't it, girls? We used to get together like this all the time, talk about spells and brew potions."

"The good old days." Elsie nodded. "When you were still alive."

"Molly, tell her to stop doing that. I don't need to be reminded every five minutes that I'm dead. I *know* I'm dead. I can look right through my hand."

She held it up and peered through the transparent semblance of her former flesh.

"Let's focus," I said. "This is serious magic that can have very bad consequences if we don't do it right."

"Kind of like what happened to Cassandra." Olivia tried to get her own back by making fun of Elsie's magic.

"No. Not like that," I disagreed, not convinced that Cassandra was really hurt by it. "That was magic gone awry. This could be much worse. We could call something we can't control. We could hurt Brian."

"That would be terrible," Olivia added. "I know you don't like him, but he really *is* a very nice young man."

"Give it a rest," Elsie sniped. "Even if he didn't kill you, he's not a *nice* young man! And maybe if you had better taste in *nice* young men, we wouldn't be here tonight!"

"It's almost midnight." I took off my jacket. "Let's get started."

"Ooh! You look fabulous, Molly!" Olivia soundlessly clapped her hands. "I haven't seen you dressed like that since we did the spell that helped Joe propose to you."

"Joe was already in love with you," Elsie said with a roll of her green eyes. "You must have something to work with. No one can truly make someone love you. Lust after you, be obsessed with you—yes. But not *love*."

"I know *that*!" Olivia scoffed. "I've done my fair share of love spells and potions in my day."

"But no love spell worked for *you*?" Elsie guessed.

Olivia floated through the trapdoor and the rug.

"She's really getting the hang of being a ghost," Elsie remarked.

I lifted the trapdoor to the cave and started down the stairs. "She won't have anything else to do for a hundred years."

"I've heard that's the life span of a ghost," Olivia said.

"Really? A hundred years?" Elsie shook her head. "At least she won't need plastic surgery."

"Why are you being so mean to me, Elsie?" Olivia circled the roof of the cave. "The dead have feelings too, you know."

"Time to end the chatter, ladies." I stood near the cauldron. "Elsie, call the fire."

It was important for us to be actually based in our elements. I had filled the mop bucket with water. I planned to stand in it to get the best effect from my element.

Elsie drew her sword. She stood as close to the fire as she could.

Olivia's staff was with us, even though I wasn't sure it would do any good for it to be there. I didn't see what it could hurt either, and it made her feel that she was part of this important spell.

The flames made dancing shadows on the cave walls. Olivia floated near the ceiling and tried to restrict her movements so we wouldn't be distracted.

Elsie raised her sword and began the incantation Olivia had recited for us. We had already discussed what order we would use.

I followed with the same incantation until our voices mingled.

The fire roared as it reached for the ceiling. The heat from it was stifling. My face was hot and sticky.

The water in the mop bucket began churning around my feet like a spa. It had been cold to begin with but quickly heated. There was a slight trembling to the ground. Small rocks danced around us as our voices got louder and stronger in the spell, as though shaken in a huge sieve.

We repeated the incantation five times before we stopped. It was exhausting. I wanted to collapse on the ground but held my place with my feet in the water bucket.

"We did it!" Elsie's voice cried out as the chant echoed away.

I opened my eyes, and there was Brian, standing in the cauldron. The fire raged around him. He was protected only by the balance of our elements—and Elsie's control of the flames.

He was wearing blue boxer shorts with a sports emblem on them. I didn't recognize the team name, but that was okay. We'd found a way to get his attention.

"What's going on?" He was suddenly aware of his surroundings. "Why did you bring me here?"

CHAPTER 29

Tell the truth—you cannot lie.
This spell defies you to decry.
Black or white, big or small.
The truth will come—or naught at all.

"We need your help to find Dorothy." I thought we might as well get to the point. She was the immediate problem. "I want to collect on the debt of honor that you owe me."

"So soon?" He scratched his head and yawned. "I have a big test in the morning. Can't we do this later?"

"No! The rogue witch took her. She could be dead by morning."

"Are you sure? What would someone like that want with an untrained witch?"

I'd asked myself that a hundred times since Dorothy had disappeared. The only answer I could come up with seemed ridiculous, but I said it anyway. "The witch wants her magic."

He laughed. "Yeah. The Big Bad wants that little-kid magic Dorothy can do. That doesn't make any sense."

"Any magic is better than none, if the witch is really trying to live forever," Olivia added.

"And she has absolutely no defenses to overcome."

"I have a small problem, Molly," Elsie whispered. "I

really have to pee. I think it was all the excitement. I'm sorry."

"Seriously?" I sighed. "Didn't you go before we came down here?"

"No. I didn't have to go then."

"But you control the fire," I reminded her. "Either it will die out completely while you're gone, or it will get even hotter and possibly roast Brian alive."

"Hey!" Brian gave us a nervous but winning smile. "I don't know where Miss Witch-in-Training is, but I'll help you find her. Have the old chick release the clarion spell."

"Old chick?" Elsie glared at him, and the flames roared even higher. "Can't we roast him? I don't like his attitude."

Olivia came down from the ceiling. "Girls, he said he's willing to help. Give him a chance to prove himself to you."

Brian glanced up at her. "Thanks, Olivia. You were always very sweet."

She giggled and pirouetted near the sandy floor.

"All right, Elsie," I said finally. "Let's release him. Then you can go to the bathroom."

It was a lot easier to let go of the spell than it had been to use it. I felt the effort leave me. I took a deep, cleansing breath before dragging myself to my chair and collapsing.

Elsie scooted upstairs quickly for a woman her age.

Brian sat in Olivia's chair, obviously comfortable despite his lack of attire. I could see what had attracted Olivia to him—he had a very *athletic* body. "So you think this rogue witch is scared of you two?" he asked in a doubtful voice.

"No. I can't explain why he or she would be worried about Elsie and me. But why else threaten us and take Dorothy?"

"Maybe you have something the witch wants," he suggested.

"That could make sense, except that we don't have anything of great value to a witch with that kind of power. The witch didn't ask us for anything. And this is the second time we've been attacked."

"Third, if you count my murder." Olivia pouted.

"How do you plan to find her? If the witch is as powerful as you say, she could cloak herself."

"We needed a third witch for a locator spell with Dorothy and Olivia gone." I didn't plan to tell him that we couldn't remember one. Needing another witch to make it work made sense too, without the embarrassment.

"Sure." He got to his feet and took stock of our cave. "Sweet spot down here!"

"Thanks."

"Why do you think this witch wanted your spell book?" he questioned.

"I don't know. The witch is collecting items of power from our community. Even the council isn't sure why." I glanced at Olivia. "All we've heard is what Olivia said. The witch is trying not to die. Killing Olivia is part of that, I suppose. What happened that night?"

He shrugged. "We went out and had a few drinks before dinner. Then we ate."

"And we danced!" Olivia swirled around the cave.

"Then we went to a few other bars." Brian's forehead furrowed. "One thing led to another, and we went back to my apartment—"

"I get the picture." I stopped him from relating any other details I'd be sorry I heard. "I still don't understand why you were in that alley, Olivia."

"Well, I forgot something at the last bar we went to. I can't think what it was right now. I went back to my place after I'd left Brian. Once I realized, I went right back out to find it."

"You didn't drive. Your car was still at your house." Elsie rejoined us.

"Yes. That's right. I was a little tipsy. I called a taxi, and the driver took me to the bar."

"And then what?" I asked.

Olivia thought about it. "I don't know. I was in the alley, and someone came up behind me. I fought, but I wasn't strong enough. It was terrible. All I could think about was that I would never really know my baby girl."

"Which is why you called her name." Elsie nodded.

"Yes." Olivia tried to wipe a tear from her eye. "I can hardly bear to think about it."

"It sounds like the same spell that brought me to the tavern by the waterfront," Brian said. "I didn't know why I was there either."

"Maybe the witch planned to kill you too," Elsie said.

"Maybe." He considered the idea with an uneasy expression.

"Let's get started on the locator spell," I suggested before we got too maudlin to do anything useful.

"Yes." Elsie picked up her sword. "I hope you know a good one, Brian, my boy, because none of us can remember *any* of them at all."

He grinned. "You're joking, right? A locator spell is easy!"

"Not if you don't know one," Olivia said.

"Okay. Whatever."

He glanced at me, but I didn't say anything. I was sticking to my original assessment of the situation. It would be good to have a third witch. Brian was an air witch like Olivia. Elsie and I were used to working with that element.

"I'll need my wand," he said. "It's back at the apartment."

"And you'll have to put on some clothes," Elsie observed. "Something spiffy."

"Too bad," Olivia murmured.

"I could use a ride to my place." He pointedly stared at me. "It would be faster than calling a taxi. I don't exactly have my car with me.

"All right. But let's hurry."

We didn't speak at all on the way back to the apartment Brian shared with the other young men near the community college. My mind kept straying to Olivia going to this crowded, probably messy apartment, to have sex with the young man beside me. She was definitely the wild one of the three of us.

Elsie had stayed at the shop with Olivia until we got back. She was breaking out the elderberry wine that we'd made last summer. So much had happened; summer seemed a lifetime away.

"Cheer up, Molly," Brian finally said as we pulled into the parking lot for the complex where he lived. "We'll find Dorothy."

"Thanks." I wondered if the rogue witch would give her up that easily. It struck me that *finding* Dorothy might be the least of our problems. Brian's magic was young and strong. I could feel it racing through him like quicksilver. It would give our spell a boost that Dorothy's untrained magic wouldn't have.

But using a locator spell to find Dorothy was one thing— confronting the powerful witch who'd taken her was another. If there was a spell that could compel the rogue witch to give up Dorothy, I didn't know it and had never tried using one like it. I supposed that was the price I paid for using magic to take care of housework and make my life easier.

"Have you ever done anything like this?" I asked him, alone in the car with the night and the rain. I didn't want to sound like a silly old woman, but I felt like one.

"You mean confronting a wicked witch who kills and steals for power?" He laughed. "Sure. All the time."

"Seriously." Was everything a joke with him?

He sobered. "I think only members of the council have done this kind of thing before, Molly. I don't know why they aren't here doing it now."

"Yeah." I looked out the side window. "Me either."

"Come on inside," he invited. "You probably shouldn't be out here alone with the rogue witch running wild."

I wasn't really scared to stay outside and wait for him—until I thought about how Olivia was killed. Going inside, now that he'd mentioned it, seemed a safer choice.

There was loud music playing in the stairwell. Footballs and kissing couples occupied the spaces between stairs. Brian hailed some of the people, fist-bumping a few as we went.

Once we'd reached his apartment, jackets, bikes and old food littered the living room and kitchen. We zigzagged through all of it and found the bedroom. No doubt it was Brian's—his name was on the door.

We went inside and closed the door behind us. I thought that a wand could be a fragile thing, difficult to find in the ruins of a student's life.

But it wasn't a problem. Brian's room was as neat and orderly as the other rooms were a mess. The wand was perched on a table beside the bed. It was made of willow that had been shaped and cut to bring out the most power in it.

"My dad gave me this on my tenth birthday." Brian lifted it. "We started training when I was really small. He and my mother are both witches. They wanted me to be strong when I grew up."

It suddenly occurred to me who this young man was. "Abdon Fuller? Are you related?"

"Yes. He's my grandfather."

"He's been a member of the Grand Council of Witches forever." I worried that we'd said and done too much around Brian.

"He has," he agreed with a smile. "Or at least longer than anyone else can remember."

"I didn't know."

"Yeah. I'd rather no one put us together, you know? Every witch in Wilmington hates the council. I do too, even though he's a member. To tell you the truth, he and I don't get along all that well. You don't have to worry about me talking to him about all this, Molly."

"Thanks." I was beginning to agree with Olivia about Brian. The more I got to know the true man, he seemed like a very nice person. A little more ego than I liked to see in a witch of his age, but not as bad as I'd feared.

"No problem. Guess I should change. Elsie wants me to come back *spiffy*."

"I'll wait in the car." I didn't want him to confuse me with Olivia. "I'll be fine."

He frowned but didn't argue. "I'll only be a minute. This is actually about as spiffy as I get!"

I went downstairs and stopped before I went outside. I hated that my town and my life had begun to make me nervous. I'd never been afraid to be out late at night by myself on the streets. I was a witch. Who could hurt me? But it seemed my glory days were well behind me.

I waited at the foot of the stairs, near the outside door. There was no point in taking foolish chances. Olivia was dead. It could have been me.

Brian was as fast as he'd said. He was wearing jeans and a nice red satin shirt. I knew Elsie would like the red satin. He didn't say anything about me waiting inside for him. I was grateful that he didn't make fun of me.

Rain was coming down even harder on the way out. We'd had to park in the back of the building and walk around. I was soaked by the time I reached the car, but the rain was a wonderful, uplifting magic for me. Brian wasn't as happy with it, though air didn't truly conflict with water. Elsie would have been very upset.

We got in the car, prepared to leave, when a dark sedan pulled up beside us. It was so close that I wouldn't have been able to get out my door. My heart started racing. I couldn't pull forward. There was a car parked in front of us.

Someone shone a flashlight in the window. I rolled down the glass as I gripped both my amulets. Brian took out his wand.

"Molly?" Joe's face was wet, his hair plastered to his head. "What in the world are you doing out here?"

I felt my breath catch in my throat. "You startled me."

Lisbet was with him. She was wearing a heavy yellow poncho and a big rain hat. "I guess so! What in the world are you doing out here at this time of night?"

"I brought something to a friend of Mike's. You know students—they either have no money or they've forgotten that they need to eat this week. I offered to bring some food by."

Joe peered more closely into the car. "Who is that with you?"

"Hi." Brian leaned forward into the flashlight's beam. "I'm Brian Fuller. I'm a student. Friends with Molly and Elsie."

"Funny." Joe glanced at Lisbet. "We're actually here to see *you*, Brian. Would you mind stepping out of the car?"

"Me?" Brian's gulp was audible. "What for?"

"We finally found a videotape of Olivia going into a bar," Joe answered. "She was with Mr. Fuller."

CHAPTER 30

Fret not thyself with evildoers.

Brian and I ended up at the police station with Lisbet and Joe. I called Smuggler's Arcane with Brian's cell phone to let Olivia and Elsie know what was going on. I was disgusted and nervous about the new direction of Joe's investigation. While we were there, not able to tell Joe the truth about Brian, Dorothy could be suffering somewhere in the night.

Joe and Lisbet split us up. I'd been hoping Lisbet would go with Brian so I could have a moment alone with Joe to clarify what was happening. That didn't happen.

Lisbet and I sat down together in a small room. She offered me coffee—I said no.

"Why were you with Brian Fuller tonight?" she asked.

I'd thought about this on the way over. I was ready. "Brian is an old friend of Olivia's. He wanted to talk to me about her death."

"What about them going out for a drink on the night she died?"

"They frequently went out. The three of us go out together, at least we did."

"Was Brian the man you said Olivia was dating—the one you saw on the boat, Molly?"

I laughed. "Goodness, no! I could have told you his name if it was! I want you and Joe to catch Olivia's murderer, Lisbet. She was a very dear friend."

Her eyes narrowed. I knew finding me with a suspect was another nail in my coffin—so to speak. I'd sort it out later with Joe. Once he understood, he'd stop harassing Brian.

I just hoped it wouldn't be too late for Dorothy.

"Excuse me." Lisbet smiled and curtly nodded before she left me alone in the room.

I waited, impatiently, for a long time. Finally, I took out my compact and attempted a spell to find out what was going on.

I held my amulets in one hand and stared into the compact mirror. "Guide me to the one I seek," I whispered, staring intently into the reflection.

A light haze covered the mirror. Fog swirled in the glass.

I concentrated harder. An image began to form.

It was Dorothy! That hadn't been what I meant when I'd said the spell, but what a joy to know she was alive. I couldn't talk to her. She was sitting in a chair, crying. My heart broke when I couldn't comfort her or ask where she was.

Fog swelled in the glass again, and this time I was able to see Brian and Joe.

Brian smiled and winked at me. He knew I was watching.

"Something funny about my questions?" Joe asked

"No, sir." Brian focused on him. "Just wondering when I get my phone call."

"I'm not arresting you," Joe responded.

Brian got to his feet. "Then I'm going. If you have any other questions, let me know."

Lisbet walked in, and I shut the compact.

I mimicked Brian by getting to my feet. "Am I under arrest?"

"No." She smiled. "Of course not, Molly."

"Then I'm leaving. You know where to find me if you have any other questions."

She nodded. "Okay. But be careful who you hang out with. You don't want to end up like your friend."

I told her I would be careful and held my head high as I walked out of the room. Joe was in the hall. I told him that I'd see him at home and hurried out to the car. Brian was waiting for me.

"Your husband is a *cop*?" He raked his fingers through his damp hair. "That's as bad as my grandfather being on the council!"

"He's really not that bad." I opened the car and we got inside. "I saw Dorothy!"

"Yeah? With the mirror spell, huh? Good! She was alive, I guess."

"Yes. I didn't see who was holding her or where she was."

"Too bad."

We discussed the rogue witch as we drove back to Smuggler's Arcane.

Brian agreed that this was no ordinary witch. "This witch must be formidable. I've only heard of a few witches being killed by their own. The council has always gone after them with a vengeance."

"I know Olivia wasn't a significant witch, but I don't believe the council would've stood for her death at the hands of another witch if they'd thought there was anything they could do about it."

The very idea of the witches on the council not being able to control another witch who was bent on murder and stealing as many magic artifacts as she could find was terrifying.

I knew my limits, or at least I thought I did. I knew I couldn't handle such a witch.

And Joe was caught in the crosshairs investigating the case. I wanted to run home and take him and Mike away somewhere safe until all of this was over.

I didn't feel secure again until we were back in the shop and I had locked the door behind me.

"We've got the wand." I started down the stairs to the cave. "I hope we can find Dorothy now. I saw her in my compact mirror. At least she's still alive."

There was no response. The words echoed inside the cave. I reached the rocky floor and then noticed Cassandra, waiting by the fire.

"Looks like we don't need it," Elsie said. "We've been busted."

Cassandra was in a high fit of anxiety. I'd never seen her this way, although I'd never seen her as much as I had the last few days either.

She was tapping her foot on the ground. "What are you *thinking*? Twenty years of peace with the werewolves, and now they're up in arms. No witch-on-witch violence—and now we have a witch who was murdered and has become a ghost."

Mr. Brannigan was back too. "Cassandra's right. Things are badly askew here."

"We've tried to tell both of you that there was a problem." I didn't back down from either of them. It didn't mean I wasn't afraid of Cassandra and what she might do. It only meant that I was too frustrated and angry to care.

"So you took it upon yourselves to solve the problem." Cassandra's white brow was actually furrowed in indignation. "You should have asked the council for help with this matter."

"We *did*," Elsie reminded her. "You were no help at all. That's why I turned you into pottery."

Olivia and I both glared at Elsie for talking before she thought.

"Sorry." Elsie put her hand over her mouth.

"Oh, that was nothing." Cassandra's laugh tinkled around the cave. "I was going on vacation anyway. It meant I got to leave early."

"In the middle of this crisis?" I demanded.

She studied her fingernails. "I had reservations."

"Well, you could've told *us*. Now we have dust upstairs everywhere." Elsie glared at her.

"Can we please find my daughter?" Olivia requested.

Cassandra didn't look at her. "Send your ghost away—or I will."

Olivia *humphed* but scurried upstairs with the cats.

"That's so much better." Cassandra smiled benignly at the rest of us. "I can understand that you're mourning your lost friend, ladies. But going against the express orders of the council and dragging another witch into it is inexcusable."

"What's *inexcusable*," I raged, "is the council doing nothing while another would-be witch may be killed. I understand that you didn't realize this rogue witch was capable of murder. Now that you know, what are you going to do about it?"

"I tried to tell you to stand down. I warned you that the council was worried and might not be able to help." Cassandra defended what she'd done. "You kept coming up with schemes—like this one tonight."

"I want to be transparent about my part in all of this." Mr. Brannigan cleared his throat to speak.

"Never mind. What's done is done. Don't think the rest of the council doesn't know."

"Good." I challenged her. "Let's go see them right now. I'm tired of this game. Let's see what they can do about it."

"Your mother's amulet has made you daring," she purred.

I felt the amulet grow warm on my throat. I didn't know what it was capable of. I had to back down. "My quarrel isn't with you or the council. I only want to keep my family safe. I want to know who killed my friend and why. And I want Dorothy back."

"I think this discussion is over." Cassandra stared at me.

I saw fear and uncertainty in her beautiful eyes, but before I could remark on it, she was gone.

"Are they always like that?" Brian asked. "I don't have many dealings with them."

"Always." Elsie yawned. "I don't know if I can do a locator spell now, Molly. I'm exhausted."

"What happened with Joe and his partner?" Olivia came in close.

I gave them a brief rundown of what had happened. "They didn't want to arrest Brian. I'm sure Joe didn't know what to think, but they let us both go."

"Probably only until they can find more evidence against me." Brian pulled out his wand. "But they'll have a hard time finding *me* again."

"Mr. Brannigan." I stared at him. "Can you help us with the locator spell since Elsie can't? We need to find Dorothy right away."

He held up one hand. "Absolutely not! You heard what Cassandra said. If you persist in going against the council, none of you have a very bright future."

Elsie grabbed my arm. "Are you sure that's the best thing to do?"

"Never mind him," Brian said. "Let's try it with you and me, Molly. We might be strong enough together to pull it off."

"Before you try it," Mr. Brannigan said, "the council has decided to take possession of your mother's amulet, Molly. This would be for safekeeping until the thief who took your spell book and the other local items is brought to justice. It seems that the amulet has some ancient power that the council wasn't aware of."

"No!" I put my hand up to it. "This belongs to my family. The council doesn't need it."

Mr. Brannigan waved his hand. "Allow me."

The chain stayed where it was. He frowned and tried again. "Molly! You can't defy the council!"

"I can until we find Dorothy. If you're not going to help, you can leave."

"I'm going to tell Cassandra! And you better hope the amulet doesn't fall into the wrong witch's hands." After that stern warning, Mr. Brannigan stalked up the rickety stairs and was gone.

"Let me have a look at the amulet," Elsie said. "You never said you had something of great magical value."

"I didn't know. I told you about it a long time ago. I've just never worn it because it's so gaudy."

I tried to get it off. The clasp wouldn't open. Elsie tried too. Brian also had a go at it. The amulet and chain stayed around my neck.

"I guess you're wearing it whether you want to or not," he said. "Let's try the locator spell, Molly. If that thing has so much power that the council wants it, we might pull it off."

Brian and I concentrated together after he reminded me of the spell he knew. There were hundreds of locator spells. We held hands and joined our magic. It didn't work. We tried standing in our elements again. The spell still didn't work.

"Let me try to help," Elsie said. "I might have enough energy to make a third witch."

But her face was so pale—and her hands shaking so—that I decided we shouldn't try it. She could barely stand upright. I didn't want to risk her health.

"I can do it, Molly," she softly protested.

"Not tonight," I told her. "I want to find Dorothy as much as anyone, but I want you to live until Boca."

"And far after," Olivia added with a concerned face.

"What about taking a look into the mirror again?" Brian suggested. "I know the mirror spell is limited, but maybe we can get an idea of where she is."

Instead of pulling out my compact again, we went upstairs to our large, antique mirror that we'd always used for spells. Brian and I joined hands and whispered the spell for sight.

Olivia and Elsie watched from the table as the mirror turned hazy and then cleared. The same room I'd seen earlier appeared, but Dorothy wasn't there.

"Maybe the witch moved her," Brian said. "She might have known you were watching, like I did."

He'd barely finished speaking when the mirror went black. "Spying on me?" a raspy voice asked. It was the same voice I recognized from the shop when the witch had snatched Dorothy. "I *hate* spies!"

It was as though a huge, powerful hand reached out through the mirror and knocked Brian and me off our feet. I couldn't see anything at all. It had to be a spell but not one that I recognized.

"Are you okay, Molly?" Elsie asked.

"I'm fine." Brian helped me to my feet. "I've never felt that kind of strength or malevolence from a witch before. How will we ever take Dorothy from her?"

We were all silent on the way back to Brian's apartment. There was nothing else we knew to try that night. We agreed to meet back at Smuggler's Arcane again tomorrow night, hoping Elsie's full magic—with mine and Brian's—would be able to make the locator spell work.

Elsie sagged in the front seat beside me. Her head rolled on her shoulders as she fell asleep.

I'd talked Olivia into staying behind at the shop. I knew she'd be safe there. I wasn't so sure about anywhere else.

"I hope Elsie will be okay," Brian said when he got out of the car at his place.

"I'm sure she will," I said with a smile. "Thanks for your help. I'll see you tomorrow."

"Yeah."

I watched him walk away into the thick mist that had come up after the rain had stopped. I fought with myself to keep from breaking down and crying.

I didn't know if Elsie would be okay. I could only hope. I didn't know if Dorothy would survive the night. My world was falling apart. I was terrified.

I closed my eyes and held on to my amulets before I left the parking lot. I needed all the strength I could muster.

Elsie woke when I parked the car at her house and went around to the other side to help her out.

"You know it will be a miracle if we pull this off," she told me as we walked up to her house. "Even when we were in our prime, the most complex spells we ever did were keeping our cars clean and grading school papers."

"I guess we're both having a midlife crisis."

"Midlife?" Elsie laughed. "I'm not prepared to live another seventy years. This is fine for you and Dorothy—even Olivia if she hadn't died. I'm a lot older than you, Molly. I'm not sure I'm up for it."

I smiled and touched her hand. "You were the most powerful witch in Wilmington at one time. Your worst is probably better than most witches' best."

She rolled her eyes. "Flattery will get you everywhere. I'm not saying I won't try. I hate being the weakest link."

"I think you have some untapped strength. You'll just have to call on it."

"Can I call long distance?" She smiled as we reached her front door. "I thought I'd be in Boca right now. Who knew all this other stuff would happen?"

"You said you aren't sure about retiring," I reminded her. "Maybe this is your kick in the pants."

"Maybe so." She gazed up at the stars. "I feel terrible being the reason we have to leave Dorothy out there."

"I know. Tomorrow, we'll try again."

"And the council?"

"Maybe they'll thank us for finding the witch they're afraid of."

"Fat chance!" Her smile trembled on her lips. "Good night, Molly."

I drove home, knowing I still had to conjure up another bubble to tell Joe what was going on. I wasn't looking forward to it.

I parked and went inside. The smell of pizza assailed my senses. I dropped my bag and jacket on a stool. I was starving, but not hungry enough for cold pizza. A person could only eat so much pizza. I found some milk and cereal and took out a bowl.

"There you are." Joe came into the kitchen with an uncomfortable look at Mike lying on the sofa playing video games. "I was wondering if you were ever going to get home. Let's go in the bedroom."

I left my cereal untouched and went into the bedroom with him.

He locked the door. "Haven't had to do that in years. It used to be a big thing when Mike was little."

"It was," I agreed with a smile. "We've been spoiled since he went away to college."

"It won't be long before he's done with school and has his own place. Then we can canoodle in the kitchen, if you like."

"Canoodle, huh?"

He kissed me and whispered, "I'm a nervous wreck about this whole magic-bubble thing, Molly. Can we get it over with?"

I invoked the enchanted bubble again. Our words were protected from the ears of the witches' council. I explained again how dangerous it would be for them to find out that he knew about magic.

"Whatever you have to say has to wait for us to be in the right place to discuss it." I took his hand. "You can never mention that you know about magic, even casually, without the shield. I don't want to lose you."

"I guess these people don't play around, huh? You know, it's hard to get used to the idea that my wife is a real-life witch. I'll make sure I keep a low profile."

"I'm sorry it has to be this way. What happened tonight?"

Joe explained how they found a videotape of Olivia and Brian walking into a bar together. "I couldn't believe you were there with him when we went to pick him up."

"Brian is a witch too. He's helping Elsie, Olivia and me try to find Dorothy."

"Olivia?"

"She's come back as a ghost—probably only until we find her killer. The killer is a powerful witch, Joe. You have to stall until the Grand Council of Witches can deal with her. If you try to take her with just you and Lisbet, you'll both be killed."

I also explained that Dorothy had been kidnapped by the rogue witch.

"Maybe that's something I can help with," he said.

"No. You have to stay away from this. You don't understand what's involved."

He nodded. "Okay. We have some clues that we can look into. That could keep us busy, I guess. The ME found some black fibers on Olivia's body. Some were lodged under her fingernails and in the wound on her neck. We think the fibers came from something her killer was wearing."

"What kind of black fibers?"

"Polyester and cotton with rayon. The ME thinks it could've been a ski mask, disguising the killer's face. That might mean that Olivia knew who killed her. Even though she was killed from behind, the killer may have wanted to be extra cautious."

"Just take it nice and slow. Don't be in a hurry. Give us a chance to find Dorothy and notify the council."

He didn't look happy about that. "Magic or not, Molly, I don't like the idea of you going toe-to-toe with a killer. You said Olivia was a witch too, but whoever it was killed her anyway. Is there some way I can be around when you bring the killer out?"

"You don't have to worry. All we plan to do is keep him or her in one place for someone from the council to take care of. If they don't actually take him somewhere else, maybe they'll render him harmless so you can arrest him."

"Warlock, right? A male witch is called a warlock."

"No, sweetie. A male witch is still a witch."

"Okay. Not happy with this setup, but I guess you know what's best when it comes to witches." He frowned. "Mike isn't a witch, is he? Does it run in families?"

"It does run in families, but it passed him by. I'm glad in some ways."

"Well, let me know if I can do anything to help. I kind of feel a little useless right now. Do you have some way to protect yourself?"

"We do have protections," I assured him. "I think we'll be okay."

"I love you, Molly. Be careful. I'd rather you be alive than care what your council thinks about me knowing you're a witch. Remember that."

"I will." I kissed him. "I love you too."

I dispersed the enchanted bubble. Like Joe, I wished it could be out in the open too, but that wasn't the way the council wanted it.

"So, pizza again tonight, huh?" He grinned.

I shuddered. "Not for me. I'm eating cereal."

We went back into the living room. Mike had gone to bed. I hated that our relationship had been so strained. I'd been so caught up in everything else going on that I hadn't been able to talk with him about school. That was going to have to change.

I missed Isabelle's presence in the house. She added a calming factor that always soothed my jangled nerves. I knew I'd be glad when this whole nightmare was finished and my life could get back to normal. I wasn't cut out for intrigue.

My heart ached for the old days and for the loss of Olivia. Even though she was a ghost, I couldn't pick up the phone for a late-night gab session. We couldn't go shopping and laugh as we tried on clothes we would never really wear outside the dressing room.

I realized that my life was never going back to normal again. Those days were gone.

I tried again to remove the amulet. The stubborn clasp wouldn't budge. I looked at it in the bathroom mirror, wishing it had come with instructions.

"Come to bed," Joe called.

I went in, and we cuddled until he fell asleep. I knew there wouldn't be any sleep for me that night. I faced the blackness with eyes wide open, hoping we'd find Dorothy the next day.

CHAPTER 31

I invoke the power of the universe.
I call on every known source of help.
Guide me in this time of trouble.
Lift my eyes to see the light!

I picked Elsie up in the morning, as I had countless other mornings on my way to Smuggler's Arcane. She'd brought homemade shortbread cookies with her, but she'd been able to sleep for a while too. Her magic felt stronger.

We got to the shop to find Olivia and all three cats waiting by the front door.

"Oh, girls, I'm so glad you're back! It's been the longest night waiting and worrying about Dorothy. If I weren't already dead, I would be now. I don't know how I'm going to survive waiting until midnight to find her."

"We'll be stronger then, and there will be less human interference," I reminded her. "We don't want to try and fail again."

Elsie made tea and put the cookies on the table. "I don't know about the two of you, but I'm thirsty and starving."

I fed the cats. They were nervous and fidgety. It's always hard being away from home and following unfamiliar routines. I assured them that it would be over soon as I stroked Harper and Isabelle. Barnabas pestered Elsie for attention. I would do in a pinch, but while she was there, he only had eyes for her.

Hemlock still didn't like or trust anyone but Dorothy. He hissed and drew away when I tried to touch him. I left him alone.

The three of us sat down for orange spice tea and short-bread cookies.

"You know"—Olivia hovered over her empty cup and saucer—"it's odd that you can be dead and still feel physical things like hunger and exhaustion. I wonder if that goes away with time."

"Maybe it's like phantom limb pain." Elsie picked up a cookie. "People feel their amputated legs and arms long after they're gone. You have phantom hunger pains."

Olivia looked longingly at the cookies. "You know, the one thing that puzzles me is why anyone would want our old spells."

"Excuse me?" Elsie interrupted.

"I don't mean it like that." Olivia's form fluctuated a little with her agitation. "You know what I mean. Our magic has never been anything special. Even our mothers' and grand-mothers' spells were all about avoiding storms and making children happy. Why would this horrid, powerful witch the council is afraid of want it?"

"Olivia has a point." Elsie munched as she spoke. "Why does she want it, Molly?"

"Maybe it doesn't matter what the spells are." I was only guessing. I didn't understand either.

"Well, if I were going to steal someone's book, I'd want it to have great spells in it like disappearing and shape-shifting. A spell like refilling a flat tire would be meaning-less to me." Olivia swirled through the shop.

"Unless it didn't matter because it was just one magic

item out of dozens, and I was going for quantity." Elsie dunked her cookie in her tea.

I stopped eating my cookie and pushed back my chair. "That's true of the witch, but what about her accomplice?"

"We don't know for sure that the witch has one, do we?" Olivia asked.

"You know," Elsie said, "a few years back, when I was a teenager, there was a group of thieves that stole similar things for their collections."

"A *few* years back?" Olivia hooted. "I'd say that's more than a *few* years."

"You know what I mean." Elsie waved her hand. "Don't make me turn you into a puff of smoke."

"As if you could do that," Olivia taunted her.

"Ladies, I think we may be onto something. We know there's a black market for magical items. Maybe that's what's feeding the accomplice. Finding that person could lead us to the witch."

"How would we figure that out?" Olivia asked.

"We could go out to Oak Island and see the Bone Man." Elsie clapped her hands. "Road trip!"

"Oh you silly goose!" Olivia said. "Oak Island isn't that far at all, if you don't count the ferry ride."

The Bone Man was a trader between the worlds of magic and mundane. He wasn't a witch or any other magical creature—at least not as far as I knew. He was a dealer in magical items that were hard to get for witches. We'd bought unusual things from him several times before.

"They say his mother was a witch, and his father was a pirate," Olivia said. "He's got the *worst* reputation—and the sexiest eyes I've ever seen."

"The council frowns on him," Elsie warned. "We're not supposed to have dealings with him."

Right now, the council frowns on *everything* we do anyway," I reminded her.

"Better bring the cookies then, Molly." Elsie snatched them from me. "Is there still a thermos here that we can put tea in?"

"Dealing with the Bone Man can be very dangerous." I picked up my handbag. "We have to keep our wits about us."

"Don't lose hope." Olivia flitted around the room like a fairy. "Be careful."

"You're going too." I grabbed her staff. "What have we got that we can take to him for a trade? I have a few things in my bag." I went through it. "Joe found a real silver half dollar that I've kept with me for a while. I have a broken gold bracelet that belonged to my grandmother. I had been thinking about turning it into cash."

"He'll want your amulet, Molly," Olivia pointed out. "The way Cassandra and Mr. Brannigan went after it last night, it must be very valuable. I'm sorry I told you to wear it. I think it was a mistake."

I shuddered. "He can have it if he can get it off without *touching* me!"

"You'd give that up?" Elsie asked.

"To save Dorothy—yes!"

Olivia said, "You know, I left my old diamond ring behind the counter when I washed my hands the day I was murdered. You could take that with you to trade."

I got the ring and put it into my bag. There was no way to know what the Bone Man might want for the information we needed.

"I still have my old gold crown that fell out of my tooth a month ago." Elsie took it out of her big green bag and looked at it. "The dentist didn't want it. I should've known it was a warning of trouble to come."

"Eww!" Olivia scrunched her face.

"I have a few other things." Elsie started putting them on the table. "A shark's tooth, and an old, dried lizard that my daughter found behind the sofa. Poor thing must've gotten trapped back there." She showed us the flat, dried lizard. "I've also got a snail shell and a piece of fool's gold. Maybe one of those would interest him."

"Does anyone remember what we traded for the dodo feather?" Olivia asked.

"It was a whole bag of toenail clippings," I answered. "Remember, he wanted clippings from dead men's toenails. We had to sneak into the hospital morgue using Joe's police pass to get them."

"Oh, *yes*! We needed an extinct bird's feather to make that potion for the woman who was being haunted by her amorous husband's ghost." Elsie smiled at the memory. "The good old days."

"Except that Joe got called about going into the morgue. He didn't know what was going on. He never suspected it was us, thank goodness. I think he always thought it was a prank that Mike and his friends did."

Elsie kept rooting around behind the counter until she found a travel mug for her tea. "I'm ready to go. Molly, I'll let *you* do the talking."

CHAPTER 32

Rain slash and thunder rumble,
Elements! keep me out of trouble.
Cold night and warm day,
let nothing stand in my way.

It took about an hour to follow the coastline to the ferry landing that would take us to Oak Island. We passed the North Carolina Aquarium and the Confederate historic site Fort Fisher on the way.

The gray Atlantic crashed on the shore after a night of wind and rain. Seeing the ocean so close made me yearn to go into it. The water called to me—the deeper the better.

But there wasn't time. I had to be content seeing it, stretched across the horizon, as the conversation in the car swirled around me.

"I think we last went to see the Bone Man when we were making a charm for Regan Thomas," Elsie said.

"Regan Thomas?" Olivia wrinkled her forehead as she tried to think who that was.

"She was the teacher at the high school who took the basketball team to the state finals," I reminded her. "Mike was a senior that year. He was on the team. We looked up a spell to help them, and it needed a shell only located at the bottom of the sea."

"That should've told us something right there." Elsie shook her head.

"Did the team win?" Olivia asked. "I can't recall."

"Oh, they won," Elsie said. "But the coach lost all her hair. I think that was when we first noticed that our magic wasn't what it had been."

Olivia laughed. "We've had such adventures together. I'm glad that's not entirely over because I'm dead."

This reminder of her present state was depressing. There had been banter and chatter about it since the event that I'd ignored. This one pushed deep into my soul and created a hole there that I knew would never be filled.

I pulled the car up to the gate where the tickets for the ferry were issued. The ferryman told us it would be about twenty minutes until the boat was ready to leave again. We were welcome to pull the car into the parking lot.

"You should feel right at home on Oak Island since it's haunted." Elsie grinned. "Maybe you can find some of your own kind to play with, Olivia."

"I'm still a witch, even though I'm dead," Olivia protested. "I don't want to hang around with any ghosts."

I pulled the car smoothly into the parking space. We got out and brought umbrellas with us since it still threatened rain. Elsie and I walked around the boat, looking at the ocean splashing up against its hull.

Olivia was peering at the bearded captain in the wheelhouse, practicing writing her name in the mist on the window.

"I didn't have a chance to tell you," Elsie whispered. "I left Brian with a little surprise this morning. He'll be back to see us in the next few days."

"What did you do?"

She giggled. "I put some itching powder in his hand when

he shook mine. It's time-released so it won't show up right away. He'll come to us when it does, and you'll have your chance to pitch him joining our coven."

"That was a sneaky idea. Good, but sneaky. Maybe we can retire even if we can't find the spell book, if we find the witches to take our places."

She looked into the deep water. "I don't know. If we can find Dorothy, and Brian will join us, I'd like to stay here. We wouldn't need the book. I could guide another pair of young witches around the pitfalls of magic."

"It would be all right to retire, Elsie. Hundreds of witches do it every year. It won't be the end."

She shrugged. "It's okay for you—you have Joe. I'd be alone without a coven. I know my magic isn't what it used to be. Maybe I can find an amulet like yours to recharge it."

"You could have mine, if I could get it off."

"I can't believe your mother didn't say anything to you about its power."

"I don't think she ever wore it. Maybe not Grandma Faye either. I don't think they knew what it could do."

We both stared out at the horizon, as though the answer to our problems were there in the quickly moving gray clouds and rolling sea flecked with white.

There were still only two other passengers on the ferry when they closed the boarding ramp and started making way.

Olivia found us. "This is *really* exciting. I'm so glad I came now. I can't wait to get to the island."

Elsie and I huddled under our umbrellas. The air was cold once we'd started moving. But it was filled with tiny drops of rain that the wind occasionally blew back at me. It lifted my spirit out of the doldrums where it had come to rest.

"I'm a little nervous about going to meet the Bone Man again." Olivia flitted back and forth across the boat. The wind didn't move her incorporeal form. "I remember hearing that he doesn't like ghosts, and that he got rid of a few on Oak Island when he took up residence there."

"I'm sure he'll be fine with you," Elsie said. "If he's not, we'll protect you."

"Maybe I should stay on the boat. I don't want my half-life to be any shorter."

"A lot of what we've heard about the Bone Man probably isn't true." I wanted to make less of the man's reputation. I didn't want any of us to be scared of him when we got there. That could spell disaster.

"Such as?" Olivia was willing to be reassured.

"Well, those bones he wears, for example." Elsie's eyes narrowed as she thought about it. "I've heard the bones belong to his enemies. He took them when he killed them."

"How is that supposed to make us feel better?" Olivia demanded.

"I don't know." Elsie shrugged. "I just thought it was a good story."

"Think again."

"I'm sure there's a lot of mythology about him that's not true." I pulled my coat closer against the cold. "He can't possibly live up to the reputation everyone has given him."

Elsie nodded. "I think he can, Molly."

"Well, the two of you are no help at all!" Olivia circled around the boat and came back to us. "I'm glad Dorothy isn't here today. At least *she* isn't scared of the Bone Man."

"There's the island," Elsie pointed out. "Too late to turn back now."

"Just remember—no magic on the island if we want to trade with the Bone Man. He's got a thing about it."

"I'll be good, Mom." Elsie laughed. "Look how *good* we were last night with Brian. It was like reeling in a big fish. I could feel him pulling back, but we held on to him. What a moment!"

The ferry bumped against the rocky shore of Oak Island.

It had been a pirate hangout for many years and a smuggler's hold for many more. The lighthouse still stood sentinel to the wild forces of the Atlantic, protecting ships passing by. We weren't far from the Graveyard of the Atlantic, where so many sailors had lost their lives for generations.

"We have to find the old cemetery." Elsie's whisper was whipped away by the stiff, cold breeze.

Gulls wheeled and turned in to the wind, crying out for their breakfast. The pungent smell of fish permeated the area, enticing them.

No witch would come here unless she needed something. The Bone Man knew that. Among his many myths were tales that he lived in the old cemetery that was hidden in the sparse trees that grew on the island. It wasn't a public place, although travelers had sought it out for generations. This was where you came for love spells and spells to make your enemy vanish.

The Bone Man might *not* be a witch, but he had the reputation of one.

"There are some who say he's dead." Olivia repeated another story. "Maybe now that I'm a ghost, I'll be able to tell."

We got off the boat and trudged along the sandy paths that would lead where we needed to go. Each of us was lost in our own thoughts. I held Olivia's staff in one hand.

Olivia's mind was on Dorothy. "She's a fighter, like her mother, you know. I'm so sorry I missed out on all those years with her. On the other hand, I bypassed the smelly diapers and the baby drool. Maybe it's just as well. Now she's a lovely young woman who's neat and clean and smart. We have to get her back, Molly."

"We will. You did what you had to do. Once she's finished with her training, it won't matter if she runs across her father."

"Do you really think so?" she asked in a scared little-girl voice. "I feel so guilty."

"I would've done the same thing," Elsie said. "In fact, I'm sorry I didn't have that opportunity. It might have been nice *not* to have a daughter at all."

"Oh, you don't mean that," Olivia chided. "You love Aleese. I know you do."

Elsie sighed. "I'm sure you're right. I wish she were a witch though. I'm jealous of you having Dorothy."

Olivia preened a little, in ghost fashion. "Thank you. She *is* very special."

The wind felt colder out here on this tiny scrap of land. It whistled around us as it blew across the stony outcropping. The angry waves continued to fall against the shore, foam puffing up where the water left the sand.

The cemetery wasn't a long walk from the dock, but Elsie and I were out of breath by the time we saw the familiar old headstones. We'd always been too frightened by the thought of meeting the Bone Man again to take the time to look at the names carved into those slabs of stone.

I believed there were witches buried here—not witches that he'd killed, but those who'd lived here hundreds of years ago. I'd once read about a colony of witches who had settled here in the 1400s to get away from the Inquisition in Europe.

Nothing was really known about them. History stopped being interested in them after they got here, it seemed. I wondered if the Bone Man was one of their descendants. That would explain why he lived here—and his abilities.

The ghost stories might not be true at all. Many ghost hunters had fantastic tales to tell about their adventures here. I didn't believe them, even though tales of hauntings had circulated through the area for years. Witches and ghosts usually didn't mix. This place was hallowed ground for magic. It seemed unlikely ghosts would want to be here.

"Keep your thoughts clear," I whispered as a reminder. "We don't want the Bone Man reading us like the Sunday paper, or we'll lose our bargaining power."

Elsie did the mime trick of zipping her mouth and throwing away the key. Olivia stared at the cemetery before us and nodded.

Together, we started into the cemetery, passing the old headstones. There were a few sculptures of sleeping angels and crosses. I remembered them well. The path was always a little overgrown. The sand snagged at any unwary foot.

I held Elsie's hand in mine. We were both cold and trembling. I wanted to be strong—the anchor for our coven—but the truth was that I was terrified. I knew Elsie was too. I wished that Olivia weren't a ghost but were still there with us, flesh and blood. With three of us, it always felt safer coming here.

A small whirlwind of brown leaves suddenly rose up before us. Out of it, the Bone Man appeared.

"Ladies. How may I be of service today?"

CHAPTER 33

Bless the morning,
Bless the day.
Bless the tide,
Bless my cares that float away.

Olivia disappeared for a moment, and Elsie drew in a frightened breath.

I clutched Elsie's hand tightly. My heart was pounding, and my legs felt like rubber, but I knew I had to hide my fear if I wanted to negotiate with the Bone Man.

"We've come to make a trade." I released Elsie's hand. Being the recent mother of a teenager and the wife of a homicide detective had made me an expert in being terrified and hiding it.

The Bone Man stood at least seven feet tall. He was emaciated, joints sticking out prominently. His head was barely a skull, too small for the rest of him. His hands and feet were very large and bony too. He wore no shoes or gloves. His mouth was stained red.

His black eyes appeared larger than they should have been, like a painting out of correct dimension. They stared right through me. The wind rattled the dried bones that hung from around his neck and accentuated his worn black suit.

It looked as though he'd taken it from a corpse in the cemetery, of a fashion I'd only seen in books from the 1700s.

He rubbed his hands together. "Always willing to make a trade. What have you got for me?"

Elsie brought her hoard out of her pocket, her hand trembling so that she dropped her dried lizard.

He eyed her offerings. "And what do you want from *me*?"

"We want to know who kidnapped our friend Dorothy Lane. We think it was a person who trades in magic antiquities, not a witch." My voice was a little shaky, but it came out okay.

"Kidnapping, eh?" He grinned, showing rotted teeth. "Bad business."

"So you'll help us?"

"Not for that meager fare." He spit on Elsie's trades and pushed them aside with his foot. "What else have you got for me?"

We put everything we'd brought with us on the ground at his feet. He looked all of it over with a jaundiced eye.

"Either you don't know what's going on or you think I'm a fool." He laughed, the sound shivering through us. "Since I know you don't think I'm a fool, I'll say good-bye now, and no harm done."

"Think of something, Molly," Elsie urged in a tiny voice.

"I don't know what else to offer. This is all we brought."

The Bone Man swiveled on one long, thin leg to face us again. "*All?* I don't think so."

I wasn't sure what he meant and was a little flustered. The last time we'd traded with him, he'd barely said two words to us. We'd gone back for the toenails, and he'd given us what we needed.

Having a real conversation with him was unnerving. My instinct was to run away as fast as I could rather than look into those cold black eyes again.

"What is it *you* want?" I thought he must have something in mind that we weren't considering.

"Now we're ready to trade." He stepped close to me, one eye squinted almost closed.

I could smell death on him. His bony finger reached out and pointed at the amulet around my neck but didn't touch me.

"I'd like that fine piece." He stared at my throat. "But only blood can take it. Even you can't gift it."

I was glad he didn't want it, though I would've given it to solve the mystery of who had Dorothy. His words were puzzling. What was it about the amulet that made everyone want it?

Unfortunately, asking that question would've meant another trade that we didn't have payment for. Maybe another time.

I marshaled all my resolve and got past how close he was to me. The feeling of snakes and spiders crawling over me lingered as I met his gaze. I knew there wasn't enough hot water and soap in the world to get rid of that.

"What then? What will you take for the information we need?"

"There's only one thing you have that is worth the price of what I can tell you." He nodded at the staff in my hand. "That will do it."

"You can't have her," Elsie protested. "We don't need your help that much."

"He's talking about my staff." Olivia's voice was shaky. "He wants *me*."

"No!" Elsie grabbed the staff and clutched it to her chest. "You can't have it."

The Bone Man shrugged and started to walk away again.

"Wait!" Olivia called him back.

"No. We can't do this." The wind was blowing Elsie's faded curls into her angry face. "We can't give you away. Without the staff, we'll never see you again."

"You have to do it." Olivia kept her loosely held form

between us. "We have to know what happened, not just for me, but for Dorothy. You have to find her. Find my killer too!"

"I don't want to lose you." I realized that I was sobbing, tears dropping off my chin. "We'll find another way. There's got to be another answer."

"Don't be that way, girls. Maybe there will be something you can trade later and get me back. If not, I've lived my life." She smiled, but I could see ectoplasm tears running down her face. "Come on. Let's do this now and find Dorothy. Take care of the problem, Molly. Don't worry about me."

Her sacrifice made horrible sense to me.

Maybe because we were desperate.

Maybe because we were standing in the middle of the graveyard with the Bone Man.

In hurried words, I persuaded Elsie to trade the staff for the knowledge. Olivia kept urging us to do it before it was too late.

"Wait." I stopped the Bone Man before he could disappear. "We'll do it."

He grinned as he turned around. "Give it here then."

Crazy courage that I didn't even know I had made me call him on the deal. "You'll get it when we have what we need."

His corpselike face grew as angry and fierce as a storm on the ocean. "You doubt my word, witch? I have *never* gone back on a trade."

"And we are trading the spirit of our beloved sister to you for the information we seek. We won't do it until we hear what you have to say."

I didn't think he was going to do it. I thought he'd walk away and we wouldn't see him again. In some ways, I wished that would happen. I wanted to get Dorothy back, but the price was too high.

Instead, he pushed his face near mine. "You're a rare one, aren't you? Or is it the amulet talking?"

I could barely breathe. The stench was overwhelming, but that was mild compared to my utter terror at looking into his face. There were shadows in his eyes that no one should ever have to see this side of the grave.

In a voice that was almost lost in the wind, I answered. "I don't know what the amulet does. I don't know why everyone wants it. I do know that my friend's spirit is tied to this staff. We don't want to give that up. But we will—if you can prove to us that you have what we need."

He backed up and spit in his palm. "Done."

I swallowed hard and shook his icy claw.

"Don't worry," Elsie whispered, "I have hand sanitizer in the car."

I held the staff. Olivia stayed close beside me. "What can you tell us, Bone Man?"

"There is a dying witch who will do anything to taste immortality. She has already killed and stolen magic from countless witches. She wears many guises but none so innocent as the human without magic who aids her. She has promised a taste of magic that the human was not born to. It is a trick, but her slave is not aware."

"How do we find this witch?" I asked.

"You cannot find her. You can, however, find the one who serves her. It is she who took your friend's life and your spell book. She will lead you to the witch who has stolen Dorothy Lane."

"How will we know her?"

"Follow the trail she has left behind."

I opened my mouth to ask for something less vague. Surely after the sacrifice we were making, we deserved more detailed information.

"And come back, Molly Addison Renard, if you'd like instruction on the use of that amulet. I'm sure you could find *something* to trade for it."

He laughed, the sound echoing around us in the trees.

When I looked up, he was gone. Olivia and the staff were gone with him.

"Is that it?" I raged to the open cemetery. "That trade wasn't worth it. We want our friend back."

Elsie was softly crying, wiping tears gently from her eyes. "She's gone. I feel like Jack, getting beans for Olivia, my cow."

Despite my rage and frustration, I smiled. A bright shaft of sunlight broke through the dark clouds above us. The cold wind suddenly smelled like roses after a summer rain.

"It's going to be okay," I told her. "We're going to find Dorothy. We'll come back for Olivia."

"But, Molly—" Elsie could barely speak. "We can't just leave *her* here."

"It's what she wanted for now. We have to go home and find Dorothy. That's what's important. That's why Olivia gave herself to the Bone Man. Let's go."

We walked quickly out of the cemetery. The ferry had returned when we reached the dock. Elsie and I got on board. We stared at the ocean as we left the island.

"That was too vague." Elsie pounded her fist on the side of the boat. "How are we supposed to know who this woman is? It's not like we haven't looked around. It could be any woman in Wilmington."

"We're strong." I put my arm around her. "Our magic will lead us to the woman, and we'll know what to do."

Elsie shook her head, her lined face defeated. She walked across the boat to stand on the other side, watching as Oak Island disappeared.

Did I really believe that we'd come back for Olivia?

I had to. It was the only way I could bear to leave her.

CHAPTER 34

I find inspiration in the fire.
I find inspiration in the air.
I find inspiration in the water.
I find inspiration in the earth.
Elements: Inspire me!

The car was so silent on the way back to Wilmington that I turned on the radio. I switched it off just as quickly when loud 1970s music pumped out of it.

I looked at Elsie. She was staring blankly out the window. I wished that there were something I could say to reassure her. I wished there were something someone could say to reassure *me*.

Either we'd left what there was of Olivia on Oak Island for sketchy information, or it had been a good trade that would lead us to her killer. Either way, we'd left her there with the Bone Man. It wasn't a pleasant thought.

"What do you think he wants with her?" Elsie asked. "Was it actually the staff he wanted, or Olivia?"

"I don't know." Truthfully, I didn't want to think about it.

"This was a terrible thing to do." Elsie's voice cracked. "Forget what I said about wanting to stay a witch until I die. I wish I could renounce my magic right now!"

"We'll get her back," I promised. "We'll find something the Bone Man will trade for her."

"What would that be?" Elsie stared at me. "We wouldn't have had to do any of this if the stupid council had done their job!"

There was another long silence between us until we reached Wilmington. I felt defeated, as Elsie did. I didn't want to agree with her out loud. I was afraid we'd both get mired down in sorrow so deep that we'd never find our way out again.

"We have to follow the plan." I turned on Front Street to head back to the shop. "We locate the person helping the witch, find Dorothy and the council shuts them down.

"Oh. Is that the plan, dear? How exactly are we going to do any of that?"

I pulled into the front parking space at the shop. A sharp, new black Corvette was parked next to us. The personalized license plate said "WCHYMAN."

Oh brother!

It seemed to me that Brian had grown up with little or no guidance too. What was the next generation of witches going to be like if their parents didn't take the time to train them? Brian's parents and his grandfather surely knew that he was running wild. Why didn't they help him?

"Oh look!" Elsie pointed. "It looks like my itching powder has done its job. There's Brian."

"You're a miracle worker."

"Not so much, but it's nice to feel successful about *some-thing*."

I put the car keys into my bag. "I guess we'll build on that!"

Brian was standing on the stairs. His frown was monumental on his handsome, young face. He held up the hand Elsie had doused with itching powder. It was bright orange and twice its normal size.

"I guess you know how this happened." Brian looked directly at me. "I thought we were a team."

"Sometimes these things happen for a reason," I told him. "In this case, there's something we'd like to talk to you about."

"So you spelled me?"

"No, of course not." Elsie was trying to break the locking spell on the door—not very successfully. "I noticed that orange moss in the cave last night. Some must've gotten on you, but we can clear it up like it never happened."

She winked at me as I moved to help her with the door. Brian stayed where he was.

"I can't believe you people did this to me." He was still complaining. "What did I do to you? You asked for my help. I tried to give it. I almost got arrested for you."

"It's what we can do *for* you," I assured him. "Have you ever thought of joining a coven?"

"So that's what this is all about." He nodded. "I knew you didn't deform my hand and steal my wand for no reason."

"Steal your wand?" Elsie shrugged as she looked for the antidote to the itching powder. "Don't look at me. I never touch another witch's tool. That's my motto."

"Come on. I know one of you did it." He stared at me. "You knew where I kept it, Molly. I should never have trusted you to come with me."

"I didn't take your wand. We've been out on Oak Island all morning." He was acting very strangely. Maybe I was too hasty thinking about inviting him into the coven. We'd watched Dorothy for months before putting the summoning spell on her.

"Look, this is getting old." His voice deepened. "I *want* my wand."

I thought about the string of magic thefts. This was probably one of them. Of course, we weren't any closer to finding our spell book. I didn't think there was anything we could do to help him.

"Here it is." Elsie found the cream that would take away the effects of the itching powder. "Hold still a minute. This won't hurt at all."

"Was there a protection spell on your wand?" I watched them. "Otherwise, anyone could have taken it."

"I've never had a protection spell on it," he said. "I never needed one. But I have a finding spell on it. I don't care who took it, I just want it back. My grandfather will kill me if I've lost it."

"A finding spell!" Elsie clapped her hands. "Brilliant! If the same person who took our spell book took your wand, we can help each other."

The insolent pup had the nerve to look at us as though we were beneath him. "No offense, but I don't see what help you two could be. We couldn't even do a locator spell last night!"

"We were able to conjure you here last night and hold you," I reminded him.

He rolled his eyes. "Okay. I get your point. That's the only thing good about a coven—they work together and the magic is stronger. But this doesn't mean I want to be part of yours. I work on my own. I'm better that way. I'm only doing this because I owe you, Molly."

I was leaning toward agreeing with him. I didn't know who his parents were, but they'd given him an enormous ego for someone so young. It probably went along with council association.

"Let's pinkie swear." Elsie held up her pinkie finger. "I know it's not real magic, but isn't it fun?"

Brian held up his orange hand. "I'm missing a pinkie. When is that stuff gonna work?"

We talked about the finding spell Brian had used on his wand. It had never occurred to me to put a finding spell on our book. The protection spells we'd placed on it had seemed good enough.

The finding spell was set up to trace his wand from his room to the person who possessed it. I told him about our visit to the Bone Man.

"Look at the board over there." I showed him the spot. "There are dozens of witches who have had their magic tools stolen."

He looked at the notices on the board. "I get it. This witch's accomplice is stealing the items, either for the witch or to sell. Either way, she doesn't have any magic. We can take care of her easy."

"I think it makes sense that the witch is protecting her helper. That's why Olivia didn't feel anyone sneak up on her in the alley that night."

"Or the witch did the deed herself." His gaze searched the room. "Where is Olivia?"

"We traded her for this information." Elsie sighed. "The Bone Man has her."

"The Bone Man." He shuddered. "What does he want with her?"

"We don't know," I admitted. "She told us to leave her and find Dorothy. That's what we did."

"Do we have a plan for what we're going to do if we find the dying witch's thief?" Brian asked. "Just wondering before we get to that point."

"I thought we could coerce the thief into telling us where the witch is." I sat down with Isabelle on my lap. "Do you have any ideas?"

"I do have an idea." Brian punched one hand into another. "I take back my wand and do something really bad to both of them. Maybe I'll use some of Elsie's itching powder on them."

I urged caution. "We know the thief isn't a witch, but he or she is probably dangerous anyway. We should be prepared for anything."

"This could be the only chance we'll have to catch her," Brian added. "Let's not screw it up."

Elsie laughed. "I don't think we have to worry about some random street thief. We have a lot of magic on our side. She'll tell us what we want to know, or we'll fix her little red wagon."

He laughed. "How do you come up with these things? I wish my grandmother were as cool as you."

"Why, thank you." Elsie's green eyes sparkled. "It's not often that a witch my age is told that she's cool."

I felt like part of one of the movies frequently made in Wilmington as we walked out of Smuggler's Arcane together. The lady at the bookshop next door smiled and waved and then apparently thought better of it as she got a good look at us. She darted behind her shop door and stared.

"You can ride with us, if you like," I suggested to Brian.

"Are you kidding?" He ran his hand across the shiny surface of his Corvette. "A gift from my father when I graduated from high school. I never travel without it."

I waved as I started the car and followed Brian out of the parking lot. I hoped our newly formed coalition would work. We'd known Brian for even less time than we'd known Dorothy, and what we knew about him wasn't exactly heartening.

I knew he was sneaky and a bit underhanded. Maybe that could work in our favor. Elsie and I could be a little *too* aboveboard. It had never mattered before, but it might matter now. This witch and her accomplice weren't playing fair, but we still kept acting like they were.

Brian's magic was intense air magic, much stronger than Olivia's had ever been. Still, it should be easy to tune our magic to his.

That was a good thing, because I didn't expect Mr. Brannigan, Cassandra or any other member of the council of witches to show their faces while the real work was being done. They'd probably find some way to take credit for it later. I didn't care as long as we got Dorothy back.

We approached the old apartment building where Brian lived. I followed him into the parking lot behind it. I wished Joe could have been there to help us with this part. He would've known what to do with a criminal who wasn't a witch. But I still couldn't ask him for help. Not as long as the witch behind it was involved.

"I hope you're ready." I turned to Elsie.

She took out her sword. "As ready as I'll ever be."

Brian was out of his car and searching the parking lot with worried eyes. "Maybe we should go somewhere we won't be interrupted."

"What about that little group of trees over there?" I pointed to the berm that had been planted to separate this parking lot and the one next door. There were a dozen tall pine trees and some smaller shrubs that might disguise us from prying eyes.

"That seems okay." Brian led the way toward the trees. "You know, I put the finding spell on the wand, but I'm not sure how to invoke it."

Elsie giggled. "I *knew* you needed us."

"Just this one time." His ego acted to protect him from the idea that he might always need help. "I know what I'm doing."

"It sounds like it." I didn't want to be hard on him. If he stayed with us, he'd learn the right way of doing things.

We huddled close together in the island of trees between the two concrete seas. The three of us invoked our magic tools to find Brian's wand. He muttered the enchantment he'd used, and we all took up the call to find what was lost.

The cars in the parking lots were stationary. No one came out of the buildings on either side of us. I could see the beginning of a fine, glistening thread of magic stretching from us and outward. It moved in the breeze like a spider's web, catching the sun and growing toward the missing wand.

The thread of the finding spell reached out. It settled on a single person who was wearing a black jacket. We watched as that person walked into the parking lot and looked around, as though wondering what had brought her out there.

The amulet felt warm in my hand, but I didn't need its magic to know who it was. "Lisbet?" I whispered, and saw her head turn toward me.

CHAPTER 35

I call the storms. I summon the rain.
Hear me: bring the clouds again!
Lightning flash and thunder rumble.
Strike my enemies with your trouble!

"That's the woman who works with your husband!" Brian pointed.

I kept my eyes on her. "I know." She'd been right in front of me the whole time, and I hadn't realized.

"Is it all right to kill her?" he asked.

"Of course not!" Elsie sighed. "The council frowns on that kind of behavior."

"She's the one who killed Olivia." Brian said in a menacing tone.

I put my hand on his arm. "You don't want revenge as much as *we* do. But for now, we have to let her live if we want to find the witch who really caused all of this."

"What do you have in mind?" Brian asked.

"Let me talk to her. She knows me. I hope she trusts me."

"Does she know you're a witch?" Elsie watched Lisbet, who watched us.

"I don't know. It's possible. I'll go with the assumption that she *does* know. The witch she works for has broken every other council rule. Telling her about magic would be the least of what she's done."

"Be careful, Molly." Elsie grabbed my arm. "I can't stand the idea that something could happen to you too."

"I'll be careful." I hugged her. "Keep your sword handy."

Brian nodded at me. "I could come with you."

"Thanks, but I think I'll do better on my own. My husband always says it's good for the bad guy to think she has the upper hand. That way she thinks she's in control."

"So you can pounce and kill." Brian held his thumbs up. "Sweet!"

I started walking down from the berm where we'd been hiding. I wasn't sure what I was going to say to her. I had to swallow hard on my anger, thinking she might have been the one who killed Olivia.

I'd known Lisbet for ten years. She was involved in every aspect of our lives. I knew she wasn't a witch. What had happened to make her this way? Had the witch spelled her?

She looked at me as I reached her. "What are you doing here again, Molly?"

"You *know* why I'm here."

Lisbet's inquisitive eyes swept the area. "I don't know what you're talking about. You should go on home now. I'm sure Joe is wondering where you are."

"I know what you've done. I know *why* you've done it. No harm will come to you if you take me to the witch you're working for."

The smile on her thin face faded. "No, Molly. Please don't get involved with it. I'll leave town. I don't want you to get hurt. You and Joe are like family to me. Leave it alone."

"I can't. She took someone dear to me. I want Dorothy back. You know where she is, don't you?"

"No." Lisbet shook her head. There were tears in her dark eyes. "She'll kill me. She'll kill *you*, Molly. I could never face Joe again. You have to leave it alone. She'll release the girl when she's done with her. When she's back up to her full strength from absorbing all the magic, she'll leave here. It will be over."

"We can't wait that long." I put my hands on her arms as she sobbed. "You have to help me get her back before it's too late. Her mother, my best friend in the world, is already dead. Dorothy can't die too."

Lisbet was sobbing, hanging like a rag doll. "No. Please don't ask me to do this. I've done so much already. I didn't want to kill your friend. *She* said it was the only way."

I swallowed hard. She'd killed Olivia. "There are witches around us who want to kill you, Lisbet. You have to do as I say."

"I'm not afraid of witches," she sneered. "*She* protects me."

"Unless she's here right now, I suggest you listen carefully. You could be dead long before she could defend you." I tipped my head toward the berm. "They're waiting for your answer."

A lightning strike came out of the otherwise clear sky. It struck so close to us that the ground shook beneath our feet.

I wasn't sure how Elsie and Brian had managed it, but it was a nice touch.

Lisbet almost jumped out of her skin. The terror in her eyes was enough for me to know that she didn't believe she was safe anymore.

"What was that?" She spun in a circle, trying to discover what had happened. "They can't do anything to me. I'm protected."

I looked at the amulet she wore. It was dead. If there had been magic in it, it was gone. What about the witch she worked for? Why didn't she have Lisbet's back? Did she realize we were closing in on her?

That could be dangerous for Dorothy. Panic seized me, but I had to stay calm.

"I tried to help you because of our past relationship. If you won't listen, you'll have to face their revenge." I started to walk away.

"Wait." She squinted, trying to see where her adversaries were. "I'll take you to her. Maybe you can bargain with her for your friend's daughter. I can't make any promises."

"Smart girl." There was no way to guarantee this wasn't a trick. We had to take a chance for Dorothy's sake. "Let's go."

I got in my car. She climbed into the passenger side. "Where are the others?"

"They're air witches. They have their own means of transportation."

I thought a little magic myth was in order here, even if it wasn't completely true. Of course they wouldn't get on their brooms and meet us there. I hoped Elsie and Brian got the idea.

"What in the world is she doing?" Elsie asked as she watched my car pull out of the parking lot.

"I don't know. But I'm following her," Brian said. "Come on!"

We drove into the old town part of Wilmington, near the river. This wasn't an area I'd pegged as the lair of a rogue witch. The buildings were in disrepair—windows broken and doors hanging open. It didn't even look like anyone was living here.

"She's lived here for five hundred years," Lisbet said. "She's seen the whole world change. She wants to stay alive. I don't blame her."

"How did you get involved with her?"

"She offered me something no one else could—magic and power. I couldn't say no. She showed me a whole world that I didn't know existed. She opened my eyes."

"And that was enough to kill my friend?" My voice shook, and my hands trembled on the steering wheel.

"I didn't have any choice, Molly. She needed your friend's magic and your spell book. Your friend wasn't the only witch I've had to kill. I'm sorry for that—but not for what I've seen and done. You can't know the freedom and excitement of real power until you've felt it."

I wanted to strike her down. I'd never entertained that thought before. We would never even sell items needed for a death spell or potion at Smuggler's Arcane. This was different. I wanted her to be dead like Olivia—her throat slit in a dark alley.

I had *never* used my magic to hurt anyone in my life. I had never even thought about it. But at that moment, if common sense hadn't prevailed, I would have killed her.

I quickly pushed those thoughts aside. I didn't want Lisbet to see me that way. She was trained as a detective to pick up on those signals. Revenge had to wait.

And there was the witch to deal with. I fingered my amulet, not at all sure I could face such a creature. The only thing that kept me keep going was reminding myself about Dorothy and Olivia. I had to finish this.

I parked the car outside the sagging redbrick building. All of the windows were painted black. The front door was barely on its hinges. There were runes scratched into the wood at the windows and doors. This close, I knew that a witch protected this place.

And yet those runes were as useless as the amulet Lisbet wore. Was the witch so close to death that she couldn't maintain her spells?

I hoped so. It might be the only chance I had to stand up to her.

"She's in here." Lisbet glanced around the deserted alley and then grinned. "I hope you know what you're doing, Molly. I don't think she's going to like that I brought you here."

"I'm sure she won't. On the other hand, she's infuriated the witches in Wilmington, not to mention the werewolf community."

Her eyes were enormous in her sallow face. "There are *werewolves* in Wilmington?"

I didn't answer. "Shall we go upstairs?"

I could feel Elsie and Brian behind us, even though I couldn't see them. A witch can have relationships that are strong enough to make her aware when those people are near. I hadn't known Brian long, but he was already one of those people.

The door creaked as Lisbet opened it. The foyer of the old building was disgusting with garbage, filth and dead rats. The stench almost made me vomit. I covered my nose with my hand and kept going.

We walked around the debris, and I set my foot on the groaning stairs. Around me, paint was peeling from the walls, and the ceiling was dripping with moisture. It had been a long time since the witch who lived here had done anything, magic or not, to maintain the place.

We came to a landing at the top of the stairs. The structure was set up more like an apartment building than a house. There were several doors off the landing. Underfoot, the carpet was threadbare and covered with mold. Where I could see it, there were holes in the wood floor beneath it.

"Careful where you walk," Lisbet warned as she danced around the pitfalls. "It's this way."

I saw her open the door that led to the witch's hidden sanctum. Terror so sharp I could taste it almost stopped me.

I could hardly force my feet to move forward. My whole body shook with it.

Anger had sustained me to this point. Now—alone and about to face a monster—I could scarcely breathe. I wished that I had a staff or some other bulky item to hold on to. Holding the tiny cauldron and the amulet in my hand wasn't enough.

I put one foot in front of the other carefully to follow Lisbet's tracks. I silently urged my friends to be coming up the stairs behind us, even though I knew they weren't that close. I hoped I could find something to distract the witch until we could face her together. I couldn't do this alone.

"What's taking you so long?" Lisbet called from the doorway. "Not *scared*, Molly, are you?"

I set my chin and stared her down. "I'm not afraid of your witch."

"Great! Come on inside then. My *mother* is waiting."

Her *mother*? Lisbet's mother was the rogue witch. Lisbet had no magic. Her mother had promised her magic if she could keep her alive. It was a lie—a lie that had cost more than one witch her life. Magic couldn't be gifted. But Lisbet obviously didn't know that.

The odor coming from the apartment where Lisbet had disappeared was even worse than the hall and stairs. It was dark in the room, with the windows painted over. The stench of mildew and mold added to the smell of decay. I wanted nothing more than to run in the opposite direction. Every nerve and muscle was trying to pull me away.

When I was completely inside the apartment, the heavy door slammed closed behind me. I tried not to panic. Running would only make me seem weak at a time when I needed to appear strong, whether I was or not.

Panic is our great enemy, Elsie had once told me when I was very young.

Illusion is a witch's best friend.

There was a candle burning beside a bed with a huge, moth-eaten canopy over it. I saw a figure pushed up on several large pillows, a black comforter pulled up to her chin.

I stepped closer to get a better look. I couldn't feel any life here at all, and no magic. I realized why when I was finally beside the bed.

The rogue witch was dead. I couldn't be sure for how long. She'd certainly been alive the night before when we'd cast the mirror spell. Her head was thrown back, mouth open. She looked as though her last act had been screaming at the world. A heavy boline, perhaps the one that had been stolen, was protruding from her chest.

"Mother is angry," Lisbet whispered. "She wants you dead too, Molly. I'm sorry."

Clearly, Joe's partner had lost it. The situation was too dangerous to remark on her loss of reason. Even though the witch was dead, Lisbet's predatory insanity closed around me like a smothering cloak.

"She doesn't look angry." I peered into the dead face. My knees were knocking, teeth chattering. "She looks at peace. She promised you magic?"

"That's all I ever wanted," she said. "I would have done anything to be like her. I wasn't born a witch, but she said I could be one if I helped her. It should have been my birthright, like you and your friends."

The pathetic plea in her voice—not to mention the dead witch before me—rendered me speechless.

Lisbet came up close to me. "Do you know what she said to me this morning?"

I swallowed hard. "What?"

"She told me that she'd lied to me. Can you believe it? She said she couldn't give me magic. I suppose you already knew that, huh Molly?"

I nodded. "No one can make you a witch if you aren't born with magic."

"Interesting." She jerked the boline from her mother's chest. "She also told me that the amulet you wear is very ancient and powerful. But there's only one way to remove it once a witch has put it on. You have to die."

CHAPTER 36

Life is fragile.
Protect mine, all ye elements of the universe.

I felt the knife at my throat and her arms wrapped around me. She was small and thin, but she was whipcord strong.

Staying calm wasn't an option anymore. This was the way she'd killed Olivia. I could feel her hot breath on my cheek. One of her hands was in my hair, pulling my head back for the cut.

I gagged on fear and the stench around us. I couldn't even think of a spell that could help, much less form the words for one.

"Hold it right there, Lisbet."

I hadn't even heard the door open behind us, but suddenly Joe was there. I could barely make out his familiar form.

I don't think I've ever been so glad to see someone.

"I'm your partner, Joe." Lisbet's voice was normal and pleasant. "You won't shoot me."

"Let Molly go," he said. "Put the knife down and let her go."

"Why are you even here, Joe?" She didn't move at all. "You're supposed to be on the other side of town."

I could feel her tears flowing onto my face. Her heart was pounding, and she shook all over. Seeing Joe there had changed everything.

"We've been investigating you, Lisbet. You've been crazy since we started this case. I was almost too close to it to see what you were doing. I found the mask with Olivia Dunst's blood on it at your apartment. The fibers matched the ones we found on her. I was waiting to see what your next move was. I didn't expect this to be it. There are officers waiting downstairs. I wanted to come up alone and face you. You're my partner. You deserved that much."

"Joe." Her voice was barely audible. She moved her hand from my hair and wiped the tears from her face. "You weren't supposed to get involved in all this. I didn't want to hurt Molly. But I need this last kill—for her magic and the amulet. My mother is wrong. I can finally be a witch."

"No, Lisbet." His voice was gentle. "You killed someone. There's only one thing that's gonna happen now."

"An eye for an eye, right?"

"No, Lisbet. It doesn't have to be that way."

The knife had gone slack against my throat. Her arms were limp but still clinging to me. I closed my eyes and muttered a spell for protection. It was all I could do to keep my thoughts together long enough. I hoped it would work.

I put my hand on my mother's amulet and forced my will through it. It created a shock wave effect that shoved air molecules between us. It threw her away from me. I took a step back, prepared to defend myself if I needed to.

Lisbet made a growling sound in the back of her throat and leapt toward me. A single shot rang out in the dismal apartment. She dropped to the floor.

"Are you all right?" Joe came quickly across the room.

He checked Lisbet first, his gun still in his hand. "She's dead."

He put his arms around me and held me tight.

"I'm fine." I put my arms around him and hoped I'd never have to let go. "You really came without backup, didn't you?"

"How did you know?"

"There's that sound in your voice. I can't describe it, but I can always tell when you're lying."

Elsie and Brian plunged through the door.

"Are you okay?" Elsie pinched her nostrils tightly together with her fingers. "What's that *smell*?"

"I think it's this dead witch." Brian was staring at the body on the bed.

"Quiet," Elsie warned. "There are people *without* magic in here too."

I turned to Joe. "I think Dorothy is here somewhere. We have to find her."

We searched the whole disgusting building and finally found Dorothy asleep on a cot in the basement. She was cold, but she still had a pulse.

"I think Lisbet murdered her mother before it was the right time to perform the ceremony to strip Dorothy of her magic," I said with a grateful heart.

"It would have killed her," Elsie whispered.

Elsie and I kissed her pretty face and bestowed what blessings we could on her. Brian did the same with a little more gusto than was needed. Olivia wouldn't have liked it.

Joe called for backup and an ambulance.

"There are a few things we need to find before your crime lab gets here," I explained, careful what I said.

He nodded. "I'm going outside to wait for backup. It'll only take a few minutes. Make it quick."

Elsie stayed with Dorothy. I found a light switch in the bedroom, and Brian reclaimed his wand. There were some other missing magic tools there too, but many more were gone—including our spell book. We took everything with us to distribute back to their owners.

Cassandra joined us a few minutes later. "Oh good. Matilda is finally dead."

"Glad we could help out." I was annoyed and sarcastic, no apologies for it.

"She was one of the old ones." Cassandra peered into Matilda's face. "She came here with her father from Germany more than four hundred years ago. She was very strong. *Some* members of the council were afraid of her."

"So you used us to get rid of her for you," I accused. "She led us around, making us think Brian had killed Olivia."

"Not exactly." Cassandra touched Matilda's cheek. "Let's give her the send-off she deserves." At her touch, Matilda's body shook and fell apart, eventually becoming a fine gray powder. "Bye-bye."

"She killed Olivia, and no telling who else." I wished I felt better, knowing Matilda and Lisbet were dead. Instead, I just felt numb.

"She didn't actually," Cassandra explained. "Her daughter did the dirty deeds for her. Matilda hasn't been out of bed in months, but she still had plenty of magic to cloak her daughter and the tasks she sent her to do. That's why the council couldn't see what was going on."

"And you knew all this?" Elsie demanded.

Cassandra shrugged. "We suspected she was stealing magic artifacts, but we couldn't prove it. Now it turns out that she didn't steal anything or kill anyone. It's not our problem."

"No," Brian said. "She got her daughter to do it for her while you looked the other way. We all know she couldn't become a witch by stealing artifacts, but this way you and the council didn't have to do anything."

"You could have told the witch and her daughter what they were doing wouldn't work," Elsie suggested. "You could have spared us all a lot of heartache."

"The important thing is that witches weren't technically involved." Cassandra smiled.

"What about our spell book?" I asked.

"I don't know what Matilda had her daughter do with the things that were stolen." Cassandra's expression was sincere for once. "I'm sure it will turn up somewhere. In the meantime, you have other witches to recruit."

"Don't look at me." Brian turned away. "This isn't the kind of witch I want to be."

"Well, the police will be here soon. I guess I should be going too." Cassandra regally bowed her head. "On behalf of the Grand Council of Witches, we thank you for your service."

I could hear sirens coming toward us. Cassandra was gone with a puff of smoke and the scent of roses.

"How does she *do* that?" Brian scratched his chin. "I thought it was impossible."

We walked out of the old building together. Joe was waiting by his SUV.

"What are you going to say?" I asked him.

"I'm going to say that Lisbet came at me when I confronted her with the facts about these deaths. She was out of her mind. I'll be on desk duty for a while." He shook his head. "I can't believe she was going to kill you. What happened to her? I don't understand."

The sirens were getting closer. "I'll tell you what I know later. I love you."

"I love you too. Get out of here."

I didn't like leaving Dorothy, but I knew Joe would see to it that she got good care. I hoped she would be all right. Elsie was already trying to conjure flowers we could take to her hospital room.

We drove away from the house of horrors before the police arrived. I watched Brian leave before me and thought we'd never see him again.

But he met us back at Smuggler's Arcane. "What?" he asked when we saw him. "I needed some time to decompress before I faced anyone else. Not that anyone is gonna believe me when I tell them about this."

"At least we have Dorothy back again." Elsie made chai tea that smelled heavenly.

"That's right." I looked at Brian. "It was your idea to use the lightning bolt, wasn't it?"

"Yeah." He shrugged. "It's the only trick I know. I'm not sure I could've done it without Elsie. It only seems to work when I'm around a fire witch. Maybe someday I can do an earthquake or something. That would be good in a case like this too."

"I'm thankful nothing like *this* ever happens to us." Elsie measured tea into cups. "We aren't those kind of witches."

"Good." Brian was checking out our books. "I'd hate to think I had to face this kind of thing every day."

I glanced at Elsie. Did that mean he was staying?

There was a pounding on the shop door. Brian jumped. We muttered a protection spell together.

The door burst open anyway. Olivia's staff appeared on the counter as the door slammed closed again.

"What now?" Elsie's eyes roamed the shop.

"Oh, girls!" Olivia appeared with a rapturous expression on her ghostly face. "You aren't going to *believe* what happened. The Bone Man had some interesting ideas about things he and I could do. That was all he wanted from me."

"Huh!" Elsie shook her head as she put the tea and cups on the table.

"That's right. Even dead, I've still got it." Olivia laughed as she circled the room. "And that old Bone Man has it going on too."

"That's amazing." I sat at the table with Isabelle. "We have plenty to tell you too. It's nice to have you back."

"It's nice to be back," Olivia said. "Did you find Dorothy?"

We called that night to check on Dorothy. She was sleeping. The nurse said to call back in the morning. We called back in the morning, and Dorothy was gone. The doctor had released her.

That was when the real worry started. We called everywhere and went to her apartment and Olivia's house. We couldn't find her. She wasn't at the library. She wasn't answering her cell phone. Even Hemlock had no idea where she could be.

"Do you think this is part of the spell the witch had her under?" Olivia fretted. "How could she just disappear?"

"What about a lost spell?" Brian suggested. He'd surprised us by showing up at the shop that morning. "Or a finder's spell?"

We were about to head down to the cave when the door chimed as it opened.

"Dorothy!" Elsie and I got to our feet.

She smiled. "Hello. I'm here to collect those old books for the library that you wanted to donate."

Elsie squinted. "Is that all you have to say to us? What happened to you, child?"

She looked fine. Not a hair was out of place. Her clothes weren't even wrinkled.

But her brown eyes were blank. She stared at us and at the shop as though she'd never seen us before.

"The witch took her memory," Brian said. "She doesn't know us."

"If it's not too much trouble," Dorothy said pleasantly, "could you get those books for me? I have to get back to the library."

"I'm not sure what books you're talking about," Elsie said. "Where is your stone?"

"Yes!" Olivia clapped her hands soundlessly. "If she has her magic tool, she might regain her memory."

"You called about some books." Dorothy was beginning to sound suspicious. "If you don't have the books, or you've changed your mind, that's fine. I'll come back later."

"Wait." I thought of an old spell that was supposed to restore lost things. I wasn't sure if Dorothy's memories would qualify as lost things, but it was worth a try. "We were about to have tea. Elsie will look for those books. It should only take a few minutes. Won't you join us?"

I could tell she was uncomfortable with the idea, but being Dorothy, she didn't want to be rude.

"I guess that would be okay." Her eyes roamed the shop again. "You know I've seen this place lots of times on the way to Two Sisters Book Store. I've thought about stopping in but never did."

"Please, take a look around," I invited. "I'll make your tea."

Olivia couldn't wait. "Dorothy! Don't you recognize me? I'm your mother."

Dorothy took off her jacket and put down her purple bag. She walked to the bookshelves and thumbed through our old volumes.

"I don't think she even hears me anymore," Olivia mourned. "This is *worse* than death."

I put on the kettle and crouched next to the bottom of the cabinet. "I think I know a spell to find missing items that might work."

"Restore lost things!" Brian joined me. "I know that one."

"That's not for people's brains," Olivia complained. "You'll mess with her head. She might be a zombie or something."

Elsie came behind the counter too. "What kind of books do you want me to look for?"

"We're not *really* donating books," I whispered. "It's a ruse until we can think of some way to restore her memory."

"Really?" She looked pleased. "That's a wonderful idea. I'll *pretend* to find books."

"You can't do it, Molly," Olivia continued. "There could be consequences."

"There will be consequences if she can't remember anything," Brian said.

The kettle started whistling, and I took out the cups. I left Olivia's star-shaped cup behind the counter.

"That's my cup, Molly!" Olivia pouted. "I want some tea."

"You can't drink tea anymore," I reminded her. "It's okay to pretend when we're alone. But if I put out a cup for you too, that might send Dorothy screaming into the street. She's already not sure about us."

"Oh, all right. I'll hang around like an old tapestry until she remembers. You'd think ghosts would have more abilities than this. I miss my magic."

I didn't comment on her loss. I was sure there were other things ghosts could do. I'd never known a ghost, but I'd read and heard the stories. No doubt Olivia was still acclimating to her new existence. We'd have to deal with what she could do as a ghost later.

I put the tea, cups, honey and milk on a pretty flowered tray. "The tea is ready. I hope you're thirsty."

Dorothy stopped exploring long enough to join Brian and me at the table.

Elsie placed three books next to the tray. "Here are those books we promised you."

Dorothy seemed surprised. "I thought you had boxes of them. That's why the library sent me over to collect them."

"Have some tea." I shook my head at Elsie. Couldn't she find more than that?

"Oh I love chai tea." Dorothy sat down. "Do you have any sugar? I'm allergic to honey."

"Yes." It was the perfect opportunity for me to work on the spell while she was waiting. I stepped behind the counter and acted as though I were looking for the sugar as I murmured the restore-lost-things spell under my breath.

The door chime sounded again. I hoped it wasn't a customer. This was a bad time to bag up herbs or hunt for a specific book.

Instead it was Mike—which was much worse.

"Hey, Mom," he greeted me. "What's up? I thought you might want to do lunch."

Mike's gaze found Dorothy's, and the rest of us were forgotten. "Hi, Dorothy. I was hoping I'd find you here."

She stared at him with the same blankness. "Hi. Do I know you?"

Mike's smile went away. "We had coffee, remember?"

"No. I'm afraid not. You must have me confused with someone else."

I needed more time to work on the spell. I couldn't be distracted or lose my concentration if it was going to be effective. I ignored Elsie's and Olivia's beseeching looks. I put my hand on my amulet as I focused on the spell to find Dorothy's lost memory.

Brian joined me behind the counter and covered my hand with his. "Let's see if we can speed things up, huh?"

Elsie finally picked up on what was going on. "Mike, have some tea. We have some wonderful chai, and I love the mint."

Mike put his hands in his pants pockets and hunkered down in his jacket. "I'm not thirsty, Elsie. Thanks anyway."

"I'm sorry I don't recognize you," Dorothy said to him. "I'm sure I'd remember if we had coffee."

"Is this some weird way of telling me you don't want to see me again?"

"No. Really. I don't know if I want to see you at all since I don't know you."

Elsie made a hurry-up gesture with her hands. I closed

my eyes and tried to ignore the drama. Brian did the same. I could feel his strength joining mine.

We'd gone through the repetitions of the spell twice. It didn't seem to have any effect on Dorothy. We repeated it once more. I put one hand on the amulet and one on the cauldron around my neck. Brian tightly held his wand with both hands.

There was a popping sound that was followed by a rattling noise. I didn't look to see what it was, still trying hard to make the spell work. *Come on. I need this. Work for me.*

"Oh my stars!" Elsie said with a laugh. "So it was *here* all the time."

"What's this?" Dorothy bent over and picked up the old emerald cull she'd found by the river.

Hemlock howled loudly and ran to her.

"Oh." Dorothy blinked a few times and peered around herself. "What happened? The last thing I remember was the witch grabbing me."

"Witch?" Mike jumped. "You saw a *witch*?"

We managed to laugh off the part about a witch grabbing Dorothy. Mike seemed fine with it. I sent him off on an errand, with a promise that we'd all have lunch with him later.

When he was gone, Elsie, Dorothy and I hugged and exchanged stories about what had happened. Brian stood off to the side alone until Elsie noticed what he was doing and hugged him too.

"Honestly, it was like I was here one minute and went to sleep." Dorothy shrugged. "I woke up when I picked up the emerald, and Scooter was howling."

Her cat meowed loudly in protest.

"Oh, sorry. *Hemlock.* That's going to take some getting used to." She rubbed his back and he purred, twisting around her ankles.

When our jaws were tired of telling our stories and

speculating on where our spell book could be, we decided to call it a day.

Elsie emailed Larry the werewolf to let him know it was safe to come home. Dorothy took the staff and her mother, and they went to explore their new house.

I went to my house, hoping Joe could fill me in about what happened after we'd left the witch's apartment. I hoped he wasn't wrong about trying to protect me from the police proceedings that would come with him killing Lisbet.

When I got back, Mike was searching for detergent so he could wash a load of clothes. "I'm going back to school, Mom. I've thought about it, and Cindy isn't worth giving up my life for after all."

I found the detergent and started the washing machine. "Cindy? You were leaving school because of a girl? You never even mentioned her."

He shook his head. "Not just any girl. I thought she was the love of my life—until I met Dorothy. There's something about her, right?"

I started putting his clothes into the washer. "Absolutely."

"I don't think she'll care about our age difference, but I know she wants me to finish school. We talked about it. She even offered to come up and visit sometimes."

I stared at my son. I loved him, but I hoped he would grow up soon. "I'm sure you're right."

"You mind if we have something besides pizza tonight?" He grabbed an apple from the counter. "I know you and Dad love pizza. I'm a little tired of it. How about some Chinese instead? My treat."

"That sounds good." I hid my smile behind the laundry room door. There were some things a witch just had to live with.

Joe was home early thanks to what had happened that day. His boss, Captain Phillips, had sent him home after the cursory questions into Lisbet's death. He hadn't been suspended, but he would be on desk duty for two weeks during the investigation.

His face was pale and troubled when we went to bed that night. I created an enchanted bubble so we could tell each other everything we knew about what had happened. If nothing else, it would give him a place to start to understand Lisbet and what she'd done.

After we departed the bubble to talk of more normal things, he put his arms around me. "I was more scared today than I've ever been. The idea of losing you almost stopped my heart. Let's not *ever* do that again."

I kissed him, and put my hand on his worried face. "Never again. But I'm glad you were there."

"Me too. I'm exhausted. Let's go to sleep."

When we were snuggled up close together, I was so grateful for my family and my life. The spell book was important, but not as important as being with the ones I loved. Maybe my life had changed forever, but it was still good.

I kissed Joe's cheek with my arm around him. "Are you asleep already?"

"*Mmm-hmm.* Feels good. You should try it."

I smiled. "Good night, Joe."

"Good night, my little witch."

M7G0610